PRAISE FOR
EXILED SOUTH

"History. Well, along with the characters, we discover anew what a loaded word it can be, manipulated to benefit its acceptable version at the time. No one can stop history from repeating itself. This revelation is at the heart of the story. There are many secrets to anyone's past, and if we choose to search for shards of *truth* (another loaded word), we will likely find them like gold coins hidden beneath the floorboards. This is a tale of courage and reckoning, of a woman's life turned upside down and then righted, or righted *enough*, a story whose pages will not stop turning because Lizbeth will not let them.

"Cannon gives readers just what they want from a historical, yet superbly contemporary, novel: stay-up-until-the-sun-comes-up reading."

—Mary Lou Sanelli, Author of *Every Little Thing*

"Harriet Cannon's novel *Exiled South* rips the cover off traditional Southern sagas and takes you on a riveting international journey across a century, exploring the hidden trauma and deep wounds of three generations of one family following the Civil War. Hats off to Cannon for her bold and exciting new work in a field of multicultural relationships that she knows well. The story Cannon tells reveals that we are all connected in ways we least expect."

—Eleanor McCallie Cooper, Author of *Dragonfly Dreams* and *Grace in China*

"In her excellent debut novel, Harriet Cannon has created the rich, textured portrait of a woman caught between her family's mysterious (possibly stained) past and a tumultuous, sometimes tragic present. Cannon constructs a mesmerizing emotional geography for her protagonist, Lizbeth Gordon, a woman determined to fully discover—and to ultimately come to terms with—her ancestral history, while simultaneously navigating her new, unexpected life as a widow and ex-patriate. Cannon's settings are wonderfully hypnotic—you can almost smell the pluff mud of the South Carolina Lowcountry or hear the strains of 'The Girl From Ipanema' wafting over a warm, Rio de Janeiro beach. Lizbeth Gordon is a memorable character on a remarkable journey, and we're invited to accompany her. And we're damn lucky to have a writer like Harriet Cannon as our guide."

—**Scott Gould**, Creative Writing Department, SC Governor's School for the Arts and Humanities, Author of *Whereabouts*, and *Things That Crash, Things That Fly*

"When Lizbeth Gordon leaves the Pacific Northwest for the sunshine of a South Carolina beach, she's seeking peace, comfort, and a way to put her life back together. Unexpectedly, her new location gives her the chance to investigate family history and family secrets. Lizbeth seizes the opportunity to explore a past filled with fascinating details about life under siege in Civil War Charleston and the tough post-war choices faced by survivors. *Exiled South* deftly explores the ways that decisions in the past impact lives in the present. Be sure to check it out for great book club discussion topics."

—**Rebecca Hodge**, Award-Winning Author of *Wildland* and *Over the Falls*

Exiled South

by Harriet Cannon

ISBN 978-1-64663-546-7

Published by

 köehlerbooks™

3705 Shore Drive
Virginia Beach, VA 23455
800-435-4811
www.koehlerbooks.com

EXILED SOUTH

a novel

HARRIET CANNON

VIRGINIA BEACH
CAPE CHARLES

For Grandmama and Mere, story tellers extraordinaire

PROLOGUE

Lizbeth Gordon and Dan Keller fell in love on a Mexican beach in 1988. She was at loose ends after three years in the Peace Corps. He was celebrating his MBA, getting by on his good looks and a few Spanish phrases. They swam and shopped village tiendas and had amazing sex.

One night as they sat on a sand hillock admiring the moon over the Pacific, he teased, "If you are from South Carolina, why don't you have an accent?"

She decided to test his mettle with the truth.

"I dove into social justice my last year at high school, so I wanted to go to a liberal university up north where I could do more." She shot him a half smile. "I danced around the house for hours when the scholarship to a college in New Jersey arrived." She nodded to herself, remembering her naiveté.

"But I hadn't reckoned I'd get harassed for my small-town Southern accent. One guy in English class was a ruthless jerk. He smirked at the way I talked, said my Daddy was probably Ku Klux Klan."

"That's harsh."

"It was. It pissed me off when people from Ohio or New York judged me for where I'm from instead of the person I am." She smoothed the frayed edge of her cut-off jeans to keep focused. "I made up my mind life would be easier if I fit in. I've a good ear for languages. By June, I sounded like a Mid-Atlantic television reporter." She'd meant to stop there but changed her mind. "Truth be told, there's more to why I don't say much about being Southern."

"Tell me."

Lizbeth sucked in a breath and cleared her throat. "My circle of friends believed we could usher in a new age of rainbow races and cultures; we brought speakers to campus, danced to Michael Jackson's Thriller album, and celebrated when Alice Walker won a Pulitzer Prize for *The Color Purple*. Remember those days?"

"I do."

The warmth of his exhale ruffled her hair.

"My senior year I signed up for a course in African American History." She remembers the charismatic visiting professor's easy smile like it was yesterday. Those who wanted a decent seat in the theater style classroom arrived early.

"A girl often sat near me. One day our eyes locked across the aisle. On the way out of class, she introduced herself as Angela, but we didn't chat again."

Lizbeth's voice faltered. Suddenly her throat was full of phlegm. Goddammit, she'd started her story, and she was going to finish no matter the consequences. She cleared her throat.

"Angela waited for the perfect moment to drop her bomb. The syllabus topic that day was 'politics of reparations for enslaved people.' During question-and-answer time, Angela stood. She introduced herself as Angela Gordon, a proud Black woman. She pointed at me. 'Over there is Lizbeth Gordon, my White cousin whose ancestors enslaved mine in the Piedmont area of South Carolina.' I was appalled. My Granddaddy Gordon was from the Piedmont."

Lizbeth covered her heart with her hand, to keep it from bolting from her chest. Retelling the story was like being back in that classroom, bathed in a shower of shame. She sucked in air until she could continue with a steady voice.

"The professor invited Angela and me onto the stage with him. He made a big deal of facilitating a reconciliation conversation on the spot. I said the institution of slavery was a low point in human history and apologized for my slaveholding family. That wasn't difficult. It's what I believe. But standing at the podium with Angela while she and a couple hundred of my peers fired off questions about my White Southern family crushed me."

"Why didn't the professor intervene when it got nasty?" Lizbeth felt Dan's arms draw her close.

"I don't know. Angela had seized the spotlight and was on a roll. She produced a photograph of a mixed-race woman, 'my granny's mama,' and passed it to the professor and then around the room."

Lizbeth bit the inside of her cheek remembering the triumph in Angela's voice when she said, "Enslaved women can't say no to the master."

"Angela grabbed my hand and raised our arms up in a salute to the class. Behold the cousins! The class clapped. A few even whoop-whooped."

Lizbeth sat up and rolled her shoulders, wishing she could roll that afternoon out of her life. "Angela produced a camera and asked the professor to snap some pictures. She pulled me in close." Lizbeth's lips twisted in a grotesque smile. "Cheese please Angela said and, I complied like a puppet. No one noticed Angela's thumb and index finger like a crab claw at my waist. I had a bruise for a week."

"Wow."

"Yeah, it was awful." Retelling the events of that afternoon made her nauseous.

"Did you know your ancestors were slaveholders?"

"Well, kinda, but not specifically." Lizbeth wet her lips. "Slaveholding before the Civil War wasn't exactly dinner table conversation at home, but yeah, I heard stories. Yeoman farmers like my people could buy a slave if they had a couple of good harvest years. I don't doubt Angela's story. We could be related. I get her anger. She must have experienced racism, as well as her family stories of enslavement."

"It's odd she would want a picture of the two of you."

"Angela wasn't finished with me." Lizbeth shivered and Dan gently folded the edges of their colorful Mexican beach blanket around her bare legs. "The next week she and I were on the front page of the newspaper with a caption that read, *Angela Gordon, student with enslaved ancestors, finds her cousin, Lizbeth Gordon, fellow student and descendant of slaveholders.*"

"That was mean-spirited."

"It was," Lizbeth said through pursed lips.

"An editor at the paper had called me for permission to print a picture of 'the reunited cousins.' I knew, if I refused the editor's request, Angela would have spread the word I was a racist." Nightmares of those isolated last months at college still plagued her.

"I spent the rest of my senior year pinned with a scarlet letter, watching my liberal friends pass by on campus like I'd developed a peculiar body odor." She reached into her pocket for a tissue.

Dan pulled Lizbeth deeper into the crook of his shoulder and kissed the top of her head. "Did you talk to Angela again?"

"No. I dropped the class. After graduation, I didn't go home to Neely, South Carolina. I worked as a waitress in Charleston until I got a job as a Peace Corps volunteer. Now it's time to head back to the States, get a job, and get a life." Lizbeth looked into her lover's face. Her lips quirked in a wistful smile.

Dan squeezed her shoulder and returned her smile. "Why don't you come home to Washington State with me?"

PART ONE

The past is never dead. It's not even past.

William Faulkner

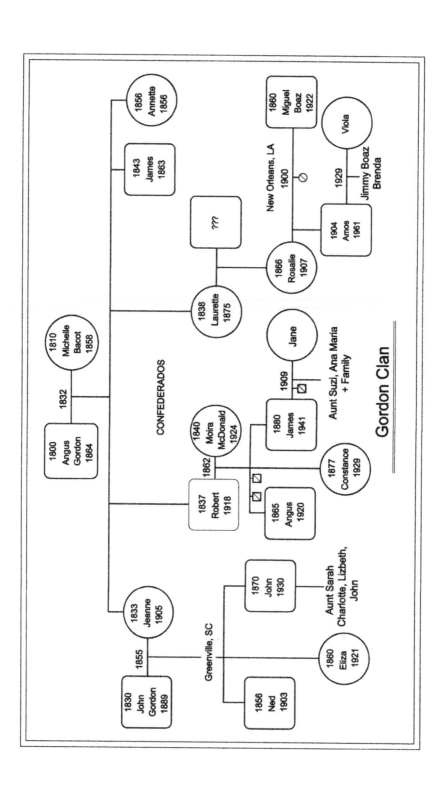

Gordon Clan

CHAPTER ONE

Olympic Peninsula, Washington State, December 2009

L izbeth Gordon reheats last night's chili, fills her wine glass with merlot, and sits alone at the kitchen table reading the *Sounding News*. It sooths her to pore over local news and gossipy letters to the editor late in the day. Between school district politics and a depressed student in her office this afternoon, she needs soothing.

Where's Dan?

At seven-thirty she calls his cell, which goes directly to voice mail. She leaves an upbeat message. Dan's become touchy when he's tardy. Is he punishing her by sending her calls to voice mail? That seems a little paranoid, but, well, his behavior has been odd lately.

Last week they'd argued about his long hours. Then he did a 180 and teased her, like the old days, "Lizbeth, my darling, you're stalking me. Life is more fluid with Josh and Robbie at college. Lighten up."

"I worry when you're late."

"Don't."

Dan's been her rock for twenty years. How can she doubt him? Six weeks after they arrived in Washington State, the home pregnancy test confirmed her suspicion. She had trepidations about starting a family with a man she'd only known a couple of months, but Dan organized a party and passed out cigars.

They settled in artsy Port Benton. Dan started his dream business as a marketing consultant for Native American casinos and small resorts propagating like mushrooms on the pristine Olympic Peninsula. When Josh and Robbie entered kindergarten, Lizbeth entered graduate school. Family life and work were a dream come true with only a hiccup after the twins left for university. She'd burst into tears while stirring spaghetti sauce for two instead of a crowd of teenage boys. Dan had hugged her till she smiled again. She'd rallied by starting a counseling practice after school hours. And yoga three times a week that did marvelous things for her butt.

But lately, she's been wondering what's up with Dan's evening meetings.

Lizbeth knows she's a master at facilitating conflict resolution in everybody's life but her own. Dammit! Something's fishy.

She gets up and dumps her dishes in the sink. Dan can clean up. She tops off her wine glass, takes a sip, changes her mind, does up her dishes, wipes the counters down, and starts the dishwasher. The rain pounds like a gorilla clogging on the roof. Concerned, she opens the door onto their front yard and breathes in the heavy, wet scent. The wind whips her exhale into white smoke. In the glow of the porch light, thick drops dance on the front walk.

She hugs herself standing in the glassed-in porch of their 1940s-era home and floats in memories. When Josh and Robbie were young, the porch was full of boots standing in hunks of dried dirt, piles of sneakers, and scooters that belonged in the garage. Now the shelves Dan built to provide some order are empty except for her gardening boots, a couple pairs of Dan's running shoes, and a small bag of bird seed.

She stares into the angry storm, takes a sip of wine, and speed-dials Dan's cell again. It goes to voice mail again. Dan had a meeting in Port Angeles. He'll be traveling on a rural road with a reputation for landslides and wrecks. She's got to distract herself until she can wrap her arms around her husband and know he's home safe.

Cell in hand, Lizbeth ascends to their upstairs TV room with each step pounding a note of frustration. Dan still teases her as he always has and brings her flowers on Friday nights like he always has, but lately he prefers reality TV instead of classic country music to relax. Exactly when did mindless entertainment replace their shoulder-to-shoulder time on the couch dueling over *New York Times* book reviews and politics? And yet, when the lights are low, and the music is right, they satisfy each other in bed like they did at twenty-something. They're fortunate to have that in middle age, right? All kinds of stories including husbands with wandering eyes and partners with porn on the computer drift around the teacher's lounge.

Lizbeth decides there's no reason to micromanage Dan's intentions. She clicks the television on.

CHAPTER TWO

On the Keller-Gordon front porch, Officer Brian Warwicki sets his face in a neutral pose, straightens his shoulders, finger-combs his military-cut salt-and-pepper hair, and presses the bell.

Lizbeth is well into streaming a rerun of *CSI: Miami* and feeling a sleepy buzz from the wine when the doorbell chimes. Odd. Could she have locked Dan out? No way. No one in this small community locks the door. There it is again. Definitely the doorbell. She takes the stairs down two at a time and yanks open the door to find their neighbor, Brian, in full uniform, standing in the front porch.

"What's happened, Brian?" Lizbeth takes in the police cruiser in the driveway. Her heart speeds up, beating a tempo of Oh my God. . . . Oh my God. . . . Oh my God. . . .

"May I come in?"

"Yes, of course." She steps aside, waving him toward the living room, closing the door. Her mind an iceberg of fear, her body moves on automatic pilot as she follows him into the living room.

"Please sit down, Liz."

Lizbeth lowers herself on the couch by the fireplace, sinking into the overly soft cushions. She escapes momentarily from whatever is coming.

"I really should get these cushions re-stuffed."

Tension thrums through her body. She laces her fingers, nails digging into the back of her hands, forming half-moon indentations. She waits.

Warwicki takes a seat in Dan's favorite wing-backed chair, his lips set in a grim line.

"I've got some hard news, Liz. Please hear me out. Then I'll answer your questions." Brian clears his throat. "Dan was in a terrible wreck on Highway 20. His injuries were profound." Warwicki's eyes hold Lizbeth's prisoner. "In spite of Fire and Rescue's best efforts, Dan died at the scene."

His words shoot into her heart with paralyzing pain.

"No," she says. Then, "No, no, no . . . that can't be true." She begins rocking back and forth like a religious student at prayers, closing her world off from everything. A low keening escapes her lips.

Brian's firm hand on her forearm brings her back.

"Look at me, Liz. I'm so sorry. Dan was my friend and a wonderful guy." Brian threads his fingers through Lizbeth's to get her attention. "I want someone to sit with you. Who shall I call?"

"No, no, no . . . Take me to Dan. I need to see him!" Her heart is beating like it's going to explode out of her chest. Lizbeth jumps up, searching the room with wild eyes. "Where's my purse?"

Brian stands, gently wraps his hands around her upper arms, and draws them both back down onto the couch.

"I hate to have to tell you this, but . . . state law requires an autopsy be performed after a fatal wreck. Dan's body has been taken to the Levitz Funeral Home. It will be several days before the pathologist files a report with the county coroner. Then Dan's body will be released to you. There is no way you can see him tonight."

"PLEASE, Brian. I need to see my husband."

"I'm sorry, Liz. That's not possible."

Lizbeth pinches her eyes closed, willing herself to another planet or at least back to yesterday so she can create an alternate reality to this one.

She feels Brian's arm tighten around her shoulders, bringing her back.

"I need to hear it all, Brian. Tell me everything." Her eyes search Brian's deep blue ones as she squares her shoulders.

"Are you sure, Liz?"

"Tell me, Brian," she whispers with an exhale.

"No one actually saw the wreck. A citizen passed by shortly afterward and called nine one one. By chance, I was patrolling nearby. I was the first cop on the scene." Brian runs his hand over his hair. "Questions remain about how and why it happened. We'll do an investigation, of course. At this time, we estimate Dan was driving around seventy miles an hour in a forty-five-mile-an-hour zone, through those S curves near Anderson Lake Road."

Lizbeth gasps and slaps her hand over her mouth.

"What are you saying? Dan's not reckless. He loves that Mustang like a third child." Is she going to faint? She never faints.

"I agree."

Brian stops for a moment. She notices him notice her hands, white and bloodless, gripping the couch cushion on either side of her knees. She swallows hard, trying to stay calm.

"Tell me the rest, Brian."

"Are you sure you?"

"Yes"

"I found Dan unconscious at the scene. His car had run up a bank, flipped over and skidded on its roof. His seat belt held him suspended upside down. I want you to know we believe Dan lost consciousness as his Mustang hit the rocky bank."

"This can't be real!" Lizbeth stares into Brian's face, willing him to agree.

"Lizbeth, listen to me. I can't stay long, but I won't leave you alone. Who can I call to be with you?"

"My cousin Charlotte," Lizbeth chokes out. "She's on speed dial on my cell." She swipes at tears streaming her cheeks. Her body begins to shake like a sapling in a Nor'wester.

"How soon can she get here?"

"I don't know." Lizbeth hiccups. "She lives in Greenville, South Carolina."

"You can call Charlotte later. Right now, let's get someone from the neighborhood."

"Oh my God . . . Josh and Robbie. What will I tell them?" Lizbeth is hyperventilating.

Brian takes her by the shoulders.

"Look at me, Liz. Where do you keep your paper bags?"

"In the pantry," she says, gulping air, pointing toward the kitchen.

He returns with a brown paper lunch bag, blows into it to expand it, covers Lizbeth's nose and mouth, and tells her to breathe deeply.

Minutes pass. Lizbeth drops the bag and stares at her neighbor.

"Please, let me wake up from this nightmare!" Her breathing is normal, but her body is shaking. Is she going into shock?

Brain grabs a crocheted throw from the arm of the couch and wraps it around Lizbeth's shoulders.

"I'm going to call Susan Munoz from down the block." They both know reliable Susan, the sixty-something neighbor and grandmother, known for her big-hearted community volunteerism.

Lizbeth hears Brian's low conversation with Susan as if it is coming through a tunnel. Susan arrives and takes Lizbeth into her arms. His hand on the door, Brian says, "You know where to find me if you need me," he salutes a wave as he slips out.

Susan holds Lizbeth on the couch until she has no tears left. Later, Lizbeth phones her sons and Charlotte.

Susan pours cups of herbal tea and stays until Josh and Robbie arrive in a borrowed car from college, two hours away.

CHAPTER THREE

Greenville, South Carolina, to Port Benton, Washington,
December 2009

C harlotte Gordon Beal books the first available flight from Greenville to Seattle. It's no surprise when Lizbeth volunteers Josh or Robbie to collect her at the airport.

"No way, darlin'. Keep your babies close to home now."

"Are you sure, Char?"

"Absolutely. I've reserved a Mercedes coupe. You know I'm particular about my ride."

Charlotte has made the sixty-plus-mile drive from the Seattle-Tacoma International Airport to the Olympic Peninsula before and is prepared for the trek. After the Hood Canal Bridge, the scenery gets very rural very fast. Skyscraper-size Douglas firs line the two-lane highway, while peekaboo views across small organic vegetable fields and livestock pastures show off the rugged snowcapped Olympic mountains in the distance.

The locals don't bother with much road signage, Charlotte recalls. Selling ice cream and beer to confused tourists who wander country roads with spotty cell phone coverage is good for the rural economy. That may have been fine on her last trip west, but Charlotte is in no mood to waste time when one of her favorite people in the world is in crisis. Her rental car comes with a high-end GPS.

The two cousins have been as close as sisters since Charlotte can remember. People who see them together take them for siblings; both are taller than average, have wavy, ginger hair that frizzes when it's humid, fair skin that freckles in the sun, and the Scottish Gordon nose.

Navigating the back roads, Charlotte ruminates on how, as a kid, her cousin was feisty, all-in for causes, fighting injustice—until that nasty event her last year at college got Lizbeth sidestepping confrontation. Even so, with her history of gumption, Charlotte believes her cousin can step up when she needs to.

Charlotte can't resist a smile remembering the year Lizbeth's parents took a sabbatical to London and hired a graduate student to stay with their twelve-year-old daughter. A week after they left, the student's video-game-addicted, cigarette-smoking boyfriend moved in. Incensed, Lizbeth used her babysitting money to buy a bus ticket to Charleston, two hundred miles away. Lizbeth walked from the bus station, carrying two suitcases, and surprised Charlotte's family sitting at dinner. She refused to return to Neely until her parents were back in South Carolina. Fortunately, Charlotte's room had twin beds.

Using razor sharp observation and empathetic hugs, Lizbeth has always been a loyal friend. In high school, Charlotte fell in with a fast crowd and partied with guys she met in the afternoons, drinking beer on the beach. Lizbeth knew why—Charlotte was in agony watching her father's vitality eaten up by cancer—Lizbeth dogged Charlotte until she came clean.

Years later, Lizbeth was the first one Charlotte trusted to tell she'd joined the fellowship of Alcoholics Anonymous.

Charlotte has lessons learned during fifteen years of sobriety, like keeping mum, at least initially, when the people she loves aren't thinking straight. Dan's death in a strange accident has Charlotte's mind hopping. The last time Charlotte saw Lizbeth's husband, he seemed oddly distracted, off kilter, and moody.

But on the phone yesterday, her cousin had called Dan "my forever one and only." Charlotte suspects Lizbeth's intuition is away with the fairies on the subject of Dan Keller. Approaching the first traffic light in thirty miles, Charlotte slows the Mercedes. Even in the short, dark days of December, the Victorian-era town overlooking Benton Bay is a rare jewel in the Pacific Northwest.

A year and a half ago, she and her daughter, Penny, celebrated Josh and Robbie's high school graduation with the Keller-Gordon family. One afternoon, they took an Old Town tour guided by a barrel-chested man with a nineteenth-century handlebar mustache. He regaled them with tales of his great-grandfather, an infamous tavern owner in the city's heyday as the prosperous customs Port of Entry for Washington Territory. He'd twirled his waxed mustache and told of the rough waterfront, where men were shanghaied and women walking alone could be kidnapped into slavery. To show how the city's gentry lived, they strolled past logging barons' Victorian mansions with breathtaking views of the bay.

He went on to tell the group how the good life ended in 1889 when Seattle won the bid for the Transcontinental Railroad's Northwest terminus. After that economic blow, Port Benton limped along with a small paper mill and a modest commercial fishing fleet until the 1970s. The guide had described how nature lovers, hippies, and boatbuilders restored dilapidated Victorian buildings into bed-and-breakfast hotels and small businesses. Port Benton embraced the arts; tourists swarm the waterfront galleries and parks during the summer months, filling the coffers of entrepreneurs.

When Lizbeth and Dan fell in love with the small town and found careers to sustain them close to nature, it didn't surprise Charlotte. But Lord have mercy, the climate is nasty, rainy, and cold October to June, and the water temperature still in the mid-fifties in August! Ugh. And at this time of year low, gray clouds kiss the bay and days are so short one wonders if full daylight will ever arrive. Charlotte shakes her head to throw off the worry bug. In addition to grieving Dan, Lizbeth needs to pull up her big girl panties, and sort out her feelings about being Southern. Otherwise, her dear cousin will stay stuck . . . belonging where?

As Charlotte makes the last turns into Lizbeth and Dan's neighborhood, she finalizes her strategy to entice her cousin to Folly Island, to the Low Country Carolina cottage on twelve-foot stilts their grandparents had built with a wide, screened-in porch facing the sea. Weathered by decades of storm surges and hurricanes, permeated by salt air so thick you can almost chew it, the place survives. It's Charlotte's vacation home now.

CHAPTER FOUR

Port Benton, Washington, December 2009

Charlotte parks and ambles up the walkway, knocks once, and opens the door.

"Hallooo, Lizard!"

Lizbeth is sitting cross-legged on the couch, her laptop open on the coffee table, and staring at nothing. She tries on a smile, fails, and opens her arms. Charlotte slides in close. They hug long and deep, finally releasing each other to scrub away their tears.

"I just got off the phone with Dan's parents." Lizbeth rolls her wide, red-rimmed hazel eyes and squints at her cell phone on the table like it's a poisonous snake. "They want to come immediately to 'help plan' the funeral. Meaning, they want to take over. Control freaks!" She spits through clenched teeth, her voice low, so the twins in the kitchen won't overhear.

"Howard and Lillian are devastated, of course. Their beloved one and only could do no wrong. Me, not so much as you know." Lizbeth gives her cousin a crooked smile and shrugs. "I've been the difficult daughter-in-law since the day I announced I was keeping my Gordon surname."

Lizbeth stares at the graphic swirls on the offending computer screen in sleep mode, willing it to type out instructions on dealing with conservative in-laws. A tear rolls down her cheek. "I've put them off a few days, but I've got to book them a hotel soon or they'll show up here and I'll be on a cot in the den."

"Leave it to me, cuz."

"I'm a zombie, Char, like in the TV show *The Walking Dead.*" She sniffs and grabs a tissue from the box on the coffee table.

Charlotte squeezes her cousin's hand.

"I bet there's a hole in this couch in the shape of my butt, after two days sitting in the same spot. People call with sympathy, but you know the small-town thing: We care . . . and we want to know everything." She hugs her stomach.

"Are you hungry?" Char asks gently.

Liz looks blank. "I haven't been able to eat." She shakes her head, returning to the hazards of small-town life. "The gossips would devour me whole if they could."

"Uh-huh. You gotta take some space for yourself, darlin'."

"If I can't take care of myself, how can I help my boys?"

Charlotte smooths unwashed bangs from Lizbeth's forehead, taking in her cousin's rumpled clothing and the purple half-moons under her eyes.

"Darlin', it looks like you need care-taking, big time."

Lizbeth's cell rings. Charlotte grabs it and answers, "Keller-Gordon residence, how may I help you?" With the phone tucked between her shoulder and ear, Charlotte wiggles her fingers at Lizbeth's protest while rummaging in her voluminous shoulder bag for something to write on and a pen.

"She's not available right now. I'm her cousin Charlotte from Greenville, South Carolina, here to help out. As you can imagine, the family's plenty busy. Yes, indeed, I'm taking your name and number as we speak. Rest assured the family will get your message."

After Char hangs up, Lizbeth glances at the name on the pad and pulls a face. Another vulture. "Oh, God. Patty Peterson."

"Lizard, my dear," Charlotte continues, "I am taking over as your personal secretary, starting now. Leave the well-meaning friends, casserole queens, and curiosity seekers to me. I promise to keep a list of every little thing that can wait and grab you for the important stuff that can't. Meanwhile, you are in serious need of some beauty rest, so you can do what you need to do. Trust me."

Lizbeth meets her cousin's gaze. "I do, Char. Thanks."

Charlotte gives Lizbeth another once-over. "That outfit you're sporting is way past its due date, darlin'." She rummages in her bag again and plucks out a bottle of lavender shower gel. "Take this upstairs and don't come back until you are a new woman." Lizbeth hugs her cousin hard and walks to the stairs, gripping the railing as she ascends. Her limbs feel like the toy clown with spring legs her boys loved when they were toddlers.

The voice of an excited sportscaster draws Charlotte to the kitchen, where Robbie and Josh, shoulder to shoulder, are watching football replays on a laptop.

After a long group hug, Charlotte looks up into their sad, handsome faces.

"College must be good for you boys. Y'all have grown two inches since Penny and I were out here last year. So, who's taller?"

Josh smiles. "Me, by an inch. And he's my older brother by twenty minutes."

"But I'm better-looking," says Robbie with a leer.

"You are both drop-dead gorgeous." Secretly Charlotte agrees with Robbie. It's hard to tell the twins apart from across the room, but up close, Robbie's eyes are robin egg blue while Josh's are gray. And Robbie has that engaging little gap between his two front teeth, real chick-magnet appeal. Charlotte notices Robbie's hand in a bowl of granola and gives him the stink eye. "That your dinner?"

"Guess so."

Dishes are piled in the sink and the untouched pan of some kind of fruit dessert sits on the counter. Charlotte opens the fridge and spots a lasagna casserole. She admonishes tongue-in-cheek, "You've got food, boys!"

"Susan from down the street brought it by a while ago. She offered to stay and straighten up, but we sent her away." Robbie shrugs. "We don't want anyone except family around right now."

Josh nods. "Yeah. When I was out this morning, people in line at the post office stared. It sucks. They kept sneaking looks but I was glad when they didn't say anything." Charlotte could almost see his teeth clench as a muscle worked along his jaw. "I want to be left alone. Just us family, and a maybe a couple friends who won't ask twenty questions."

Later, Liz drifts downstairs, dressed in fresh sweats and trailing a scent of lavender.

"OK, confession time," Charlotte announces. "I brought proper sustenance from home. And I stopped at Safeway for what I couldn't haul on the plane. All y'all gotta eat some Southern comfort food, whether you think you're hungry or not."

She goes out to her Mercedes and returns with groceries in a blue cooler bag. They all talk about nothing while Charlotte fries up bacon, simmers grits, grates cheddar, and flips eggs over easy. Lizbeth eats her first real meal in two days and smiles while Josh and Robbie vacuum their plates clean like they haven't seen food in a week.

After dinner, Charlotte digs melatonin gummies out of her tote bag and insists Lizbeth take two before she tucks her into bed.

One of the twins' high school buddies stops by. The boys retreat to watch a movie, relieved to sidestep the subject of their father for the evening.

In the morning, Charlotte fries up leftover grits with cheese, a meal the boys make fun of until they dig in. Lizbeth lugs all the family albums into the living room. They spend the day retelling family camping stories and Carolina beach adventures, laughing and crying while Josh and Robbie pick favorite pictures of their father for a memorial video they will set to his favorite music.

Late in the afternoon, Charlotte jumps off the sofa in time to grab her cousin's phone before it goes to voice mail. It's the coroner. Josh and Robbie have wandered into the kitchen for a snack, so she signals Lizbeth over with a wave and hits the speaker-phone button.

"I'm sorry for your loss, Ms. Gordon," the coroner says. "I understand your husband was well respected in our community. I wanted you to know as soon as possible that the pathologist's report is in and I've accepted it."

"What killed Dan?" Lizbeth whispers so softly Charlotte has to repeat the sentence to the coroner.

"The report states Dan Keller's death was caused by head trauma and internal injuries. His driving was not impaired by blood alcohol content above the legal limit."

Lizbeth looks at her cousin like a deer frozen in oncoming car headlights. Charlotte jumps in, "Thank you for letting us know, sir."

"I've released your husband's body. You're free to contact the funeral home and make decisions about the remains."

Lizbeth blurts, "I don't understand. What caused the wreck if he wasn't drunk?" She slaps her hand across her mouth, then withdraws it. "Oh, my God! I didn't mean it that way. Dan was not a drunk. Please tell me what more you know." She starts to shake and feels Charlotte pull her to sit on the couch.

"Contributing factors to the cause of your husband's wreck are inconclusive. The report revealed Mr. Keller had a stomach ulcer. It is possible acute pain could have caused poor judgment."

"Thank you for letting us know, sir," Charlotte says again, and disconnects.

"I had no idea Dan had an ulcer." Lizbeth pushes herself to a wobbly stand. "What else don't I know?"

Charlotte puts her arm around her cousin's shoulder. "Steady now, girl."

"I need to see Dan now! I won't believe I'm not stuck in a sick dream until I see him." Lizbeth starts hyperventilating and melts back down on the sofa. Charlotte goes to the pantry for a paper bag.

∞

When the panic attack passes, Lizbeth calls the funeral home.

"You're welcome to come this afternoon, Mrs. Keller," the funeral home director's carefully modulated voice oozes.

Lizbeth hisses through gritted teeth, "My name is Ms. Lizbeth Gordon, not Mrs. Keller, and I'm coming to see my husband now."

The funeral director ushers the cousins into a well-appointed room with overstuffed mauve leather furniture. "Sit for a moment and we'll go through to the viewing when you are ready." He hands them Styrofoam cups of herbal tea from a carafe on the sideboard. Lizbeth takes a sip, puts the cup down, and stands. Between the muted lighting, the soft music, and her mood, she feels like an actor in the old television show "The Twilight Zone."

"I want to see my husband now."

"Please know, it will be most unsettling, madam. Mr. Keller's body sustained grave trauma. In addition, there are disfiguring surgical incisions from the autopsy."

He guides them through a side door, down a long hall, and into a chilly room that smells vaguely antiseptic. Odd-looking, stainless-steel equipment of undeterminable function hangs on wall hooks and a large industrial sink spans the far side of the room.

The funeral director crosses to a draped gurney in the center of the room and reverently uncovers Dan's head, neck, and shoulders. Charlotte wraps an arm tight around Lizbeth's waist, keeping her steady as they move toward the gurney.

"Oh, Dan," Lizbeth whispers as she touches his cold, stiff cheek. She turns to Charlotte and continues with a weak smile. "He would hate for anyone to see him like this. Even me. I always teased him that looking good mattered too much."

Charlotte squeezes her waist in response.

Lizbeth's attempt at levity evaporates as she stares at Dan's body for a minute that seems like an eternity. She goes white, pivots, and flees back down the hall and out of the building. She barely makes it to the parking lot before throwing up.

∽

Josh and Robbie insist they want their father's memorial service as soon as possible.

"It's awful around the house without Dad," Josh says. "Everything I do, everywhere I look, he's here." A muscle jerks in Josh's jaw exactly like Dan's used to when he was stressed.

Eyes full, Robbie agrees. "My friends at school will be there for me in January. Josh and I have each other. It'll be easier not to think about Dad twenty-four seven with winter quarter classes to focus on." Lizbeth gives them a small smile. "OK. You win." She pinches her thigh hard under the table to keep from uttering the bitter words she's thinking: You'll be together at Western Washington University, and I'll be alone here in Port Benton, trying to remake my life.

⁓

Meanwhile, Dan's parents, the Reverend Howard Keller and his wife Lillian, press for a "proper funeral" at the First Methodist Church where they worship on visits to Port Benton. The twins counter by renting a room for a memorial at the Hurricane Ridge Visitor's Center, a favorite family jump-off spot for hikes in the Olympic National Forest.

With her heart pounding over escalating conflict, Lizbeth uses every trick in her counseling playbook to facilitate a compromise. They settle on a "celebration of life" at the chapel at Blakely Park, land that was an early twentieth-century US Army fort built to protect Puget Sound. The park's forest trails and beaches are steeped in Gordon-Keller memories, and the chapel meets the senior Kellers' demands for propriety. They all agree the choice would please Dan.

Two weeks to the day after Dan's death, friends and family pack the chapel to standing room only. There isn't a dry eye during Robbie and Josh's video slideshow of their father's life, the images set to music with infinite care. Howard's homily on Christian charity is perfect way to honor his son's annual leadership in the Habitat for Humanity fund drive. Neighbors tell stories of friendship and Dan's devotion to coaching Little League baseball.

Lizbeth cherishes her spot between her sons, each holding tight to one of her hands. Still, on and off, she feels like she is floating, out-of-body, an observer rather than a participant at her husband's memorial.

After the service, friends arrive at the Keller-Gordon home for a potluck. By the time the last mourners are waved off into the evening, Lizbeth has a splitting headache. All she wants is to get into bed and pull the covers over her head for a week. Or a month.

Before she can climb the stairs, Charlotte pulls her aside.

"I didn't want to mention this until we were alone. Some woman named Janet Lee from First Olympic Bank left you a voicemail while we were at the chapel. Apparently, Dan's missed two payments on your line of credit. December's payment is due the thirtieth. She wants to talk to you ASAP."

Lizbeth stares at her cousin. "That's crazy. We don't owe money on our line of credit!" Her voice sinks to a whisper as she continues, "Dan insisted we get one last year, in case the boys had an emergency, but we've never used it."

Charlotte takes Lizbeth by the shoulders and holds her gaze. "Apparently Dan did."

CHAPTER FIVE

In the morning, Lizbeth and Charlotte sit in the Mercedes outside The First Olympic Bank. An employee unlocks the front entrance and disappears back inside.

Lizbeth gets out of the car, slamming the door. Charlotte hustles to catch up as they pass through the double doors and pause at the teller's counter. Lizbeth cuts the young woman's cheery greeting off before she can get a full sentence out. "I need to talk to Ms. Lee."

The teller, too surprised to push back, points to the rear of the room, where a well-fed thirty-something woman, garbed in an expertly tailored navy blue pantsuit, sits glued to the monitor on her desk.

"Ooooh my, my," Charlotte says under her breath. "No one dresses like that in this little town. That woman must be on the corporate climb."

"Hush," Lizbeth whispers as they cross the well-appointed room.

Taken aback at being approached without warning, Ms. Lee rises. "Do you have an appointment?"

"I'm Lizbeth Gordon, Dan Keller's wife."

Ms. Lee switches seamlessly to a saccharine smile.

"Please be seated." They all sit. The banker's face reflects both sympathy and satisfaction as she holds Lizbeth's gaze. "I'm terribly sorry about your husband. I understand he was a popular figure in this community." She gives the cousins another practiced corporate smile. "However, we do have a problem. Payment on your line of credit must be attended to." Ms. Lee pulls up a spreadsheet and angles the screen so Lizbeth and Charlotte, sitting on the other side of her desk, can view it together.

"Your line of credit has been maxed out for months," Ms. Lee says, with a look that reminds the cousins of an aggravated elementary school crossing guard. "Your husband made payments in a timely fashion until recently. Look here." Her finger hovers over the year's entries and the past-due column in red. "We sent your husband multiple notices. We need October, November, plus December's payment by month's end or your home will go into receivership. We don't want that to happen, do we?" Ms. Lee's lips curve in a smile that doesn't reach her eyes.

Lizbeth's heart is hammering so hard she's sure the bitch across from her can hear it.

"There must be some mistake!"

"It's all correct and well-documented, as you observe on the screen, Ms. Gordon. A complicating problem is that during the recession, we estimate your home's value dropped $150,000, perhaps more."

Ms. Lee shifts her gaze from the monitor and locks eyes with Lizbeth. "This is not a good time to get in arears on your line of credit. Your home is in a nice neighborhood. If you catch up on payments, given time, I believe your equity will return to its former valuation."

Lizbeth swallows multiple times to keep from heaving up breakfast on Ms. Lee's desk. To gain some modicum of control, she stares at the old-fashioned Regulator clock ticking on the wall. Heat begins at her neck and spreads to the roots of her hair as she uncrosses and recrosses her legs. Ms. Lee fiddles with a pen and leans back in her swivel chair.

Charlotte jumped in.

"Thank you, Ms. Lee. We're going home to discuss options and will get back to you in a couple of days."

Charlotte helps her cousin to her feet with a hand under Lizbeth's elbow. They exit the bank, into a frigid December morning drizzle. Charlotte drives aimlessly around town for an hour, windshield wipers slapping, while Lizbeth cries and curses and beats her fists on the dashboard until she's spent. When Charlotte finally pulls into the Keller-Gordon driveway. Lizbeth's car is gone. The twins are out.

"What am I going to say to Josh and Robbie? They love their father like some kind of superhero. And now this."

"Yeah, this is bad, cuz. Breathe. We'll figure something out."

"Go get a coffee in town, Char. I need to be alone for a while."

Lizbeth pushes the front door open and stalks directly to Dan's office. Rifling through the top desk drawer, she finds his address book. Its soft cover reminds her how she always teased Dan about being loyal to a leather-bound volume when the rest of his office was made up of the latest technology. Her mind races to their finances. What in hell was Dan was up to? He made a big deal out of crowing when he paid the Mustang off the end of last year. As far as she knew, they had no debt other than their mortgage.

Now she thinks back to those guys nights out, how Dan made dates to try out different casinos around the Olympic peninsula. That time Dan bought her diamond earrings with his winnings. She'd been flattered at the time. Good God, how could I have been so naive?

She phones her husband's two best friends. Dave doesn't pick up, but Sean does. She skips all the usual opening pleasantries. "Did Dan have a gambling problem?"

Sean hems and haws and finally confesses, "He might have."

"Talk to me." Lizbeth's grip on her phone is shaking. Her entire body is vibrating with horror. Before her knees cave, she plops into Dan's desk chair and holds the receiver steady with both hands.

"One night about a year ago, Dan, Dave, and I dropped too much cash at the casino and went home feeling lousy. We decided to set a budget for guys night out, so we wouldn't be stupid about egging each other on. After that, Dan seemed to lose interest in gambling with us. From hints he dropped, I gathered he was gaming alone so there'd be no questions about the size of his bets. I didn't challenge him, though I probably should have."

"Why didn't you say something to me?" Lizbeth shrieks. "We might have stopped him! You have no idea what he's done. I'm probably going to lose the house." Lizbeth slaps her hand to her mouth. Oh, Lordy. What have I said? This news could be all over town by dinnertime!

Sean starts to respond, but Lizbeth cuts him off, saying, "I've got to go." She doesn't pick up when he rings right back.

After her conversation with Sean, Lizbeth remembers Josh and Robbie's eighteenth birthday. Dan had been mysterious about a coming-of-age surprise at the celebratory family breakfast. As the three of them pulled out of the drive, Lizbeth waved, a smile covering her hurt at being excluded from a male-bonding adventure.

When they returned, Josh and Robbie were high on having won more than they lost gambling at Tall Cedars Casino. Lizbeth went bananas.

"How could you have chosen gambling as an initiation into adulthood?"

"It seemed like a good idea for some fun. Chill, Liz. It's not like I took them to a brothel. But yeah, I get your point." He seemed contrite at the time. To keep the peace in front of the boys, Lizbeth left the discussion at that.

What a clever guy her husband was! Lizbeth slammed her fist on the desk. She always trusted him with their finances, and why shouldn't she? He was the one with the MBA. They discussed money openly. They went over their joint tax return every year before signing it. He was never weird or secretive about what was on his computer in the home office. It never occurred to her Dan would use their home equity loan as his personal bank account.

As Lizbeth prints out a year's worth of family and business account statements, her mouth drops open and her hand goes to her heart when she finds a checking account in Dan's name only.

"Bank of America?" she shouts. "We bank at First Olympic! How dare he?" Big money flowed in and out of that Bank of America account, with the last statement balance of $42.70. Bile fills her throat.

Mind racing, she tallies the financial statements spit out from Dan's printer in black and white. Dan liquidated his SEP IRA last month. There's a couple thousand in their joint savings account and another thousand and change in their joint checking. Her final paycheck for 2009 will be direct deposited next week adding a few thousand more. The truth is, other than what's in their Olympic account, her only financial asset is a 401K with the school district. Her hands scrunch the papers into a fat ball. She was a sucker. Cool and collected, calm and sincere Dan discussed savings and retirement while siphoning their savings away for a year.

Rage rises from her belly into her throat. Like a fire-breathing dragon, she blasts out a scream. "You betrayed us!"

Lizbeth lifts Dan's iMac off the desk and slings it against the wall, raising her fist in a silent "YES!" when it crashes into a shadow box full of his half-marathon medals. That shadow box was her Christmas present to Dan two years ago. He loved that thing.

She's a tornado in a disaster movie, twisting through Dan's office, systematically smashing his treasures: the desk lamp with a handmade shade by a local artist, an award from the Rotary Club, a S'Klallam mug from a tribal gift shop, on and on, until the room is thoroughly trashed.

Momentarily elated, she marches out of Dan's office, slamming the door. A few minutes later it occurs to her that there's one more mess she's got to clean up.

With Charlotte by her side, Lizbeth explains Dan's gaming debt to Josh and Robbie.

"We're ruined." Telling the boys is like running a wire brush over an open wound. "Thanks to your Dad our credit is in the toilet. You two will have to help finance college with loans next year." When she sees the shock and disbelief on their faces, she wishes she'd used a softer tone.

Josh pushes back. "You've gotta be reading it wrong, Mom. There must be some mistake. It can't be that bad."

Robbie jumps in. "Yeah, we know Dad loved poker and pai gow at the Casino, but he wasn't stupid!"

Lizbeth wrestles with empathy for her sons and tries to smooth the waters. "I'll figure something out," she says. Twisting her wedding ring round and round her finger, she stifles the urge to say, how dare you accuse me of not knowing what I'm talking about?

On top of everything, two days before Christmas, Charlotte gets a call from Greenville. Her seventy-five-year-old mother tripped over her beloved Scottie dog and broke her ankle. Charlotte books the next flight home.

The cousins hug hard in the driveway. "Take the bereavement leave you have coming, darlin'. When the boys go back to college, rent your house for a couple of months. Rest up at the cottage. Mama's old Volvo is there; you'll have wheels. I'll drive down to visit soon as I can."

"Thanks for everything, Char." Lizbeth wipes her eyes. "You're right, I need to get away and think. Questions about Dan are ghosting through Port Benton like ground fog." Lizbeth feels crazy with grief and rage she cannot answer or explain. "Thankfully the boys can avoid the whispers and curious looks once they're back at college."

"Come to Folly and walk the winter beach."

Charlotte blows kisses through the Mercedes window as she drives away.

Lizbeth and the twins order take-out pizza for Christmas dinner. Tightly wound as springs, they watch movies, avoiding conversations about Dan's debt and what happens next.

⁊

As a high school counselor with fifteen years of experience, Lizbeth knows the conventional wisdom; one should not make large life changes for a year after the death of a loved one. But this is not a conventional death, and she is not the conventional wife who will be working through conventional bereavement. Every time she leaves the house, she feels empathy and veiled curiosity from a friend or a sly look from a neighbor as she gets into her car. Who knows what, and who's spilling her dead husband's secrets?

On December 26, while Josh and Robbie are visiting friends, Lizbeth cashes out her school district 401K to pay off enough of their line of credit to stave off repossession. She has enough left to pay off the twin's tuition through June. She suspects Dan's parents may step up to help with college tuition next year. Dan was Howard and Lillian's joyous surprise, born to a childless couple at midlife. They cherish Josh and Robbie.

Lizbeth calls the family accountant, telling him to prepare the dissolution of Dan's business. It's a relief when he responds, "Dan was proactive about setting aside quarterly taxes for 2009."

Blood pounds in her forehead. Bastard. He let gambling bankrupt his family but didn't touch his precious business reputation.

The accountant asks a few clarifying questions. Lizbeth keeps the conversation short. "Send the necessary paperwork right away, I'll sign and return it. I'm leaving Port Benton."

Lizbeth disconnects before he could squeeze in another question. She purses her lips so tight between her teeth she tastes blood. Jeeze Louise, why did she tell the accountant she's leaving?

Lizbeth calls a Realtor whose son played baseball with Josh and Robbie. She wants her house listed for sale the first week in January. Twinges of guilt hound her; Josh and Robbie will have just a few days to choose things they want from the house before they leave for winter quarter. But she doesn't waver. She can't wait. She's outta here. Lizbeth collects clean boxes from the grocery store and piles favorite books, pictures, and photo albums into a heap on her bedroom floor. She selects a few Gordon family antiques she won't part with and schedules a handyman who will haul everything they want stored to a heated commercial unit south of town.

That leaves wrapping up things at the high school. Lizbeth lets herself into the cold building, admonishing herself for not wearing her down jacket. The furnace is always set just warm enough to keep the pipes from freezing during winter break. Biting the inside of her cheek to stay dry-eyed, she cleans out her desk, stuffing a few mementos into an old gym bag. She checks her mailbox in the office and sorts a pile of continuing education flyers, dropping all but one in the recycle bin. Years ago, she signed up for newsletters from *The International School Educator* to keep abreast of overseas teaching opportunities. She and Dan used to spend hours dreaming up international adventures to take after their sons finished high school. His recent disinterest in travel or a sabbatical overseas . . . another red flag she'd missed.

Who says I can't go international alone?

She fills out the application using the Folly Island cottage as her home address and slips it into the school office outgoing mail. Relieved the high school is a ghost village until January fifth, Lizbeth places her written resignation on the principal's desk. A tear rolls down her cheek remembering how happy she'd been as the counselor at Port Benton High.

Her next stop is the Department of Motor Vehicles, where Lizbeth transfers ownership of her SUV to Josh and Robbie. The vehicle is six years old, but the tires were replaced in September. The twins will have to figure out gas and expenses.

∽

On January third, Lizbeth helps her sons load the SUV for their drive to Western Washington University. She sets their favorite grinder sandwiches, homemade oatmeal cookies, and a thermos of sweetened coffee on the floor of the passenger seat. All eyes are moist in their traditional group hug before Josh and Robbie get in the SUV. Lizbeth stands in the street, stone-faced, watching her car round the corner.

Her life has imploded.

She turns on her heels, striding back into the house to pack. She's booked a one-way flight to Charleston the day after tomorrow.

CHAPTER SIX

Folly Island, South Carolina, January 2010

After two flights, ten hours, and twenty-nine-hundred-mile journey from Seattle to Charleston, a milk run bus to Folly Island is unthinkable. Lizbeth flags a taxi for the twenty-mile trip to the beach.

The driver, replete with tats and retro sneakers, could double for a millennial in the Pacific Northwest until he opens his mouth.

"Beautiful afternoon, ma'am." He lifts her bags into the trunk and holds the door as she settles into the back seat. "Where to, ma'am?"

"Folly Beach, East Arctic Avenue, please." At the word "beach," tension from cross-country travel slips from her shoulders.

I'm back.

Where neighbors won't look baffled when they hear my Southern expressions.

Where folks really mean it when they say, "come on over."

Where family storytelling is an art you learn at your grandmama's knee.

Where you can serve fried chicken without a lecture about lipid content.

ᐤᕒᐤ

On Interstate 526, Lizbeth watches North Charleston's industrial buildings slide by. She twists side-to-side, releasing kinks in her back, pleased the taxi has generous elbow room. There's been a construction boom in the four years since she was last in the Low Country. She's heard people complain that strip malls and multistory apartment sprawl destroy the environment. Much as she loves the marshland, good wages in manufacturing, services at the expanded airport, and tourism in Charleston County have helped thousands of people of all ethnicities rise up a notch or two. Before her thoughts get dwelling on equality in the South, she swaps them for reminiscing about childhood road trips to the beach.

In the seventies and eighties, her family drove this very route to Folly Island. Back then, it was a one-lane, potholed highway, lined with rundown single-wides and shacks with rusting corrugated roofs sprinkled among small farms. They'd pass Black folks and White folks tending vegetables, picking sea island cotton, or sitting in the shade of a loblolly pine. Country people got a bad rap in those days, and some still do. Yankees driving through the South in air-conditioned cocoons cast aspersions on "dumb crackers" and "lazy Blacks," who move slowly, pacing themselves in the heat and dripping humidity.

Lizbeth gets why folks feel nostalgic about the roadside stands offering sweet potatoes, okra, cucumbers, watermelons, and honey. Her daddy always pulled over so they could buy some of what was on offer. If no one was tending the stand, there'd be a cardboard box with a slit in the top for your money. Her parents used to say roadside stands were the only way some rural folk got cash to buy things they couldn't grow or make. With new prosperity expanding beyond Charleston, that level of poverty—as well as the vegetable stands—are rare on this stretch of four-lane highway.

The taxi heads south on the Savannah highway, then south again onto State Route 171, over the Stono River onto James Island, and southeast towards Folly Island. The land is sandy, flat as a pancake, and dotted with cherry laurel, mimosa, oleander, and palmetto. They pass a sign directing people to the hurricane escape route headed in the other direction. Crossing the Folly River, Lizbeth rolls down her window. She sucks in the salt air like a hunting dog in the back of a pickup.

The afternoon is balmy for early January. Probably near sixty. Lizbeth grins like a goofy kid, admiring the familiar web of inlets winding through spartina grass bending ever so slightly in the breeze as they cross the bridge onto the island.

Lizbeth is reminded of a continuing education class she took last summer. The teacher used guided imagery to help participants revisit meaningful places in their lives. At the end, they all shared their "Heart's Home," a place where belonging runs deep.

Liz told the group about Folly Island.

ↄ

Folly Island: 18.9 square miles, twelve and a half of which is land, the rest marsh and inlets. Folly Beach. Nickname, "The Edge of America." Latitude 32.655N, longitude 79.440W. Sixteen feet above sea level. Home to loggerhead turtles, bottlenose dolphins, sand sharks, brown shrimp, white shrimp, blue crab, sand fiddler crabs, oysters, lettered olive, starfish, sea urchins, whelks, auger snails, cockles, sand dollars, angelwings, and scallops.

Home to brown pelicans, cormorants, black skimmers, egrets, and lots of gulls: the laughing gull, the herring gull, the ring-billed gull. Also, the great blue heron, osprey, oystercatcher, and sanderling.

Home to bats, opossums, raccoons, squirrels, and skunks.

Home to dragonflies, honeybees, mosquitos, wasps, chiggers, and the "palmetto bug," a genteel moniker for a flying cockroach that grows to more than two inches long.

Folly Island. Home to 2,617 men, women, and children.

ↄ

The taxi driver parks on the mix of sand and gravel at the cottage. He pops the trunk and muscles her bags up the stairs to the outside porch. Lizbeth gives him a tip and waves as he drives off before she lets herself in with the key always kept under a flowerpot full of shells.

The cottage hasn't changed much since she was a child. Two nods to the twenty-first century are a flat-screen TV and the new gas fireplace, where the free-standing woodstove used to be.

Old magazines are stacked on the shelf below the glass-topped coffee table. The long, low bookshelf sports lore on Carolina Sea life and well-thumbed pulpy beach reads. The furniture is heavy wicker of a quality that can't be found anymore. Her nose wrinkles at a mild musty smell in what people now call "the great room." Lizbeth moves to the windows facing the sea. She cranks open the wide, salt-encrusted, louvered glass to hear the surf pounding on the beach. She breathes deeply, content for the first time in weeks.

⁓

Lizbeth hasn't slept through the night since Dan died and knows even the best makeup can't hide her bedraggled face that looks like something the cat dragged in, as Grandmama used to say. But the first night at the cottage she sleeps until sunshine through an east-facing window wakes her midmorning.

⁓

The rest of the month of January passes in a fog.

She sleeps. She walks the beach. She spends hours watching surfers in their winter wetsuits catching waves near the city pier. She sleeps some more.

She wanders the county park at the south end of the island at low tide, listening to the bottlenose dolphins exhale as they surface. She sleeps some more.

She collects shells on mornings after storms have moved the sand around. She sleeps some more.

She walks to Ken's Market and buys only the bare necessities because she doesn't care what she eats. All she wants to do is sleep.

She texts and calls Josh and Robbie. Their responses are various versions of "we're doing OK, Mom." She wants to believe them, but their telephone voices lack the old, easy banter.

She gets email updates from her Realtor in Port Benton. There's a buyer interested in her house. They've made an offer. She makes a counteroffer. Then she sleeps some more.

She writes letters laden with outrage and expletives to Dan and reads them aloud, as if she can connect with his consciousness in the energy field of heaven or whatever is out there. Afterwards she shreds the letters into teeny, tiny pieces and burns them in the heavy glass ashtray that sits on a wicker table near the porch door. Then she sleeps.

Some evenings she drinks too much wine after an hours-long weeping jag.

She forgets stuff. She remembers stuff.

And then she sleeps some more.

CHAPTER SEVEN

The first weekend in February, Charlotte drives down from Greenville. She clomps up the cypress steps in the gloaming, opens the door with her backside, unloads a bag of groceries and early daffodils by the sink.

Lizbeth is prone on the couch, playing possum with a magazine face-down on her chest.

"Uppy, uppy!" Charlotte chirps their grandmama's favorite wake-up call. Lizbeth rubs her eyes and sits up as her cousin takes in the condition of the cottage.

"Good God, Lizard! When did the hurricane blow through? What've you been doin'?"

"Sleeping."

"So I see!"

Lizbeth pulls a face and rolls her shoulders. "I haven't felt like doing much of anything, Char."

"You thought gettin' through this would be easy?" Charlotte, hands on her hips, gives her cousin a squint-eyed look.

"Well, not exactly." Lizbeth looks for sympathy. Seeing none, she takes another tack. "I check caller ID before answering the phone to avoid the ninnies in Port Benton gossiping about me, the widow that skipped town without a trace leaving an ugly scandal to smolder."

Lizbeth gets up and paces, raising a finger on her right hand to note each point she makes.

"Here's an alternate vision for my current life. The *Sounding News* outs Dan as a sweet-talking gambling addict. I get a medal from the mayor for saving me and the twins from bankruptcy. My heroine action gets picked up by the *New York Times*, resulting in a fabulous job offer with international travel. How 'bout that!"

Lizbeth stops moving and faces her cousin with a raised eyebrow.

"What if Josh and Robbie saw the error of their ways, apologized for crushing my feelings, and crowned me the best mom ever. How's that?"

"What kinda Kool-Aid have you been drinkin', girl?"

"Only the sugar-free kind."

Charlotte shakes her head like she's admonishing a six-year-old. Liz plunks back down on the couch.

"You need some serious attitude adjustment, Lizard. Lucky you: I'm here to love you up and kick your booty." Charlotte pops the top on an alcohol-free beer.

"You've had a month to sit and stew on 'those things over which you have no control.' Too much cookin' on tragedy will simmer you right down into glue."

Charlotte tosses a newspaper into Lizbeth's lap.

"I picked up today's *Post and Courier* along with fresh redfish at Crosby's on my way across the island. While I fry us up some supper, check out what's goin' on in the 'Holy City' and we'll be tourists all weekend."

Lizbeth rolls her eyes, smooths out the paper on the coffee table in front of her. "I love you, too, Char." Restless, she walks to the window facing the Atlantic, avoiding the newspaper and plans of any kind for a few minutes. Sandpipers are scrambling along the shore hunting bugs. It's a beautiful dusk with high clouds streaked with orange and purple.

"How dare nature be so beautiful, when my life is in the shitter?"

Charlotte pauses her rooting in the kitchen cupboards for the ancient cast-iron frying pan. "Let's lighten up—get some music goin'."

She turns on the kitchen radio and fiddles with the dial until she finds Bonnie Raitt's "Thing Called Love," dances over to Lizbeth, and puts an arm across her cousin's shoulders. They join Bonnie full voice for the refrain. Country songs buoy the mood while Charlotte cooks and Lizbeth wanders around picking up clothes and other detritus, redistributing things where they belong, and setting the table.

After a dinner of comfort food, they keep it light for a while, catching up on news about their children. Penny is on fire, majoring in journalism at the University of South Carolina. Lizbeth talks about Josh and Robbie's classes at Western.

The evening has turned chilly. Charlotte gets up to close the cottage door that opens onto the oceanfront. She grabs a sweater off the back of a chair.

"I'm blessed that the real estate market is waking from the recession. A BMW might be in the budget for 2010. I'm grateful for my life, Lizard."

"You've earned it, Char." Lizbeth realizes with a pang of regret she hasn't checked in with her aunt since she arrived on the island. "How's Aunt Sarah's ankle healing?"

"Mama's doing great. Her brain is sharp as ever, but that fall before Christmas proves her balance isn't. Let's us hunt up a fancy carved walking stick in Charleston. Mama would love that."

"You're on!"

Lizbeth carries their dishes to the sink and puts the kettle on for tea. When she returns to the table, her heart is pounding like a jackhammer.

"I've been saving the best news for last, Char."

"Lay it on me, darlin'. I love good news!"

"I've sold the house in Port Benton."

"What! Are you nuts? The plan was to rent it. We've just been yakking about the housing market upswing, but it's got a ways to go. Jeez, Liz."

"Well, hold on, I'm not an idiot." Lizbeth rolls her eyes, makes a crazy face like she's lost her mind, and then sits down across from her cousin, her voice deadly serious.

"Now I can pay off the rest of that two-hundred-thousand-dollar line of credit, plus the penalties. In a couple weeks I'll be debt-free *and* flat broke." Lizbeth gives her cousin a fake, beatific smile.

"Oh, wait. Correction. When the house closes, I'll have a plus or minus three- thousand dollar nest egg to deposit in the Bank of Charleston."

"Don't distract me from reading you the riot act, darlin'. Looks to me like you've sabotaged your financial self." Charlotte leans in, scrutinizing her cousin carefully. "That house was your only asset. What were you thinking?"

"I had to sell, Char. I was having anxiety attacks and horrible nightmares. You remember how I was right after Dan died? Well, it didn't get much better. I had to use the paper bag trick multiple times a day. Once I actually passed out for a few seconds. It scared me to think panic attacks were my new normal."

Lizbeth gets up again and paces.

"All around town, I got sad sideways glances. Their eyes said, 'There goes poor Lizbeth, the widow who didn't know her husband's second home was the Casino.'"

Charlotte snags Lizbeth by the arm. "Sit down, Lizard. Chill out."

Lizbeth sits.

"My family imploded, Char! Dan wrecked my life along with his precious Mustang."

To prevent a torrent of tears, Lizbeth concentrates on pushing crumbs from dinner into a pile on the flowered tablecloth

"After Christmas, I went looking for answers at Tall Cedars Casino. I found some of Dan's gambling buddies who described a man I wouldn't recognize as my husband. I also talked to Casino greeters and security guards." Lizbeth shivers thinking of the sleazy men she'd sought out.

"One man told me that the night Dan died, he argued with a guy named Buck who arranges high-interest, short-term loans. That was the last straw. I had to leave Port Benton."

"Taking a runner is more likely to bite you than solve your problems,"

Char says. "The program's got a word for what you're doing: 'a geographical.'"

Lizbeth gets cranky when Charlotte talks in slogans. Alcoholics Anonymous may be her cousin's healing force, but twelve-step talk and self-help books make Lizbeth want to run screaming to escape into *People* magazine. She slams her palm on the table, her voice tight.

"No, Charlotte. This isn't a geographical escape."

The oldies station on the radio plays the Rolling Stones classic, "I Can't Get No Satisfaction." Lizbeth squints at Charlotte and can't help but crack a smile. "Jeez Louise, even the radio is telling my story."

Lizbeth pops up, showing off a fluid beach shag dance step. Charlotte joins her.

They sit out the next song, a slow dance. "OK, right, I know where you're coming from," Lizbeth says at last. "College in New Jersey was an escape from Neely; that didn't turn out so well in the end. And, yes, following Dan to Washington state might have held a smack of geographical escape, since I didn't want to go home, and I didn't have a job lined up."

"Do go on, Lizard."

"Give me a break! You know my parents were always more into each other than they were into me. Dan and I were wildly in love. I wanted a chance for my own family; healthy and close."

Lizbeth struggles to hold back tears. Her voice cracks. "I was an involved mother with wonderful sons. Dan and I had so much going for us for twenty years, I conned myself into believing his odd behavior the last year or so was just a bump in our road."

"OK, Liz, I get it. Though your counselor's hat is making you sound like you're giving a report to your colleagues, not your cousin. How about Josh and Robbie?"

"I don't know." Lizbeth wrings her hands like Lady Macbeth during her soliloquy. "We email, we text. I can't focus on them right now. They've got each other and they've got my car. Dan's parents live nearby and invite the boys every Sunday for dinner." Lizbeth grins at her cousin. "You're the one who always says, 'one day at a time.'"

Charlotte relents. "Touché, Lizard. But someday you'll have to make

amends for the way you left Port Benton without a fare-thee-well to friends
in a community where you lived for two decades."

"My bad."

"Right. Now let's have a look at the *Post and Courier* and see what
trouble we can stir up in Charleston tomorrow. "

⁓

Saturday dawns cloudy. Lizbeth and Charlotte sit drinking coffee
on the screened-in porch. The seagulls are strangely quiet, coasting over
a glassy, gray-green sea. The tide is easing out. Wavelets race each other,
kissing the beach with the barest ripple. The weather report drifts out from
the kitchen radio. A chipper voice predicts mixed sun and clouds with a
high of fifty-five degrees.

Lizbeth lifts her hands overhead, lacing her fingers for a good stretch.
"Perfect weather for a day on our feet in Charleston."

"Let's get a move on, Lizard."

They bump out of the gravel drive onto the paved road, passing the
crab shack, various bars, and the surf shop. Without a word of warning,
Charlotte pulls over in front of The Red Dog Café.

"No offense meant, cuz, but that coffee you bought at Ken's Market
is weak and nasty. He oughta be shamed off the island for setting that
stuff out on the shelf."

"None taken." Lizbeth smiles and pokes her cousin in the side. "'A
drug, is a drug, is a drug.'"

"Hardy-har-har. Having coffee as my drug of choice won't ruin my
life or run my business into the ground. You sit tight. I'll just slip in here
and get a little something with teeth. You want anything?"

"No. I'm good. If I have more coffee, I'll fidget all the way to Charleston."

Fortified with coffee in a to-go cup, Charlotte pulls out and they are
soon rumbling across the two-lane bridge from Folly onto Long Island.
The car heater blows on their legs and the front windows are down to
inhale the pungent air from acres of tidal marsh on either side of the car.
Across the flat marsh, a few spindly rivulets open channels through the
grass. "Hammack" islands, the sand bars with ground-hugging foliage, rise

out of the water here and there like ancient burial mounds.

The marsh, with its otherworldly grasses and glorious pink and purple clouds at sunrise and sunset, never ceases to lift Lizbeth's spirits. Even winter days like this one have something that fills her with awe in the Low Country. She points out a hawk hunting over the marsh. "Wonder what's for lunch today."

Crossing the bridge onto James Island, the natural world gives way to single-story strip malls, apartments, and office buildings. Charlotte puts two fingers on the driver's side armrest. Both front windows silently ride up, finishing with a silky *thunk*.

She punches the setting for the beach music radio station, and the cousins break into song, harmonizing like they've done since junior high school. Lizbeth does the descant on the Beach Boys classic, "I Get Around." Charlotte gives her a look.

"You haven't lost your touch, darlin'. You oughta be singing in the church choir."

"Don't go there. You know I haven't been a churchgoer in decades."

"Maybe that's your problem."

"Charlotte, dear cuz, you do not want to open that can of worms this morning."

"Gotcha. Turn up the radio. We've got ten more miles to perfect our harmony."

"What's on your wish list for today? You choose. Tomorrow I want you to humor me by attending First Scots Presbyterian. Afterward, I've got a surprise."

"You keepin' secrets from me, Char?"

"Yep. Patience, Lizard. You're going to love this one."

They decide on lunch at Poogan's Porch, a Victorian-style house on Queen Street converted to a restaurant in the 1970s. They stroll through the French Quarter, a colonial Charleston neighborhood near the Huguenot Church where Grandmama used to take them to see her Huguenot ancestral graves.

Lizbeth's mouth waters as they mount the steps to Poogan's. If anything can seduce her appetite back, it's shrimp and grits and a mile-high biscuit with gravy.

After lunch, Lizbeth lobbies Charlotte to visit a favorite childhood spot. She'd read an article in the *Post and Courier* about restoration of the Old Exchange and Provost Dungeon and wants to see what the Daughters of the American Revolution, who operate the building now, have done.

Lizbeth laughs. "I'm having flashbacks of Grandmama herding you, me, and your brother, John, on her summer excursions to the Holy City."

"Lord have mercy, she stuffed her grandbabies full of Charleston lore. I remember sitting at breakfast while her stories prepared us for the day in Charleston. My favorites were the Huguenot pioneers and tales of General Washington visiting Charleston on his presidential tour of the South. I wish I'd paid better attention to Grandmama. I would have had an A instead of a gentlewoman's C in South Carolina history."

"Remember how Granddaddy rolled his eyes when Grandmama romanticized her ancestors claiming she was a distant relation of the 'Swamp Fox,' Francis Marion? Then he'd compete with her by spinning a fantastical Gordon Civil War yarn, just to get her goat." Lizbeth loved her grandparents, but she had some serious questions about their glory stories.

"I miss them, don't you?"

"I do, Char. They were a loving force in our lives when we needed one." She feels an ache in her heart. All her elders except Aunt Sarah are gone. "Our grandparents loved Carolina history, but rarely talked about their own childhoods. I never thought about that when we were kids, but now I wonder about their early lives."

"They grew up during tough times for the rural South. Especially Granddaddy, whose family managed to hold onto their land after the Civil War, barely making ends meet until the 1930s. Remember the night Granddaddy had one too many drams and told us kids about plowing corn fields behind a mule when he was eleven? That night he actually wept over how a Yankee from Connecticut who raised show horses bought the family farm in the Piedmont for a song because the Gordon's couldn't make the mortgage."

Lizbeth gets goosebumps thinking about that kind of poverty. What would have happened to her after Dan's death, without Charlotte, a graduate degree, and a counseling career she can return to when she's ready?

"Yeah. I remember Granddaddy saying he wanted to get away so bad he lied about his age to join the Marines and had a grand, wild, life—till Grandmama reeled him in."

The cousins amble up the steps to the Old Exchange and Provost Dungeon on East Bay Street. Standing in the lobby, designed to be the King's Customs Offices, Lizbeth reads the sign: CONSTRUCTED IN 1768, AS ONE OF THE LAST BUILDINGS FOR THE COLONIAL BRITISH GOVERNMENT BEFORE THE AMERICAN REVOLUTIONARY WAR.

They climb a long flight of stairs to the fine rooms—party central for people of influence in Charleston back in the day. Signage says the ballroom was where the South Carolina state Continental Congress discussed the United States Constitution.

"Wow, I remember that life-size painting of George Washington by John Trumbull like yesterday. Grandmama was gaga over it." They smile, remembering their romantic grandmother.

Charlotte elbows her cousin.

"Wanna go downstairs and visit the dungeon where John used to terrorize us?"

"Your big brother loved the goriest pirate stories. How'd he turn out to be such a decent human?"

"Got me."

They descend into the basement originally designed as a storage vault and converted to a dungeon during the Revolutionary War, when the British military occupied Charleston with an iron fist.

Charlotte shivers. "Creepy as ever—sporting weepy walls with a touch of mold and rusty chains with manacles attached. God knows how many people wore those. I was never as fascinated by this space as you and John."

"Look Char, the mannequins of the Revolutionary War patriots, pirates, and escaped slaves are still here, but they've added stories of real people too. It's fabulous."

"Uh-huh. Okay. Have you had enough history fix today? I want to check out the sale at Dillard's before we head back."

"Just give me a minute in the bookstore upstairs."

Lizbeth picks up Pat Conroy's latest book, *South of Broad.* She's read it struck a nerve, infuriating some of Charleston's old guard. She's up for something edgy.

At the cashier's counter she's drawn to a sign. HELP WANTED: TOUR GUIDE FAMILIAR WITH CHARLESTON HISTORY. She grabs Charlotte by the arm and tilts her head toward the sign. They lock eyes.

"Put an application for the tour guide job in the bag with my book, if you please."

The saleswoman gives Lizbeth the once-over from head to toe, seeming satisfied: This woman could fit in. "Yes, ma'am."

చ

After dinner, Lizbeth sits filling out forms at the cypress wood picnic table their Granddaddy built in the 1950s, while Charlotte does up the dishes.

Lizbeth slaps her hand on the table.

"You know I'm perfect for this job. They're going to love me at the Old Exchange and Provost Dungeon." Lizbeth stands. With a flirtatious smile, she curtsies. "Won't I be cute giving tours dressed as an eighteenth-century servant girl with a little white cap on my head?"

Charlotte rolls her eyes. "I don't know about the outfit to charm tourists, but Charleston colonial history is pure you. Sounds like you're fixin' to stay on in the Holy City for a while."

"Yeah. But I'll need more money than what I'm gonna make as a tour guide. Maybe I can tutor high school students struggling with Spanish for extra cash." She sighs. "I miss working with kids, Char."

"Well, I love having you nearby, darlin'. But are you sure living in South Carolina is what you want? I do recollect, with the exception of beach vacations with your boys, you've spent your entire adult life putting as many miles as possible between your sweet self and Dixie."

Lizbeth shrugs. "I don't know what I want, Char. I'm a mess. When

I was young, I thought I was a good Southern girl, and a member of the righteous youth of my generation challenging racism in America. That turned out badly when that Angela Gordon slapped me down. I haven't changed my opinion about racism, but I have no desire to explain myself to people who get in my face about my slaveholding ancestors." Lizbeth notices her fists balled tight in her lap and takes a deep breath.

"I thought I belonged in Port Benton. I was a good mom with a damn successful career, if I do say so myself. I thought I had a solid marriage, but Dan's secrets revealed his love had shifted from me to the casino, and my community judged me the fool."

Lizbeth gives her cousin a *please understand me* look. "I don't know where I belong. But, I know, at the cottage, I don't need brown paper bags for anxiety attacks and that's a start. When I get the tour guide job, I'll pay you rent." Lizbeth wipes her brow free of imaginary sweat and gives her cousin a smile. "Whew."

"OK, I get it. But listen up girl! Don't get involved in lefty politics and mess up your head. The 'New South' of Charleston is a changed place from our childhood, but you're still gonna see stuff that raises your hackles. You are not going to figure out your life unless you stay focused on yourself."

"Thanks, Mom." Lizbeth rolls her eyes. Has she ever focused on herself?

"And forget about the rent, Lizard. The place is paid for. John pitches in for taxes. As long as you don't mind company, the cottage is yours. I'll pop down. Penny will show up with friends when the weather warms. John and his family come during high season. We'll all pack in just like old times in the summer."

"Thanks, Char. I'll be your resident caretaker."

The cousins hug on the deal and then settle on the couch with mugs of herbal tea to take in a show on cable TV.

❧

In the wee hours of the morning Lizbeth wakes aching for Dan's body. She recognizes the dream she's had many times since leaving Port Benton. She and Dan are in southern Mexico, madly in love. They're traveling in a beat-up rental car through high rolling hills of the Mexteca Alta. The windows are down, a hot breeze is blowing her long hair every which way. Dan's right hand is massaging her left thigh. Unable to wait for the next village with a room to rent, they pull off the narrow road and make love in the bright sunshine.

Lizbeth startles awake.

"Damnit! Leave me alone! Why is this dream torturing me?"

She knows why. It's the pillowcase.

⁓

Dan's betrayal had taken Lizbeth low in a way she never imagined possible. To save her sanity before she left Port Benton, she'd purged Dan's clothes, books, kayak, and most of his tools. What neighbors didn't want she took to Goodwill. Her last day at the house, she discovered Dan's pillow, the one she'd thrown on the floor in the closet, the day she learned about his gambling debts. There it had stayed, lost under a pile of old clothes slotted for the garbage. Finding it unexpectedly, she was overcome by nostalgia. Without analyzing why, Lizbeth had slipped the case off the pillow and into a zip-lock bag and tucked it into the outside pocket of her suitcase.

Several times in the last month, she tromped down the cottage stairs in frustration ready to dispatch the pillowcase into the garbage bin. Each time she weakened, returning it to her bottom drawer where, in unplanned moments, she slides open the zip-lock, takes out the pillowcase redolent with Dan's spicy smell, lifts it to cover her nose and face, and inhales deeply.

CHAPTER EIGHT

The Gordon family has been Presbyterian since the Reformation. Since she was old enough to express herself in song, Lizbeth has been moved by Christian hymns. In high school, she earned a coveted spot in the Chancel Choir at the First Presbyterian Church in Neely.

In her senior year, gossip circulated about Mr. Phillips, the choir director, and his new girlfriend, a Black lawyer from Columbia. Some in the congregation elbowed each other and whispered when the girlfriend took her place in a front pew on the first Sunday of Advent. Although the lawyer had the voice of an angel, some congregants found it awkward when she continued showing up front and center every week. Mr. Phillips kept his own counsel through the holiday season, pretending not to notice when tension oozed through the congregation. In January, he gave notice and took a job in Columbia as a high school music teacher.

Lizbeth was furious at her parents, who championed civil rights at the dinner table, but didn't stand up publicly to defend Mr. Phillips, her mentor, and a highly respected musician. Her parents protested, saying their professional lives required a quieter path to social change. Lizbeth made her own statement about the quiet path by quitting the choir and refusing to attend church.

❧

Twenty some years later, Lizbeth feels like she's entered a time warp sitting next to Charlotte at Scots Presbyterian in Charleston. The men have donned sport coats, though the tie requirement seems to have eased. Women and girls are decked out in dresses or nice slacks with stylish pastel blouses. No one is wearing running shoes.

The organ warms up with the opening bars of "How Great Thou Art" and the congregation stands for the first hymn. Lizbeth holds back tears as she sings every verse at full voice without once glancing at the hymnal.

The pastor's sermon doesn't shame the congregants for their sinful behavior like she was expecting. She nudges Charlotte and whispers, "This isn't bad, cuz."

"Told you about the 'New South,' darlin'. You've been away a while. Though to be honest, you've still gotta choose your church with care. The old sermons on hellfire and damnation are alive and well in the state of South Carolina."

"Where would I be today without your honesty, Char?" Lizbeth digs an elbow into her cousin's ribs and gets a pseudo glare in return.

❧

After the service, Charlotte's surprise turns out to be Miles, an old high school friend. Lizbeth can't help but notice her cousin's energy of suppressed excitement.

Charlotte whispers, "Miles showed me something special a couple of weeks ago; wait till you see."

Lizbeth gives her cousin a "What?" look, with her eyebrows raised.

They linger chatting up old friends of Aunt Sarah. As they leave Miles says, "Bet y'all are surprised I became an upright citizen and got elected as a deacon after my days as king of the keg parties."

"You certainly were a party animal back in the day," Charlotte shoots back, shaking her head with mock criticism.

"All right, then. All y'all ready for a history lesson?" Miles takes Lizbeth's arm and Charlotte follows, grinning.

"Yep. Enlighten us," Lizbeth says.

"First Scots was modeled after a Basilica in Baltimore, Maryland, completed in 1814 to replace the original wood structure built in 1731." Miles points out the Scottish symbols in the stained-glass windows and the thistle theme on the wrought iron grilles as they move through the sanctuary.

"During the war, the famous bells were donated to the Confederate cause and melted down into bullets."

On the drive into Charleston, Charlotte had warned Lizbeth not to make any controversial comments. Miles is a Civil War history buff and participates in battle re-enactments just as his father had done.

"By the grace of God," Miles continued, "the church survived the eighteen-month siege of Charleston, but the earthquake of 1886 damaged the towers. It wasn't until 1999 that one of the towers was strengthened to tolerate the weight of the current four-thousand-pound bell. It's an exact copy of one of the originals from 1814."

"The bell's vibration resonated all the way into my bones when it tolled people to church this morning," Lizbeth says. She's taken aback by how emotionally this sanctuary grabs her gut. Eerie.

Outside in a garden of evergreen shrubs and dormant rose bushes, Miles points out the flags marking where the original wooden church stood.

"It was so tiny," Lizbeth comments.

"Twenty-five people split off from the original Congregational Round Church across the street. It seems like after centuries of religious wars in Europe, every group that arrived in the South Carolina Colony wanted their own sanctuary. Colonial Charleston had the first synagogue in the English Colonies. Y'all know colonial Charleston gave people the freedom to build any kind of house of worship they wanted."

"Our granddaddy used to joke that inviting all faiths kept people coming, while yellow fever and malaria kept killing them off like flies." Lizbeth smiles remembering how grandaddy loved a good tease.

"That's true, too," Miles says over his shoulder, leading the cousins around half buried, lichen-covered headstones, across a small lawn of pea-green spring grass, toward the far wall of the cemetery.

"A while ago, a group of us catalogued every headstone to help folks looking for ancestors. Over here's what I want y'all to see."

He stops at a pitted, moss-mottled headstone and stoops down. "See here: Angus Gordon, born January 5, 1810, Glasgow, Scotland. Died fighting fire, August 15, 1864. Beloved father of Jeanne, Robert, and Laurette."

"He's one of OUR Gordons, I'm sure of it!" Charlotte wraps her arm around Lizbeth's waist, hugging her tight.

"I can't remember anyone ever mentioning an Angus Gordon, but yeah, I remember the name Jeanne Gordon from somewhere." Lizbeth regards the headstone with its chipped corner, listing at a precarious angle. "If we had Charleston Gordons with enough status for a respectable spot in the Presbyterian cemetery, why aren't there other Gordon graves here?"

Miles has an answer. "The church garden and cemetery were in ruins after the siege of Charleston and the earthquake ten years later. In all the devastation, headstones were lost, half buried, or shattered beyond recognition. It took a hundred years to put what you see here right again."

Liz stoops to scrape at fuzzy bits of moss on the top of Angus's stone. Her fingers tingle. She bends from the waist, trying to be subtle about it, touching the velvet moss again. Since Dan died, her senses are on overdrive. She pulls her hand back and slaps it on her pant leg as she straightens up.

Charlotte and Miles, deep in conversation about a mutual friend, don't notice Lizbeth's forehead wrinkle as she rubs her thumb and index finger together, dusting off a bit of remaining green. She squints at the headstone as if it could answer her silent question. Angus, where is the rest of your family?

"After Miles showed me this stone, I mentioned it to Mama. She said she remembered the name Angus in a family Bible." Charlotte shrugs. "I was slammed with work and my social life. I didn't think to dig into what Mama knows again until you and I started reminiscing."

"So, if this Angus is one of our Gordons, why didn't Grandmama, our family historian par excellence, ever bring us here?"

Charlotte looks at Lizbeth like she's slow-witted. "Grandmama wasn't interested in the Gordon history. She was only keen on her Huguenot people and the American Revolution. Remember how she used to tease Granddaddy that his people were chasing the sheep in the Highlands while hers formed a new nation?"

"I wonder what Angus Gordon was doing in Charleston during the Civil War?" Lizbeth crosses her fingers behind her back like a superstitious child. Please no ugly secrets.

Lizbeth and Charlotte have been carrying on, forgetting Miles can't help overhearing the conversation. He gives a little cough and looks uncomfortable, as if they had just stripped down to their undergarments in front of him.

Lizbeth winces. "Sorry, Miles."

"No problem, ladies. Don't y'all be strangers now. Hope to see you again next Sunday, Lizbeth."

On the way to the car Charlotte says, "So what do you think about my Angus discovery?"

"I'm curious, yeah. What happened? Was there some kind of family argument like a macho honor duel between siblings or cousins?" Lizbeth squirms with irritation at nineteenth-century Southern chivalry.

"You know my Mama is not one who romanticizes the past," Charlotte says. "She never mentioned a stash of old documents until after Miles showed me the gravesite and I asked just that once. Then I got busy and didn't follow up. Hey! Come to Greenville for a weekend. Between the two of us pestering her with family questions, Mama will roll out what she knows. You are overdue for a visit and your Aunt Sarah is dying to see you."

"I'd love to. You being here for a weekend has gotten me off my sad duff." Lizbeth winks at her cousin.

∽

On the drive back to the cottage, Charlotte waxes on to Lizbeth about the rehabilitation of "old town" Greenville and the posh restaurants along the Reedy River.

"By the way," Lizbeth says, and winks at her cousin, "you haven't revealed the full meal deal on what possessed Aunt Sarah to sell her home and move upcountry, near you backward crackers."

"Very funny, Lizard, but you've got a point. Mama always said she never wanted to live anywhere but Charleston. But last year, she finally got disgusted by all the tourists disgorged like ants from giant cruise ships, streaming through the streets, returning late in the day to their tall white nest with fake historical tchotchkes made in China. Adding insult to injury, rich Yankees were buying up colonial-era houses in her neighborhood for second homes. So, I found her a nice condo on the Greenville Riverwalk and she's happy."

"Yeah, I can't blame her. I hope gentrification doesn't take the soul out of the Low Country."

CHAPTER NINE

After chicken sandwiches on the porch with Lizbeth, Charlotte changes into jeans and her favorite T-shirt, with *Salt Water Heals Everything* in four-inch blue script across the chest. She loads her suitcase in the BMW and stands soaking up a light salt breeze off the rolling surf.

With a honk goodbye, Charlotte pulls out of the drive determined to arrive in time for her Sunday evening AA group in Greenville. "Let go and let God" sounds easy, until your cousin and best friend does stupid stuff like accepting a low-ball offer on her only financial asset.

The traffic gods smile. She sails along State Route 26, cumulus clouds float overhead in tall, fluffy mountains, and shadows fall in stripes on the roadway when she passes a grove of loblolly pine.

Settling into the drive, Charlotte rummages in the glove compartment for her stash of Tootsie Pops. With one hand on the wheel, she selects green apple, unwraps it with her free hand and teeth. Ummmm. Perfect. She used to smoke a pack of Virginia Slims a day. At sixty calories per sucker, rolling a Tootsie Pop around her teeth is a sweet satisfaction tradeoff for the cigarettes that made her crave Jack Daniels neat.

Charlotte reflects on ways she and Lizbeth are very different, yet the strength of their friendship always wins out in the end.

As kids they shared everything: books, secrets, and strategies on how to ditch her older brother, John. Then, in their late teens, the cousins hit a rough patch. Charlotte became queen of the college fraternity parties the moment she arrived on campus at USC. She attended classes sporadically and woke up Sundays not sure what happened the night before. Meanwhile, a couple hundred miles away, Lizbeth was caught up in social activism her senior year in high school. Their dueling perspectives morphed into a crisis one weekend that Charlotte remembers well.

Lizbeth's parents went to a week-long chamber music festival in Charlotte. Thelma, their Black housekeeper who'd been their daughter's childhood nanny, was hired to stay for the week. One afternoon, Thelma's son Samuel stopped by with mail for his mother. Lizbeth had forgotten her chemistry book and had a test in the morning. She'd known Samuel all her life and didn't think twice about asking him for a lift to the high school. Much later Lizbeth would admit she ignored the look Samuel and his mother shared before he shrugged and said, "Guess so."

At the high school, Samuel stayed at the wheel while Lizbeth ran in. A few minutes later, she jogged out the door, book in hand, and slid into the passenger seat of Samuel's car. Some guys leaving baseball practice noticed and threw racial slurs, laughing and shoving each other while Samuel yelled at Lizbeth to lock the doors. He crept forward at a snail's pace as the baseball players circled the car. One kid slammed his fist on the hood. Another cracked the windshield with his bat. More bats cracked the taillights. A kid yelled, "Nigger lover girl," and raised his middle finger as Samuel took off.

Charlotte heard about it in three long voice mail messages. Lizbeth had been sobbing and venting every detail, ending with, "At school and in church we talk about Black and White friendships. I've known Samuel all my life. He's a good guy—and look what happened to his car. Now he won't talk to me. Well, I believe what I read about equality and activism. I'm going to make a real difference—starting now."

The voice mails irritated Charlotte, who was in bed holding a cold pack on her head. The next day, still nursing a tender head and tummy, she left Lizbeth a rather tart message.

"Let it go. Don't be naïve about small-town jerks." Charlotte wished she could have taped her idealistic cousin up in protective bubble wrap until she got some sense. Racism in small towns can be dangerous.

A few weeks later Lizbeth told Charlotte someone had left an obscene, threatening note in her school locker. Charlotte was scared and angry. She wanted to drive to Neely and shake safety and reality into her cousin. But she didn't. Her drinking got in the way of every best laid plan in those years.

Articles about her cousin and new activist friends appeared in the *Neely Herald*: Lizbeth at a civil rights march and Lizbeth canvassing neighborhoods with flyers for Black politicians. Lizbeth's parents called Charlotte for help after 'Nigger lover' was scratched on the side of Aunt Deborah's late model Chevy.

Charlotte drove down to Neely for a weekend. The cousins went round and round, debating social justice and activism. Although Lizbeth swore she would not be intimidated, she eventually got to where she didn't want to endanger her parents. Or their standing in the community. For the next decade, the cousins' friendship abided, with a careful chill overlay, dancing away from subjects of social activism or alcohol.

CHAPTER TEN

Charlotte leans over to punch the radio from the news channel to beach music and notices the gas gage is hovering on empty. Lord have mercy that's all I need. At the next exit she pulls into a gas station, grabs a Diet Coke from a machine while the tank fills and is back on the highway lickety-split. She runs possible scenarios on helping Lizbeth without looking like she's helping. Her dear Lizard is a proud woman, spot on with clarity finding solutions for others but lost in a fog with her own burdens.

ϖ

When Josh and Robbie were four and Charlotte's daughter, Penny, was a year older, Lizbeth's father died from a massive stroke while collecting the morning paper from the driveway. Lizbeth's mother was inconsolable. Dan was away on business. Lizbeth, swamped with grief, called Charlotte.

Charlotte and Penny picked Lizbeth and the twins up at Greenville-Spartanburg International Airport. They drove to Neely with the three children chattering like magpies in the back seat while Lizbeth sat next to her cousin, twisting a limp handkerchief in her lap.

"How am I going to help Mama? Daddy was everything to her."

"You'll find your way darlin'. Seeing her grandchildren will help."

"I feel like a crummy daughter for bringing the twins to Neely so rarely."

They parked in the driveway and entered the unlocked front door of Lizbeth's childhood home. The stuffy vestibule felt like damp cotton wool. Odd. Why weren't the large ceiling fans quietly moving air in the living room and dining room? Why wasn't the classical music Dorothy Gordon lived and breathed playing through the speakers on the main floor? Charlotte followed with trepidation as Lizbeth ran through the first floor and back garden calling, "Mama, we're here!"

Charlotte's heart was in her mouth as she followed Lizbeth up the stairs. Lizbeth yanked open the closed master bedroom door, a door always left open for air circulation during the day.

They found Dorothy lifeless, tucked up in the marital bed in her best lace-trimmed nightgown. Lizbeth's face went white. Charlotte grabbed her cousin's hands. Their eyes locked with silent knowing. Lizbeth lay down, wrapped herself around her mother's body, and wept. Charlotte noticed a prescription bottle and a snifter of brandy on the bedside table.

She kissed her cousin on the forehead, grabbed the snifter, ran downstairs, got snacks out of the cupboard for the children and turned on a TV cartoon show. Charlotte rinsed the snifter, left it in the dishrack next to the kitchen sink and headed back up the stairs to take care of her cousin.

When Lizbeth could get intelligible words out, she said, "I might have saved her if I'd lived close enough to drive home instead of the long day and two planes to get here, after Daddy died."

Charlotte held Lizbeth's upper arms, looked her cousin square in the face and said, "Your parents had a fairy tale relationship for fifty years. Nothing could keep them from being together in this life—and the next."

Eventually, Lizbeth wiped her eyes and gave Charlotte a weak smile. "You're right. My parents were inseparable, best friends." Tears flowed again. "I remember one time Mama said when she and Daddy got old, they planned to lie down and go to sleep together and not wake up. I thought she was just talkin'—you know, being dramatic." Lizbeth gave a little shudder.

"They were so close. In high school I used to be embarrassed by how they held hands on evening walks and shared kisses in the garden. But my friends said I had the most romantic parents ever."

Charlotte wrapped her arms around Lizbeth. They rocked together in a long hug. "I'm staying as long as you need me, cuz. It's gonna be all right."

Blessedly, the small-town doctor, and family friend, pronounced Dorothy Gordon's valium overdose an accident.

Lizbeth and Charlotte planned the double funeral, honoring the best of Dr. Robert Gordon and Dr. Dorothy Gordon's accomplishments. Afterward, the cousins stayed at the house for two weeks, cleaning and packing up and revisiting childhood memories. Shared history and time had smoothed the tension of a decade ago. Charlotte and Lizbeth were tight as ticks again.

Lizbeth called a local Realtor. By the time she and the twins boarded the plane to Seattle, Lizbeth and Charlotte had committed to a month on Folly Island with their children every July. They didn't miss a summer for the next twelve years.

CHAPTER ELEVEN

Folly Island, South Carolina March 2010

L izbeth stands nude in front of the full-length bedroom mirror, taking stock. She's lost weight eating only yogurt and granola because she couldn't be bothered to cook. Her stomach hasn't been this flat since before Josh and Robbie. She did crunches for months to no avail when the boys were toddlers. Dan was sweet about her extra weight, saying a couple inches around the belly is a badge of honor for carrying twins.

She exhales a long sigh. How can she both miss him and despise him? Turning to check her rear view, she's proud of her strong, shapely legs. But, hey, those tiny dimples. Ugh. Cellulite. Reminds her of Mama. Maybe a tankini and cute little swim shorts for the beach this year instead of a high-cut one-piece.

She's pale as a convict, but more beach walking can take care of that as the days get longer and sunnier. She needs a haircut and a few spring clothes a size smaller—or maybe two. When she packed up in Port Benton four months ago, warm weather clothing for South Carolina was the last thing on her mind. Four months ago, she didn't care if she lived or died.

Her job at the Exchange Building will do for now, although her wages make money a constant worry. Even when she and Dan were newlyweds, they never lived this close to the bone. When Lizbeth writes the check for her cell phone plan that includes the boys, it feels like she's lopping a limb off her body.

Recently, she had an ugly surprise. Dan's accountant called, saying the 2009 taxes were higher than estimated. If the cottage hadn't been well stocked when she arrived, she would've needed a loan from Charlotte to get through the first months. Just the thought of being that beholden makes her stomach ache.

Then there's Josh and Robbie. Lizbeth feels like she's competing in a marathon against her dead husband who crossed the finish line and collected his medal, while she slogs along behind, gulping for breath. Sometimes she wakes sweaty in the wee hours, thinking about the night before the twins returned to college in January.

Josh had narrowed his eyes and said, "How come you gave Dad's stuff away without consulting us?" Robbie swallowed a big gulp of milk and added in a tight voice, "You've made us homeless."

Buck up girl, she thinks. There are signs that the silly cards and frequent emails she sends her boys are building bridges. Last week when they Skyped, Josh and Robbie roared when she stood and curtsied, dressed in her eighteenth-century tour guide costume. It was the perfect opening for light conversation including jokes about Lizbeth hanging out with pirate ghosts in the Provost Dungeon. They reminisced about summer trips to Charleston with Charlotte and Penny. Blessedly absent were blame, and pain over the house and finances. After the call, Lizbeth sat by the phone pondering: perhaps the close relationship she had with her sons before Dan died is redeemable.

Today's a day off. One of those days when loneliness threatens to crush her. She turns the beach music channel up and dances shag steps from chore to chore as she washes salt-crusted windows and scours flying cockroach carcasses and fuzzy spider-egg pouches from around baseboards and corner crannies.

Folly Beach is her place, it was never Dan's, though she tried to entice him into loving it. The summer after her parents died, she, Dan, and the boys had joined Charlotte and Penny for a vacation at the cottage. Dan had played in the surf with the boys but grumbled about the humidity, greasy hushpuppies at the fishing pier, and how much better camping on Olympic Peninsula was compared to a hot, crowded beach on the weekend. Lizbeth didn't bother to push him to accompany her and the twins the following year. She, Charlotte, and their children began a summer beach tradition that lasted a decade. Thankfully, there are no memories of Dan at the cottage to clear away with the cobwebs.

∾

Working at the Old Exchange and Provost Dungeon has revived Lizbeth's love of Carolina Colonial history. A couple times a week, she escaped to the balm of historical research at the library. Having a cache of little-known factoids about Colonial Charleston bring compliments and fat tips at the end of her tours.

No tips accompany her school group tours, of course, but they remain her favorites. One morning recently, she'd overslept, grabbed a to-go cup of coffee, and flew out the door. She joked about her growling stomach with sixth graders from Moultrie Middle School. Humor and the creativity of kids on the cusp of their teens always made her day.

Sundays she attends First Scots, where the forward-thinking minister is easy to listen to and the music is divine. She's playing with the idea of joining the choir. At an after-service coffee hour, she met Patsy, a divorcee almost as outspoken as Charlotte, who seems like a kindred spirit.

At their first lunch date Patsy asked, "Are you open to meeting men?"

"If any man touches me, I'll knee him in the groin."

Lizbeth had slapped a hand over her heart and glanced around the restaurant to see if anyone heard.

"Sorry, guess I'm over-reactive on the subject of men."

Patsy had stared at Lizbeth, her mouth in a perfect O, her hands palm out in a gesture of peace.

"Sorry. Since my husband died, whacko things fly out of my mouth.

I keep thinking I am getting over him. Then I say something crazy and know I'm not even close."

"Did your man do you wrong?"

"He did. Someday I'll tell you the story."

☙

Lizbeth and Patsy start meeting regularly at The Hot Spot, a place with upmarket fusion food and a bluegrass band on Thursday nights. As weeks pass, it feels good, almost normal, to get out for bit of night life.

Tonight is different. Lizbeth hustles to beat Patsy to the Hot Spot and secures a secluded table. A few minutes later, she spots Patsy gliding into the low-lit restaurant, swiveling her head side to side. Lizbeth lifts her hand in a wave. Patsy winds her way through the crowded tables to the far side of the room and slides into a chair across from Lizbeth.

Patsy lifts her eyebrows, and raises her hands in a questioning gesture of *what the heck?* "Girlfriend, you know my goal for tonight is to charm that hunk of a bass player to our table for a drink when the band takes a break. How am I going to do that from way over here?"

"I need to consult you where half the restaurant won't hear my business." Lizbeth fans herself with the menu and tries on a smile. "I nearly got fired today."

"Wow. Do tell all. If it's juicy enough, I'll forgive you for foiling my evening's strategy." She winks and reaches across the table to squeeze Lizbeth's hand.

A waitress stops by with her order pad at the ready. They ask for two glasses of merlot, a plate of barbeque pork sliders to share, and a side of coleslaw. The noise level leaps as people greet friends, hollering across tables over the blue grass band warming up.

Lizbeth leans in.

"My afternoon tour was a fraternity reunion of good old boys who showed up with beer breath. They weren't looped enough for me to cancel the tour, but they definitely had a buzz on." Lizbeth shakes her head and continues. "Everything went OK until we got to the Exchange Building dungeon. Two of the guys traded racist remarks about the enslaved mannequins in shackles and another hit me up asking what was under my 'fetching' long skirt. I cut the tour short and lectured the entire group on racism and respect like they were eight years old. They complained on the way out. Now I'm on probation."

"Lord have mercy."

"Seems I've developed a hair trigger temper when it comes to the jerks of this world. Today was the second time in a week I've popped off."

Lizbeth drags her chair in closer, checks both sides and behind her before she spills her other story. "Monday at the mall, I clashed with a cashier with big attitude. After she rang me up and handed over my bag, she made a snarky remark under her breath about rich White women. I'd worked all weekend for the extra cash to buy a new swimsuit. So, I said, 'We're not all rich, you don't know anything about me.' She bit my head off with a rude comeback. I snapped at her with 'Racism comes in all colors, sister,' before I could stifle myself. Fortunately, a teenager stepped up to the counter and butted in with question about a sale. I turned on my heel and stalked off."

Lizbeth shook her head, wishing she could erase Monday afternoon. "In the heat of the moment, I was primed for a shouting match with that woman. It was that close." She holds her thumb and index finger up with an inch of air between them.

"Good grief, girlfriend. Do you think you need to see a shrink?"

"I am a shrink." Lizbeth puts her elbows on the table, closes her eyes and massages her temples. The waitress arrives and sets down their drinks. Seeing the women deep in conversation, she retreats with a wordless wave.

"You've gotta get a grip. Charleston is way different than when we were kids. But you oughta know better, with three hundred years of complicated race and class problems it's not gonna be all nicely wrapped up in a bow anytime soon."

Lizbeth feels Patsy's warm hand on her arm and looks up.

"Yeah, I know. My cousin Charlotte nicknamed me the 'equity police' when we were teenagers and I guess there are moments when I still deserve the title." Lizbeth rolls her eyes and tries to reassure her friend with a smile.

"Actually, I did see a counselor when I was in grad school. Her assessment was my limbic brain gets triggered by injustice. Jeez Louise. Turned out that woman knew her brain science, but she couldn't handle complicated real-life conversations about race."

Lizbeth pauses when she notices Patsy looks confused.

"The limbic brain, sometimes called the 'lizard brain,' directs the fight-or-flight response we're all born with. When people have good or neutral experiences with others of another ethnicity, religion, or people dressed in an unfamiliar style of clothing, the limbic brain doesn't scream danger about strangers. But if you are someone who's experienced harassment or racism or whatever trauma by someone who doesn't look like you, the limbic brain goes on hypervigilant overdrive to protect you from having another traumatic experience. So, you over-react, assuming people who don't look like you automatically mean you harm.

"Turned out, my counselor had no experience outside her safe, White, West Coast bubble. She pontificated on theories and actually didn't believe my experience; a social activist that got publicly shamed by a Black woman and shunned by White classmates because of my surname. I told her my high school and college stories, but she didn't get me and didn't want to." Lizbeth exhales a long, exasperated sigh. "I quit after a couple sessions."

"Well," Patsy says, "I didn't study limbic brains in my business program at USC, but I think I get what you're saying. But listen up, girl. When you need to make a point around town, do it with civil Southern style, or you'll end up collecting unemployment by next week."

Lizbeth feels Patsy's hard look all the way into her bones.

The waitress arrives, sets a plate of fragrant, spicy, sliders and coleslaw on their table and hurries off to take an order across the room. Lizbeth's mouth had been watering for BBQ pulled pork when she arrived, but now, even a favorite comfort food isn't appealing.

"You're right." Lizbeth shakes her head and pushes coleslaw around her plate. "My Daddy used to tell me to count to ten before I opened my opinionated mouth. I was pretty good at doing exactly that until my life fell apart last December." She folds her arms over her breasts as if she's chilled, though the room is overheated with body heat and fragrant picante barbeque.

"My future is a fog bank and that's getting to me. And now there's a new wrinkle in the Gordon history. After church on Sunday, Miles showed Charlotte and me the headstone of Angus Gordon at First Scots. I swing back and forth between excited about researching ancestors I've never heard of and trepidations about some ugly family scandal."

Lizbeth shrugs and takes a fortifying gulp of merlot before continuing. "I'm an only child. I've always fantasized being part of a big, warmhearted, extended family. Maybe I have long lost cousins in Charleston! But what if I find Angus was a slave trader, or God knows what else? After the year I've had, I don't need another dose of shame."

"Wouldn't it be better to find out what it was instead of stewing on what might have been?"

The band strikes up a popular country western favorite. A guy from the next table leans over and asks Patsy to dance. She looks at Lizbeth, who says, "Go dance, I'm lousy company tonight."

Lizbeth grabs the check.

"My turn." She swipes her sweater off the back of her chair, pays at the cash register by the door, and slips out into the night.

CHAPTER TWELVE

Greenville, South Carolina, April 2010

T he morning dawns warm and fine for a three-hour drive to Greenville. Crossing the island, Lizbeth inhales the pungent pluff mud that Low Country dwellers appreciate, and tourists complain smells like rotten eggs. Wetland transitions to houses and low office buildings with flowering dogwoods and azaleas that pop with colors from pale pinks to dark purple in a spring palette to tickle any passerby's fancy.

She is excited about a weekend away. Even if nothing emerges about the mystery man, Angus Gordon, spending time with dear Aunt Sarah will be worth the trip. Sarah had been an emergency room nurse and Lizbeth's childhood sounding board; a no-nonsense contrast to her intellectual parents and their esoteric friends. As she breezes along the highway, Lizbeth wonders what practical Aunt Sarah's take will be on Angus Gordon.

☙

Lizbeth arrives early at Passerelle Bistro and settles in at a prime table overlooking the river walk. Leave it to Charlotte to reserve the best. The Reedy River warbling past the deck lulls her into a peaceful trance until approaching voices bring her back. Lizbeth rises, spreading her arms to envelope Aunt Sarah, who moves deftly into the embrace, wielding her cane like a fashion accessory.

Sarah steps back for a good look at her niece. "Oh, sweet darlin' child, you get prettier every year. I declare, you're the spitting image of your daddy in female form. I surely do miss him!"

"I miss Daddy, too, Aunt Sarah." Lizbeth smiles as she twirls in a slow circle, palms up framing her face. "You like my new hairdo and highlights? I picked up extra cash tutoring high school students and splurged on a fancy Charleston salon."

Lizbeth gets a kick out of how easily she's slipped back into Southern decorum: serious subjects wait until conversations on the weather and social updates are complete.

After Niçoise salad and demitasse cups of coffee, the conversation turns to family history. Eyes sparkling with mischief, Sarah pulls a large envelope from her sleek leather tote bag.

"You girls asked me to find information on Gordon history. I don't have a passion for family history like my daddy, your Granddaddy Gordon. But then again, he grew up on the old family land, where back in the day people had big families and lots of tall tales. There was a mess of Gordons scattered around the Carolina Piedmont; must be fifty or so Gordon graves in the Presbyterian cemetery an hour from here if you're interested in visiting and reading family names. You two have it right though: Angus Gordon and his family *did* live in Charleston before the Civil War."

Sarah pauses, takes a sip of coffee. Pulling a face at the tepid liquid, she replaces the cup. Charlotte signals a waiter to refresh their coffee.

"Our Gordon branch shrank early in the twentieth century. Daddy left the upcountry in his teens to join the Marines and met Mama who wouldn't hear of living anywhere but Charleston. Sadly, both my daddy's brothers died young, so his ties to Greenville County shrank. I remember a few summers when Daddy's people enticed him to bring my brother, your daddy Lizbeth, and me upcountry to the annual Gordon clan reunion in July."

Aunt Sarah shakes her head and laughs.

"Folks I didn't know chatted me up with the wildest family stories or remarks on which distant cousin I most resembled. It was an enjoyable time, but I was a child, so most of what I heard from the elders went in one ear and out the other."

Lizbeth's heart pounds imagining a large upcountry family reunion and unnamed ancestors, and a flash back to Angela Gordon. Without thinking, she blurts out, "Our Gordons were slaveholders, weren't they?"

"I don't rightly know the particulars, but, yes, there were family slaves." Lizbeth notices her aunt's body tense.

"In college I met a woman who said her ancestors were Gordon enslaved people,"

"Darlin', let's not spoil this lovely lunch with a tangent on the subject of slavery." Aunt Sarah's half smile doesn't reach her eyes.

Charlotte kicked Lizbeth hard under the table, telegraphing, "Aunt Sarah does not need to hear the story of Angela Gordon."

☙

Lizbeth had kept the shameful experience with Angela in the back of her memory bank until the year of her fifteenth college reunion. A few days before the weekend festivities she had no intention of attending, Erin, a classmate with whom she had once been close, left a voice mail message.

"I'm guessing you aren't going to the reunion, but let's catch up. By the way, do you get *The Alumni News?* Did you see Angela Gordon's obituary? Call me."

Erin had remained one of Lizbeth's few college friends after that day in African American History class, but in recent years their contact had dwindled to Christmas cards. Once the boys were off to school the next morning, Lizbeth called her former classmate.

While they caught up on careers and kids, Lizbeth drummed her fingers on the kitchen counter to keep from looking like a fool pushing to hear news about Angela.

Finally, Erin got to it. "Angela's obituary in *The Alumni News* said she died in her home, alone, of a brain aneurism. How awful to die so suddenly with no one around to help."

"Yeah. Terrible." Good riddance echoes in Lizbeth's head, followed by a twinge of guilt for thinking ill of the dead.

"The newsletter said she was single. Her career was her life," Erin added, warming to the details. "*The Alumni News* had a picture of Angela accepting an award for her work with the mentally ill in Hoboken, New Jersey."

"That was it?" Lizbeth was frustrated enough to spit. Her school nemesis had died a heroine?

"Well, no. Remember Tanya, my old roommate? She and Angela used to be tight, so I called to get more info."

"And?" Lizbeth said, straining to keep her voice neutral. Jeez Louise, Erin had been one of the biggest campus gossips. Guess that trait is still alive and well.

"Tanya told me that after Angela graduated, she had trouble keeping a job. The word went around she was into drugs. A couple years later, she almost died of a drug overdose and was hospitalized."

"Wow." Lizbeth wanted to punch her fist in the air—and then felt instantly ashamed for wishing addiction on anybody. Guilt crawled up her spine.

"There's more. Wait till you hear this, In the hospital, Angela was diagnosed as manic depressive. After she was released, she turned her life around. She went back to school and became a psychiatric nurse."

"Good for her," Lizbeth said, and was a little surprised she meant it. "Bipolar disorder can be awful to live with."

Erin shared one last morsel of information.

"Tanya said some years ago Angela made a 'roots trip' that included a church in upstate South Carolina where she heard the Gordon clan was known to worship. Apparently, she wanted to find you and make amends. But nobody at the church had a record of a Lizbeth our age or which Gordon ancestor you might have been descended from, so she gave up."

Lizbeth was silent for so long, Erin asked, "Are you there?"

"Yeah. I'm here. I wish I'd known." Lizbeth felt her legs about to buckle. She grabbed the kitchen counter to steady herself.

"I didn't know either. Tanya got a job in Chicago after college, and we drifted apart. We hadn't talked more than a couple times in a decade until day before yesterday, when I called to ask if she was going to the reunion."

Erin chattered on about other classmates for a few minutes until Lizbeth found an excuse to get off the phone.

She called Port Benton High School to report in sick and went out for a long walk on a wooded trail near home revisiting every minute of that day in African American History class, wishing she had known then what she knew now.

Lizbeth knew the devastating signs of Bipolar Affective Disorder that develop in late adolescence or early adulthood. She knew how confusing the symptoms can be and how hard it can be to make an accurate diagnosis. The manic state can build for weeks, making a person feel creative, powerful, almost Godlike. Was that what made Angela so cruel? She was mentally ill, and no one knew!

People with undiagnosed bipolar disorder often use alcohol and street drugs, trying desperately to manage mood swings they don't understand that can include paranoia or psychosis, then suddenly drop into deep depression. The lucky ones get diagnosed early and continue to see a psychiatrist for medication. Some have successful lives. Others go through cycles of one relapse after another, become addicted to drugs, or land in prison for crimes due to wildly erratic, dangerous, behavior. Someone with bipolar disorder has to work hard to live a healthy, balanced life even with the proper medication. Angela was a success story.

Now and again, Lizbeth remembered Erin's call and grieved for a minute or an hour or a day, over a lost opportunity. If she and Angela had met up again as adults, might they have made peace and become friends? Could they have confirmed a common ancestor?

⁓

Charlotte's belly laugh brings Lizbeth back to lunch at the river walk restaurant.

"Mama, let's see what you've got to show us." Lizbeth admires her cousin's ease at effectively pivoting a conversation where she wants it to go.

Aunt Sarah warms to the invitation, leaning towards her daughter and niece sitting across the table. "Our ancestor—John Gordon from Greenville County—moved to Charleston to study medicine. He married Angus Gordon's daughter, Jeanne, in the 1850s. Though Jeanne and John shared a surname, I assure you both, it was serendipity, not one of those second cousins marrying each other things—so don't you two roll your eyes at me."

Sarah consults notes she's pulled from her bag. "Jeanne was my great-grandmother, though I never met her. I found a few names and dates in her Bible, passed down to me. It's very fragile. I hadn't taken it down from my bedroom bookshelf for a couple of decades until Charlotte asked about Angus."

"Thanks for looking, Mama."

"I also remembered I'd once come across a nineteenth-century Gordon family photograph in my Mama's old chifforobe. Lo and behold, I dug it out. I must say though, the musty old contents of that drawer set me sneezing something furious." Aunt Sarah pulls an old-fashioned, heavy paper folder from her tote and waves it in front of her daughter and niece.

"Now, this photograph, y'all are going to love." She sets a Victorian-era portrait on the table between Lizbeth and Charlotte.

A couple and three children—a daughter and two sons—dressed in their finest, stare at the camera with solemn faces. Lizbeth elbows Charlotte.

"The woman in that photograph could be our sister!"

Charlotte leans in and squints at the photo. "Who is she, Mama?"

Aunt Sarah turns the portrait over to reveal a formal stamp: *The William Sloan studio; 213 Main Street, Greenville, South Carolina.* Below the studio name, written in a fading flowery script: *Dr. John Gordon, Jeanne Gordon, and Children; Ned, Eliza, and Johnny, August 1875.*

"You both favor Jeanne with your height and coloring. Even in this black-and-white photograph, you can tell she's fair. And she sits as tall as her husband."

"Their youngest child, Johnny, that's our great-grandaddy, right, Mama? He looks about five in that photograph, taken ten years after the war."

Charlotte leans in, scrutinizing the family. "I remember there was a photo of Johnny as a middle-aged man on Granddaddy's desk, but I've never seen him as a child."

"The family Bible says their eldest child, Ned, died young," Aunt Sarah says. "Johnny inherited the farm; they grew corn and soybeans. That's where your granddaddy was born, nearabout forty miles from here."

Lizbeth gets goosebumps imagining the lives of people who lived through the Civil War.

"We have plenty of information on the upcountry Gordons, so why do we know so little about the Charleston Gordons, Aunt Sarah?"

"I don't know, darlin'. They left the city and joined John's family on the farm in Greenville County. After the war, people didn't talk about that suffering time with Charleston in ruin." Sarah closes her eyes a moment, lost in tales she'd heard about the past. "The names of Jeanne's parents are in her Bible: Michelle Bacot from Charleston, and Angus Gordon, from Glasgow, Scotland. But there's nothing about Jeanne's siblings except the names, Laurette and Robert."

"Certainly, being a doctor in Charleston would have been preferable to the farm country upstate. It makes no sense they'd move." Charlotte raises her eyebrows in disbelief.

Aunt Sarah adjusts her glasses and touches each of the Gordon family faces reverently. "I agree, darlin'. It's a mystery. Must have been something unpleasant made them go. Heroic stories get passed down; the ugly ones don't."

Sarah reaches into her purse for her mirror and lipstick, applies a fresh coat of Mauve Milk to her lips, snaps the compact mirror closed, and replaces both where they belong. She looks into the faces of her niece and daughter.

"Y'all remember the history your grandparents drilled into you, I hope. In February 1865, General G. T. Beauregard withdrew the Confederate Army from Charleston and Fort Moultrie to fight near Columbia, though by then he knew the war was lost. The next day, the city surrendered to General Alexander Schimmelfennig. That very day, the Federal Government imposed a martial law on Charleston that lasted nine terrible years. I was told, in the early years of Reconstruction, Yankee officers allowed their men to exact whatever revenge they pleased on citizens of South Carolina."

Charlotte turns the conversation before her mother can get going on how people lost their land for back taxes and how Yankees salting farmland caused homelessness and starvation.

"Yeah, we get it, Mama. But remember Granddaddy's heroic story about Michael Gordon, the captain who rode with Wade Hampton's Cavalry, died in battle, and was posthumously awarded the Southern Cross of Honor? One night, after a few drams, he pulled out that medal and passed it around for us kids to hold. So, we know that story was true. But some of his others, well, they had to be tall tales."

"Yes, they were, darlin'. My daddy had a right fine imagination when he was spinning a story. That's how we entertained ourselves in the evening before television and the internet."

Lizbeth wants to butt in to say tall tales or sly secrets warp relationships, but she keeps her counsel. A snarky remark would hurt Aunt Sarah, and, besides, Lizbeth's hooked. Her fear of finding ugly skeletons is overwhelmed by a compelling family mystery she aims to dig in to.

"Aunt Sarah, do you know anything more about Angus and Michelle Gordon's children in Charleston?"

"Mama's chifforobe is mostly full of Bacot family tintypes and letters, but it's possible there are a few Gordon papers other than the photograph I brought today. It's all yours if you want it."

෴

On the highway back to Folly Island, Lizbeth can't get the photograph of Jeanne Gordon and her family out of her head. She fantasizes about the missing siblings. Did Laurette and Robert Gordon resemble her and Charlotte the way Jeanne did? Why did Jeanne lose touch with her siblings? The more she thinks about it, the more Lizbeth is sure a roots journey is the perfect distraction for staying out of a funk because her comfortable life in Port Benton crashed in humiliation.

Lizbeth's already taken one serendipitous step: last month, she joined The Charleston Historical Society, thinking their lectures would add spice to her guided tours. Now she has more reason to partake of nineteenth century records.

Lizbeth's high spirits fizzle as she approaches Charleston. She blinks back tears of regret. It's her fault Josh and Robbie know so little Gordon family history. She winces acknowledging she didn't talk about her antebellum Southern family owning enslaved people when she didn't really know the history herself.

She ticks off logical points to soothe her conscience. First, her academic parents were moved by discussions on science or music. They never discussed family ancestry around the dinner table like some people did. Second, her mother was adopted, and never remotely interested in genealogy. Third, her parents lived across the continent from Port Benton, and didn't visit often. Dammit. Is she making sense, or excuses?

If her parents hadn't died when Josh and Robbie were so young, would her sons have had summer visits, played in the neighborhood park, and become friends of her old school friends' children? Why had she let her high school experiences with racism remain so influential that she denigrated her hometown as if it was a second-rate place? What kind of modeling was that? No wonder her sons didn't ask about their Southern heritage. Lizbeth rolls her tight shoulders. She let herself be co-opted by Dan's family. He was so proud of his pioneer heritage; he and his parents told and retold stories about Kellers' clearing land in the wilderness of Western Washington. She never mentioned the fact Dan's family stole the ancestral homeland of local Indian tribes. What a wimp! She'd paid a high price for admission to the Keller clan.

Lizbeth barely notices the fragrant spring flowering shrubs along the roadside as she swipes at tears. She looks down at her white knuckles on the steering wheel and carefully unwraps her fingers one by one, flexing them and rolling her shoulders again. Breathe, girl.

Although she sidestepped Civil War history, rather than get into awkward discussions about her Southern family, she hadn't been a total cultural cop-out with her children. Josh and Robbie got summer beach trips to South Carolina. She and the boys delighted in playing hide-and-seek around the old city wharfs after reading pirate stories of Black Beard blockading Charleston Harbor in 1715. On one day trip to the city, they toured places George Washington slept when he visited Charleston in 1791. Lizbeth bought her twins child-sized tricornered hats they'd worn all summer. Just like her daddy, Lizbeth took Josh and Robbie to a re-enactment at the Cowpens Battleground where rebel militia routed the "The British Butcher," Lt. Col. Banastre Tarleton in 1781. As children, her sons embraced Carolina Colonial history. Now she wants them to embrace Gordon history too. But first, she has to embrace it herself. Including whatever skeletons might be hidden in Charleston.

CHAPTER THIRTEEN

Folly Beach, South Carolina, April 2010

I t's late when Lizbeth arrives at the cottage from Greenville. She tosses some trash from the car into the wastebasket under the kitchen sink and doesn't glance at the caller ID before picking up her phone on the third ring.

Now and again, Lizbeth overrides her better judgement and picks up an "unknown" call. It makes her cranky when it's a robo call with a smokin' deal on carpet cleaning. But sometimes like last week, her colleague, Barb, called with a new phone number and Port Benton High School gossip. Lizbeth would love to hear the voice of an old friend as she puts the phone to her ear.

"Hey, Ms. Gordon, Buck Engels here. I've been looking to find you. Your man, Dan, was a gaming buddy of mine. We did a couple of deals and truth be told, he died owing me a cool five thousand. I'm thinking you might help me out."

"How'd you get my number?" Her knuckles turn white gripping the cell. "What makes you think you have the right to call me? Dan betrayed me, you asshole!" Lizbeth disconnects and throws her phone on the couch. That's it! She's got to get Dan out of her head and out of her life. She drops into one of the wicker chairs and squeezes her eyes tight. Dammit! No more!

Lizbeth heads straight to the bottom drawer of her bedroom dresser and retrieves Dan's pillowcase. Before she can change her mind, she drives to the Piggly Wiggly market and shoves it into the reeking industrial-size dumpster behind the store.

Home again, she pops a can of R.J. Rocker's Pale Ale, fills a bowl with tortilla chips, switches on the television to a flick on Showtime, and spaces out. The next morning Lizbeth visits a local phone carrier and leaves with a new cell phone and number.

CHAPTER FOURTEEN

With the plethora of historical research resources in a three-hundred-year-old city like Charleston, Lizbeth is surprised locating a couple of Civil War citizens is such a chore. She makes calls, sends emails, and has a specialist at the County Library working through a list of possibilities. The experts tell her to be patient, it can take months to find the kind of information she's looking for.

She learns that Charleston City Hall, at the corner of Meeting and Broad Streets, was within range of Federal cannons during the siege of Charleston. In August of 1863, the building suffered a direct hit. Shortly thereafter, some valuable records going back two hundred years were sent to Columbia for safekeeping. As it turned out, most those records were lost when Yankee soldiers looted the State Capitol Building and burned it to the ground.

The records that didn't go to Columbia—such as business taxes, public meeting records, and property sales—remained stored in what was left of City Hall. Late in the war, displaced people looted or sheltered whenever they could in vacant buildings. Furnishings in City Hall vanished into fireplaces. Beginning in February 1865 and continuing for a year or more,

Federal troops and Yankee civilians looted city buildings for souvenirs of conquered Charleston. Irreplaceable documents going back to colonial days were seen drifting in the city streets on the afternoon sea breezes.

After hitting one dead end after another, day after day for two weeks, Lizbeth takes out her frustration on the cottage couch cushions, putting her back into every smack with a wood tennis racquet from the nineteen-sixties she found in the closet. Spent, she falls onto the couch. Jeez Louise, what happened to Laurette and Robert?

∽

On Sunday, as the collection plate is making its rounds, an idea shoots like an arrow by one of the stained glass window cherubs, hitting Lizbeth in the heart. Why is she spending all her time in libraries when churches have centuries-old parishioner records? She gets so twitchy waiting for the service to end, the woman on her left turns to Lizbeth and says, "Are you OK?"

Lizbeth seeks out the First Scots church historian. He tells her unequivocally that not only were Angus Gordon and Michelle Bacot married at the church in 1832, but all five of their children, including the three who survived their father—Jeanne, Robert, and Laurette—were christened in the sanctuary. The deacon suspects that the headstones for Michelle and her two children who died young were among those broken beyond recognition in the earthquake of 1889.

He shakes his head mournfully. "Church records say the quake was like the devil's thunder, Meeting Street was undulating like the sea, and aftershocks continued for days."

"We know Jeanne Gordon and her family, my direct ancestors, turned up near Greenville after the Civil War. Is there anything more in the records about Angus Gordon's children, Laurette and Robert? They seem to have just disappeared."

"I wish I could tell you more," the historian says. "Because of the siege, First Scots was closed for Sunday services in July 1863, although people continued to be buried here. During that time, our congregation worshiped at the Presbyterian Church near the Charleston Museum or in their homes."

Discouraged, Lizbeth calls her Aunt Sarah to see if she remembers anything more from family stories she heard as a child.

"When Daddy gave me Jeanne's Bible, he said he'd been told Dr. John Gordon, Jeanne and their children arrived nearly destitute at the family's farm a year or so after the war. I haven't thought about the sad story in decades. Daddy's guess was, the Gordons departed the city in a hurry, perhaps their fine house was commandeered by a federal officer, meaning they would have left their furnishings behind. A healthy horse and sturdy carriage at that time would have come dear. Traveling two hundred miles over ruined roads past burnt-out farms would have been dangerous. As a child I heard stories people bartered their valuables for food and safe passage between Charleston and a less war-torn place to settle."

⁓

After repeatedly coming up short on clues to Laurette and Robert's disappearance, Lizbeth calls Charlotte near despair. "I keep hitting wall after wall. It's so bad I've been taking out my frustration by slamming the couch cushions with an old tennis racquet and swearing like a sailor. Thank God I live alone. What would people think?"

"Take a break from the archives, Lizard. Go dancing with your friend Patsy."

CHAPTER FIFTEEN

Lizbeth arrives home to find a voice mail from a Dr. David Oliviera, headmaster of Leblon International School in Rio de Janeiro. They need to fill the position of school counselor immediately. Is she available from June to December? If so, please FAX her resume and return his call with times she is available for a Skype interview.

She replays the message three times. Can this be for real? Cell phone in hand, Lizbeth wanders out onto the porch puzzling over the call. Sandpipers run along the surf line, picking up insects and other tiny edibles. The sea is calm. A soft breeze ruffles her hair.

She snaps her fingers. Got it.

On a whim, the day she cleaned out her office at the high school, she'd filled out a query from the International Education Association.

Lizbeth pumps her fist in the air, gives a whoop, and dances around the room until she can sit still long enough to google Leblon School. It's legit! She searches her Word documents for her most recent resume, puts it on a thumb drive, and drives to the Copy Mart with Leblon School's FAX number on the seat beside her.

⁓

Twenty minutes into the interview with Dr. Oliviera, two teachers, and a School Board member, Lizbeth knows she's perfect for the job. The school is desperate for a North American counselor who understands culture shock and the challenges of a multiethnic student body. They're impressed by her resume that includes Peace Corps experience in Mexico. On the SKYPE interview, she learns Leblon's' students are a mix of expatriates and Brazilians, many of whom want to attend English-speaking universities. The counselor position is for six months, with an option to renew if the fit is good. The six -month contract comes with a generous signing bonus and a rent-free apartment. Lizbeth's heart is beating like she's just finished a four-minute mile when she accepts the offer and agrees to be in Rio de Janeiro in two weeks.

She does a celebration dance around the living room. The salary is damn good, way better than the high school in Port Benton. Her wanderlust bone is vibrating. She's always wanted to go international again. She isn't naïve enough to think they offered her the job because she's the world's greatest school counselor. They're desperate. She'll have to prove herself to the staff and students. Coming in midyear will be no cake walk.

Lizbeth wants to savor her surprise before she tells anyone. She dumps her breakfast dishes in the sink and hustles to the College of Charleston bookstore before it closes Saturday at noon. She finds a set of Brazilian Portuguese Language CDs, a used text on Practical Portuguese Grammar, and a bilingual dictionary. She's good at languages. Gearing up for a new one is her kind of challenge.

On the drive back to the cottage, possible consequences of her decision jab her. She hates the thought of abandoning the search for Laurette and Robert Gordon, but hey, Leblon School is only a six-month contract. In the new year, she'll be back in South Carolina and can double down on the quest for her missing Gordons.

Lizbeth jumps when a driver lays on his horn. In her distracted state, she's cut him off while merging onto the connecter bridge that leads to Folly Island. She lifts her hand in an 'I'm sorry' wave. He raises his middle finger as he passes. Wow. Another sign to embrace a fresh start in Brazil.

A few minutes later, doubt slithers in. Will everyone think she's a nut case leaving Charleston so suddenly? Will Charlotte harangue her, saying Rio de Janeiro is another geographical escape? Allowing for a two-week notice at the Exchange Building in case she needs a good reference in the new year, means she can't take a quick trip to Washington to see Josh and Robbie. Not that she could afford one. And where would she stay? She cringes. Will moving to Rio de Janeiro weaken the bridge she's been carefully rebuilding with her sons?

⁓

Charlotte is very quiet while Lizbeth delivers her news in detail. But true to form, her cousin looks at the upside. "OK, then! Congratulations, Lizard. And leave your homecoming at the holidays to me. I'll host Christmas for everyone in Greenville."

Lizbeth sighs out the breath she's been holding. "You're the best, Char."

On a SKYPE call, Lizbeth tells her sons she's got a job in Rio de Janeiro until the Christmas holidays. She covers her hurt feelings when they seem relieved. They don't have to be the bad guys, disappointing Mom. For months, Lizbeth has been sending them *come join me* hints in the form of internet links to summer job applications at Folly Beach. Now Josh is up front: He doesn't want to spend the summer across the country from his girlfriend. Robbie shares about the internship he's been offered at an archeological dig near the Canadian border. After the call, Lizbeth notices a familiar tingle: a hollow, very alone feeling that's followed her since childhood.

⁓

Her last night on Folly Island, Lizbeth is on the couch reading a novel that started great but lost its spark by page thirty. Get off your duff and go out on the beach.

She grabs a flashlight and heads into moonlight on the strand, deciding to check on the loggerhead turtle nest tucked into seagrass on a low dune. The nest has been protected from beachgoers by four sticks and a homemade sign stuck in the sand.

Hallelujah! What timing!

Newly hatched babies are emerging from the nest. Their slightly heart-shaped top shell is about two inches across tonight; those who survive to adulthood will be over two hundred pounds and live up to sixty years. Lizbeth knows their first minutes of life, crossing from the nest above the tide line to the sea, are their most precarious. Sea birds, crabs, and fish hunt near the surf line. Hatchlings who make it past the first wave of predators enter "the swimming frenzy" away from the shallow waters to the deep where they enter what a naturalist once told her is called "the lost years." So far, there is no research on loggerheads from the time they enter the sea until they return to the coastline to forage as adolescents around fifteen years of age.

Delighted, Lizbeth squishes her toes in the wet night sand, as she walks back to the cottage high on seeing brave baby loggerheads emerging from their nest.

⌀

The international flight she's booked allows two checked fifty-pound bags. Lizbeth chooses clothing carefully, as well as small, meaningful things: framed family photos, favorite paperbacks to re-read, a coffee mug stamped with a photo of the twins in Little League uniforms, and Charleston Plantation Tea. She remembers how horribly homesick she got in Mexico after her first weeks of "honeymoon" as an expatriate. Touchstones from home will help start every day in a positive mode.

She SKYPES with Josh and Robbie before Char arrives to drive her to the Hartsfield-Jackson Atlanta International Airport. The twins confirm they are all in for Christmas at Aunt Char's and wish her luck. No one mentions Port Benton, though Lizbeth can feel the vibes. Her sons still resent she sold the family home.

Lizbeth has an hour to wander before boarding the ten-hour, red-eye flight to Rio de Janeiro. She splurges on a handful of magazines, knowing English language periodicals will be outrageously expensive in Brazil. She remembers the waves of culture shock in the Peace Corps: longing for people with facial features that resemble hers, cravings for North American comfort food, and anything in English. One day she was so homesick for something in her native tongue, she read and re-read the list of ingredients on her toothpaste tube.

Fortunately, twenty-first century technology beats the 1980s, and there's only a one-hour difference between Eastern Standard Time and Rio. Scheduling time to talk to Charlotte will be a breeze. But Robbie and Josh's unpredictable schedules, and the four-hour time difference to Washington State, will be a hurdle.

She used to know her boys like the back of her hand. She used to have confidence she could influence them towards healthy, productive lifestyles. If she's honest with herself, she hasn't a clue what they are up to aside from grade reports at the end of every semester. She thinks of her mother's muttered mantra: *Little children, little problems, big children, big problems.* At this moment, Lizbeth feels a rare resonance with her mother.

Josh loves money too much and is a risk taker like his father. Robbie is studying archeology; will he ever make a decent living? Her heart begins to race. Her breathing quickens. Stop! Breathe. She refuses to feel guilty for getting a life.

CHAPTER SIXTEEN

Rio de Janeiro, Brazil, June 2010

The steamy chaos at Galeão International Airport is mindboggling after ten hours crammed in coach. Lizbeth rubs her face to better focus on the machine lobbing all manner of suitcases onto the squeaking S-shaped belt snaking through baggage claim. Finally, she can grab hers. Where in this swarm of sweating humanity will she find the school's driver? She pushes damp hair off her forehead. Breathe. It'll be OK.

Shouldering her extra-large backpack and pulling two bulging suitcases towards the exit, Lizbeth spots a stocky, middle-aged man holding a poster with her name in bold, black letters. His receding hairline is more prominent because his salt-and-pepper hair is slicked into a tight ponytail. She sees him extinguish a cigarette under his foot as she approaches and prays his car won't smell like an ashtray.

He greets her in heavily accented but excellent English.

"*Senhora* Gordon, my name is Antonio. I will drive you to your apartment at The Royale in Copacabana."

"Pleased to meet you, Antonio." They shake hands. He takes her suitcases. Lizbeth follows him through the sliding exit doors into a bright, cloudless, sky and a riotous collection of honking horns and shouting voices.

Antonio loads her bags into the boot of a black, late-model sedan. "We want you to feel at home in our beautiful city," he says. "Doctor Oliviera directed the *porteira* to supply your apartment with some groceries so you will not have to shop directly after your travel."

"Thank you for the thoughtful welcome, Antonio." She slides into the back seat, sinking into lush, gray leather.

It's curious; Antonio has a cultured accent, and a late-model, upscale car, yet assumes the demeanor of a working-class man. Wrong political party in the last election? Black sheep cast out of the fold for marrying beneath the family's social standing? Her mouth quirks in a small smile. Welcome back to Latin America, girl, where scandalous behavior is tolerated as long as you or your family don't get publicly busted.

Lizbeth settles into her seat, cracks open a bottle of mineral water left conveniently in a cup holder by the door, and takes a thirsty slug. Antonio pulls into traffic.

After a moment, Antonio breaks the silence. "Dr. Oliviera wanted me to remind you to rest and enjoy your first days in Rio. I will collect you Wednesday at ten in the morning for a meeting at the school."

Surrounded by evidence that she's entered a world far from Charleston, Lizbeth's relieved she has time to herself before starting the new job. Antonio's airconditioned auto allows her to keep the windows closed, avoiding air thick with diesel fumes. She watches fast-moving, bumper-to-bumper vehicles shift lanes on the highway like a dance choreographed by a hyperactive demon. Men on scooters with crates of vegetables and cases of beer stacked high behind them weave and cut between cars, trucks, and buses. Not one of them wears a safety helmet, and few have working brake lights.

The vibe of Latin American cities is familiar. It looks chaotic, but there are rules. Lizbeth remembers her Peace Corps training twenty-five years ago, which set her straight on traffic.

"We have manners," a group leader said. "A harmony between pedestrians and cars. If you step out to cross a street and don't turn your head my way, it is my duty to avoid harming you. However, if I observe you craning your neck back and forth using North American rules, then it is on you to stay out of my way. You might wait a very long time to cross a street. But that's not my problem. You are in my culture now."

At The Royale, Antonio accompanies Lizbeth to the door of her fourth-floor apartment, sets her luggage inside and hands her the key. He gives her a two-finger salute. "I will be in the lobby at ten Wednesday morning, *Senhora*."

Exhausted but restless, Lizbeth wanders the apartment, opening cupboards and drawers. The place looks clean and cared for with functional furnishings. Mediocre landscapes decorate the living room walls, probably the hobby of some relative of the owner. The large 1950s-era bathroom tiled in green and pink includes a side-by-side toilet and bidet, both in pristine condition. In the bedroom, she bounces her butt on the mattress. Nice. Definitely a more recent purchase than the rest of the apartment furnishings.

Returning to the central living space, Lizbeth is drawn to the large, double-hung windows overlooking Copacabana beach. After twisting the clasp, she muscles up the middle window, wincing at the squeak of wood on wood.

The view is magnificent. The ocean spreads out forever, sparkling in the sun. Pulling a chair to the window, Lizbeth rests her forearms on the sill and pops her head out to watch the slow-moving traffic along Atlantic Avenue four stories below. Yesterday she was in Charleston sweltering in the summer humidity. Today, Rio's soft sea breeze feels divine. She guesses the temperature is in the low seventies. The southern hemisphere's winter sun is behind her building, casting a shadow on the beach. Sunbathers are gathering up towels and coolers and heading to their cars. She suspects sunrise from this window will be heart-stopping beautiful.

Lizbeth puts the kettle on and digs a box of Charleston Tea Plantation teabags and a bag of salted pecans out of her backpack. She hadn't expected a thoughtful welcome gift of fresh papaya in a handwoven basket near the sink. She slices one onto a plate, then adds cheese she finds in the fridge and bread sticks from the cupboard. While the tea is steeping, Lizbeth takes stock. She's got a couple of days to enjoy being a tourist. On Wednesday, she'll find out what she's committed herself to for the next six months.

◦○◦

After a breakfast of toast and more luscious papaya, Lizbeth consults the *porteira* at the front desk about day tours.

"My cousin José owns a small tour company" she says. "He is respected for his knowledge of Brazilian history, *Senhora*. I can make a reservation for you." She reaches into a drawer and pulls out a brochure and opens it for Lizbeth.

"His best tour visits two of our magnificent places in one day. The *Pao de Acucar* (Sugar Loaf), our conical hill icon you see on postcards, rising up where Guanabara Bay meets the ocean. And, the world-famous Christ the Redeemer, on the Corcovado. From the feet of the statue, you can see far beyond the city."

◦○◦

Monday morning Lizbeth boards the sixteen-passenger bus, taking the last available seat, which is next to a skinny teenage boy wearing a Buenos Aires team soccer shirt. The driver turns into traffic and José stands facing the passengers, hanging on to a safety bar to steady himself in weaving traffic, and begins his narrative on the history of Copacabana.

He switches easily between Portuguese and Spanish but stumbles over English as he points out sights along Atlantic Avenue. When Lizbeth laughs at his jokes in Spanish, José notices her proficiency and announces to the group he is going to drop the English translation as the only North American aboard speaks Spanish.

When they park at Urca to visit the Sugar Loaf, Lizbeth remarks to José that hearing Spanish and Portuguese one after the other is a big help with learning a new language.

"I'm nervous about getting around in Rio," she confesses.

"*No te preocupes,*" he assures her. "Brazil is the only Portuguese-speaking country in South America; we all learn Spanish at school. Most shop owners and waiters at good restaurants speak some Spanish."

The group loads onto a glass-walled gondola for the mile-long ride first to the Morro da Urca then on up Pao de Acucar. From the top, looking inland, the views are as glorious as the guidebook promised; the sun dances on Copacabana and Ipanema beaches and beyond the downtown cityscape, the mountains of Parque National da Tijuca are more vivid than a panorama from *National Geographic* magazine.

∾

The group gets off the gondola halfway down to the parking lot for a light lunch. Lizbeth chats up her seatmate, Paulo, who says he's visiting his uncle in Rio. She misses the easy banter with teenagers. When Josh and Robbie were in high school, the Gordon home was full of young male voices and merciless teasing. She'd been the queen bee, chief cook, and sounding board for her sons and their friends. A bolt of nostalgia shoots though her heart. Dammit. Stay in the present!

During the half-hour drive from Urca to Corcovado, José tells the group how the famous one hundred twenty-five-foot Christ the Redeemer was originally designed to be made of bronze but had to be changed to concrete so it could survive the elements atop the hill.

Lizbeth doesn't expect to be so taken by the iconic Christ with his arms outstretched, embracing all who seek redemption. At the tourist shop, she buys a small, hand-carved rosewood replica and holds it in her palm it all the way back to The Royale apartments.

By the time Jose's minibus drops Lizbeth in front of her building, she is feeling more confident she won't stick out like a gringa thumb. During her day tour around the city, she noticed *cariocas*, Rio de Janeiro natives, are White and Black and Asian, indigenous and mixed ethnic. Her height and fair Scottish skin aren't common, but she won't be freakish like she was in southern Mexico. She can pass for a carioca until she opens her mouth. She smiles, inviting a little swing into her hips as she walks the two blocks to the nearest grocery store to see what looks good to add to her fridge.

CHAPTER SEVENTEEN

On Wednesday, Antonio rolls to a stop in the half-moon drive, in front of Leblon International School. He opens Lizbeth's door with a flourish. Angling his thumb toward the asphalt parking lot across the street, he offers to wait for her in the shade of a breadfruit tree.

Flowering shrubs work to soften the school's street entrance, which, at first glance, looks like a flat-roofed fortress with small, high windows. The wood and glass doors whisper open as Lizbeth enters. A wide, cream-colored entry is offset by a highly polished burgundy tiled floor and a view onto a manicured courtyard. Round wooden tables with sun umbrellas are scattered here and there. A bougainvillea with magenta flowers obfuscates a serious looking chain link fence on the far side of the courtyard. The overall effect is serene and secure; a modern version of a colonial-era walled garden. Beyond the fence lie soccer fields and a tall brick building. Probably the gym. Lucky students. Somebody's got bucks. No wonder Dr. Oliviera offered such a fine salary.

Lizbeth follows signage to the administration offices. A middle-aged woman rises from her desk, extending a hand.

"Good morning and welcome." She smiles. "I'm Alicia Alverez, Leblon administrative secretary. Dr. Oliviera and the others await you." Alicia leads the way. Before knocking on the door marked Conference Room, she says, "Please stop by on your way out. I can answer practical questions the headmaster may not cover."

After a two-hour orientation to the Leblon philosophy of education and a campus tour, Lizbeth feels like her head will explode with rules, details, and policies. Thank goodness she's got a week while students are on winter break to read the teacher's manual, prepare her room, and get her professional self in order.

Lizbeth's flagging and famished. She was so ramped this morning, she'd skipped breakfast. When Alicia suggests a coffee and *biscoito*, Lizbeth jumps at the opportunity hoping a little gossip about the counselor she is replacing will go with the snack. They chat about the fine weather and motherhood and school holidays until Lizbeth finds an opening.

"What do I need to know about the former school counselor's style to get on board quickly?"

"No one wept when the Logans returned to Sidney early," Alicia confides. "Mrs. Logan was the unhappy wife of an unhappy Australian diplomat."

"It's a relief to know I'm not replacing a beloved counselor midyear." Lizbeth imagines a juicy story but doesn't push for details.

"There's something else about your arrival: It's rather exciting. I probably should wait, but I can't hold it back." Lizbeth is thinking this woman doesn't hold back on much of anything. Getting close to Alicia could be a blessing or a curse. Better tread carefully.

"One of our teachers, my friend Ana Maria Gordon de Souza, is dying to meet you. You share a surname."

"That will be interesting," Lizbeth says, feeling a little squirmy.

"Ana Maria is a lovely person. She's away visiting family, or I would connect you while the students are on holiday."

Lizbeth smiles and gathers her orientation notebook, set of school keys, and the light cotton sweater she wore in the cool of the morning. "See you soon, then."

Lifting her hand goodbye, she walks through the parking lot to Antonio's car. She raps on the driver's side window with a light touch, waking him from under the newspaper he's spread to shade his face. He stretches and pops the lock. Lizbeth slides into the back seat. She's in serious need of a nap herself. Tomorrow she'll be back to take a better look at her office and decide how to make it look inviting.

∾

In the morning, Lizbeth exits her apartment building at a good clip, hurrying to make her bus to Leblon, and smacks into a man standing on the sidewalk. He grabs her by the shoulders to keep them both upright. *"Desculpe-me, Senhora."*

Surprised by the impact, she responds in English. "I'm so sorry. I didn't look where I was going." She switches to Portuguese. *"Eu sinto muito."*

She's momentarily hypnotized by his eyes, the color of milk chocolate. His musky aftershave is divine. She recognizes him as a man she's seen reading the paper in an easy chair in the lobby. He'd smiled and murmured, *"Bom Día,"* as she passed. She'd smiled back but hadn't stopped to speak.

He switches to heavily accented English. "You are the new teacher at the international school, yes?"

"How could you possibly know that?" His hands still circle her upper arms. She steps back a pace. His smile is engaging and boyish, though he is no boy.

"Everyone in the Riviera knows Enrique Lopez rents one of his apartments to the international school. We residents notice when a new teacher arrives."

Between culture shock and orienting to a new job, it hadn't occurred to Lizbeth she might be an object of curiosity in her own apartment building. The thought makes her skin crawl a little.

"I have to be on my way, I'm running late." With a stiff smile she turns to leave. Is she acting like an ugly American with no social graces?

"Don't worry, *Senhora.* I am Joao Ramos, your neighbor from the fifth floor." Joao raises his arm, signaling a taxi that careens to the curb. "My appointment is near Leblon School." Opening the taxi's door, he invites her to join him with a sweep of his arm. "I'm pleased to drop you at your destination."

Lizbeth looks at the inviting taxi and decides to take a risk. After all, he lives in her building. She's seen him before; he can't be a dangerous stranger.

"Thank you. By now I've missed my bus. The next one won't be for an hour and I'm a typical American who doesn't like to arrive late."

"A beautiful woman should take advantage of arriving last and enjoy the attention of entering with the audience seated."

If they were in South Carolina, Lizbeth would blast him with a tart retort about machismo. But here in Brazil, she restrains herself. He'd probably use the same line on his grandmother. So, Lizbeth smiles a thank you and slips into the back seat of the late model taxi.

⁂

The forty-minute ride to Leblon School passes in easy conversation. Joao points out an upscale hotel in Ipanema where he says there'll be an important fundraising dinner the following night honoring the presidential front-runner, Dilma Russoff.

Lizbeth gets Joao laughing with her comments on the campaign process in Brazil. "The caravans of vehicles with fluttering flags, posters of candidates, people tossing candy from the windows, loudspeakers blasting recorded political messages at all hours, make it hard to get my beauty rest. Where I come from, candy-spewing cars decorated with flags are for holiday parades, not political campaigns."

"Our illiteracy rate in Brazil is high for a developed country. People learn about candidates via rallies, photographs, and those recordings you hear. Ballots have a picture of each candidate next to the name. People who can't read recognize the pictures. The system works."

Joao confides he makes international business trips several times a year and often thinks North American behavior odd. For the rest of the ride, they laugh as they share anecdotes on cultural missteps. When the taxi pulls up in front of the school, Lizbeth gathers her things and extends a hand, thanking Joao for sharing his taxi.

"Will you join me for dinner tomorrow night?"

Lizbeth goes very still in a moment's indecision. She hasn't been alone with a man since Dan died and she hasn't wanted to be. But maybe, now, in a new country making a new start, she's ready for a date.

"Dinner sounds nice. As we say in the States, thank God tomorrow is Friday!"

"I'll meet you in the lobby at nine. I have the perfect restaurant in mind."

CHAPTER EIGHTEEN

It takes days for Lizbeth to reconstruct what happened that Friday night. The evening started out perfectly. She dressed in skinny black capris, a silky floral top that floated over her curves, and strappy sandals. She dotted her wrists and behind her ears with Miss Dior. She scrutinized her image one last time in the full-length bedroom mirror before taking the elevator to the lobby. She looked fabulous! Her heart skipped in her chest, part trepidation and part thrill at breaking out of her widow's weeds as she exited the elevator into the lobby with a spring in her step.

The destination Joao chose was the Restaurante Garota de Ipanema. Once they were seated, he told Lizbeth its legend.

"The famous composer Antônio Jobim, and his friend, the poet Vinícius de Moraes, used to sit for hours at the Bar Veloso, admiring cariocas strolling to the beach. One especially beautiful seventeen-year-old girl, Heloísa Pinheiro, was the subject of much admiration. Moraes called her swaying walk sheer poetry. She was his inspiration for the lyrics to Jobim's music, a collaboration on what became Rio's signature song, 'The Girl from Ipanema.'"

"That song has always been one of my favorites." Lizbeth smiled into Joao's face.

"Astrid Gilberto and her husband, the saxophonist Stan Getz, made the song world famous in the 1960s, and their rendition is still popular here. We are sitting in the original bar, though it's been expanded and renamed for the song."

"It's so romantic. The longing for someone you can't have feels magical in the bossa nova rhythm."

"We Brazilians have a great appreciation for music and beauty," Joao says, as his gaze slid into the V of her blouse. Before Lizbeth could respond, a waiter appeared at the table.

Joao ordered a round of *caipirinhas*.

"It's the signature drink of Rio de Janeiro made from Brazilian rum, the juice and rind of limes, and a little sugar."

Lizbeth took a sip. "It's delicious: sweet and tart together."

A band on the far side of the room was warming up.

Joao suggested she order *caruru*: tender shrimp, spicy vegetables, and rice. The dish reminded Lizbeth of gumbo in the American South. They shared fried bananas for dessert. Joao held her tight as they swayed to the bossa nova rhythm and drank caipirinhas into the wee hours.

How many drinks did they order? In the taxi back to The Royale, they groped each other shamelessly in the cab's back seat.

The details of what they did in Joao's bed that night were fuzzy, but they did a lot of it. Lizbeth was sore for two days. She hadn't been with a man since Dan died. That Friday night, she gave herself completely, letting her body sing. Oh, how she had missed a man's touch.

කො

She woke alone and disoriented in Joao's disheveled bed with the scent of strong Brazilian coffee calling from the living room. How long has she slept in? What time was it? She rose slowly, head aching, and wrapped herself in the dressing gown Joao left on a chair by the door. After a stop in the bathroom, she went in search of her new man.

He was at the kitchen table reading the newspaper with his cup of coffee next to a plate of sliced pineapple and papaya. Lizbeth approached and Joao stood to greet her.

"Good morning," she said and tilted her head up to receive a kiss. Did she blush?

"Please sit. Have a coffee and toast." As they settled into chairs around the kitchen table, there was a sharp clicking sound: a key turning in the apartment door. Joao stared, his mouth half open, as the door swung inward, followed by a petite blonde woman dressed to the nines, pulling a wheeled suitcase.

"Bom dia, querido," she called as she kicked the door closed with a designer pump and turned toward the table where Lizbeth sat with Joao. Lizbeth had just a moment to register, *"'Querido?'* 'Dear?'" and her heart turned over.

The woman's green eyes narrowed. A string of obscenities as caustic as battery acid poured out of her gorgeous mouth.

She began hurling whatever was close at hand in the direction of Joao and Lizbeth. Lizbeth ducked a metal vase. Joao hurried to calm the woman (his wife?), wrapping his arms about her body, preventing more missiles from escaping.

"Por favor, meu Amor . . ."

Lizbeth slipped past them, grabbing her purse off the table by the door. She flew down the fire escape stairwell, wearing the slighted woman's dressing gown. She let herself into her apartment. Joao's wife hollered like a banshee on the floor above. Some of her words were distinct in the hall. How many residents would discuss the scandal and crashing china on the fifth floor over their morning coffee?

Dammit! Just like Port Benton. And she was the fool. Did Joao have a reputation as a womanizer, and was the latest conquest? Would the concierge tell *Senhor* Gonzales, who owned her apartment? Would she lose her job? She tried to stay rational. You didn't know he was married. You just wanted to have a good time and never meant to hurt anyone. She'd look for another apartment if she could, but she couldn't.

Her budget requires the perk of free rent. Lizbeth hides inside for the rest of the weekend. Monday morning, she takes the fire escape stairs rather than the elevator and hurries through the lobby to her bus stop.

For weeks, Liz keeps her eyes averted when she rides the elevator. She is relieved not to spot Joao reading the paper in the lobby for a very long time.

క్ు

After Joao, Lizbeth relegates men to a no-go zone. She arrives early and stays late every day of the first week of the new term. By Friday she's set up a program to ease new expatriate students through culture shock and English conversation groups for cariocas behind in their language skills. Louise, a Canadian teacher with a Brazilian husband in the classroom next door, stops by on her way home, offering advice. *Va com calma.* "Bide your time bringing in new programs. Dr. Oliviera is old school."

"What do you mean?" Lizbeth feels irritable; being busy means less time alone in the apartment stewing on Joao or other regrettable decisions she's made in forty something years.

"Our headmaster is a wonderful man in many ways," Louise continues, "but he has a good dose of Brazilian machismo. We teachers have learned to keep him thinking the freshest ideas come first from his very own head."

"Sounds like I'm going to a need mentor to get onboard."

"I know someone who might be eager to volunteer," Louise smiles.

CHAPTER NINETEEN

Rio de Janeiro, July 2010

L izbeth stops by her mailbox before the first all-staff meeting of
the new term and finds a note from Ana Maria Gordon de Sousa.
"Looking forward to meeting you." Hmm. Must be the teacher
Alicia mentioned. Hopefully not some intrusive woman expecting to be
instant best friends.

The conference room sideboard is festooned with treats and showy,
fragrant flowers from Alicia's garden. Teachers stop by to pour a coffee,
grab a sweet, or catch up on gossip before finding a seat in one of the
straight-backed chairs. Ana Maria Gordon de Sousa enters, adds a plate
of homemade *paçoca* to the snacks, fills her cup, and takes a seat next to
Lizbeth. Some seated teachers get up to snatch a piece of Ana Maria's candy
before the plate is picked clean.

Ana Maria winks at Lizbeth. "I have a sweet tooth."

"I've seen that candy on the street, but I haven't tried it."

"It's our highly addictive Brazilian peanut candy," Ana Maria says,
plunking a piece onto Lizbeth's plate. "This is my grandmother's recipe.
It's rather like the American Butterfinger bar but much better."

Lizbeth takes a tentative bite. "Wow. It melts in the mouth. Yummy." She pops the rest of the piece in her mouth.

They chat quietly until Dr. Oliviera opens the meeting with a special welcome to Lizbeth Gordon, "the new addition to our Leblon family." He skillfully leads a discussion of the semester schedule through a hotbed of priorities. A list of new students and their families is circulated, followed by strategies to help some at-risk students.

Lizbeth's never experienced a concerted schoolwide effort like this one that balances the needs of national and international students. She's impressed but feels a tingle of trepidation wiggle in her gut. Could her position as school counselor become politicized by pressure from parents who expect their children to enter prestigious universities around the world?

చి

After the meeting, Ana Maria offers Lizbeth a lift to her apartment.

"I thought you said your house is in the opposite direction from Copacabana?"

"It is, but I'm not in a hurry. It's just my husband and me at home now. Besides, we haven't had a chance to talk about our shared surname."

Ana Maria seems like a genuinely nice person, but Lizbeth feels a bit overwhelmed adjusting to her new job, and a reluctance to share her personal life. She shifts the conversation away from family to advice on shops for inexpensive local crafts to personalize her apartment.

As they drive, Lizbeth relaxes into the synergy that happens now and again when a new friendship begins to bud. By the time they arrive at The Royale, they've discovered mutual loves for ocean swimming, classic novels, and helping troubled adolescents. Lizbeth guesses Ana Maria must be sixty, but her style and sense of humor are youthful.

On the front steps of her apartment building, Lizbeth raises her arm in goodbye as Ana Maria pulls away from the curb. They've made a lunch date for Saturday.

చి

The famous Jardim Botânico has been on Lizbeth's to-do list since she arrived in Rio. She's decided on a self-guided tour wandering the gardens before her lunch date with Ana Maria.

Her brochure says the Jardim was created in the early 1800s as a location to collect flora from all of Portugal's tropical colonies. The idea was to explore growing plants for their seeds and develop economical transport throughout the Portuguese empire. The first to arrive were various species for spice and tea plant production. Next, fruit-producing and shade trees were added. Decorative and medicinal plants came next, each in its own category and locale in the Jardim. By the late 1800s, the gardens had become a botanical research and teaching facility open on weekends for public enjoyment. Now, the 140 hectares park has 6,500 species of plants and is a sanctuary for one hundred forty species of birds, like channel-billed toucans and white-necked hawks. Capuchin monkeys chatter in the trees and tufted-ear marmosets sit in wait for crumbs dropped by children.

Lizbeth wanders the packed-earth paths through the lush garden listening to a symphony of birdsong and inhaling the perfume of flowering trees. There's hardly a weed in sight. Does an army of gardeners magically appear to keep everything perfect when the decorative iron gates close in the afternoon?

It's nearly one o'clock. Lizbeth picks up her pace to arrive on time. As she enters the restaurant, she spots Ana Maria in a quiet corner. After a Brazilian double cheek kiss, they settle in dappled sunlight, eating green salads and sharing a plate of *coxinha*.

Lizbeth says, "The coxinha is delicious, but if I eat morsels of chicken covered in fried pastry dough very often, I'll outgrow my clothes in no time."

Ana Maria shares some cultural influences of Brazilian cuisine.

"Did you know, in the 1860s, immigrants from the southern United States introduced two of our favorite foods: watermelon and fried chicken?"

"I had no idea!" Odd how Ana keeps circling back to the topic of the American South.

Ana Maria smiles at Lizbeth. "I confess I'm very curious about your family history in South Carolina. I can't stop thinking we must be related."

Lizbeth, who has been trying not to wolf her lunch after only coffee and toast for breakfast, nearly chokes. She takes a sip of mineral water and swallows hard.

"What makes you think so?"

"Have you heard of the Confederados?"

"No."

"We Brazilians call people who left the Southern states after the American Civil War Confederados. Some former Confederates emigrated because they'd lost their land to carpetbaggers or because they couldn't pay back taxes. Others had been officers, blockade runners, or spies who had to live in exile after being declared traitors to the United States in 1865."

"Wow. Brazil was never mentioned in my American history classes, though I do remember something about Confederate officers escaping into Mexico to avoid prison." Lizbeth feels twitchy under Ana Maria's intense gaze.

"What made Confederates running from Yankees after the Civil War choose someplace as far away as Brazil?"

"Brazil's King at the time, Dom Pedro the II, wanted his country to compete in the industrializing world. Southern farming technology was far superior, and Dom Pedro wanted it for Brazil." Ana Maria pauses and gives Lizbeth a rueful smile. "He wasn't exactly Moses leading refugees to the promised land, but he did give away homesteads and helped settle newcomers from the American South after the Civil War."

Lizbeth is both intrigued and wary. "Why are you so keen for me to know this?"

Ana Maria reaches for Lizbeth's hand across the table.

"My ancestor, Robert Gordon, was a Confederate blockade runner from Charleston with a price on his head. He, his wife and son, as well as his sister Laurette and her infant daughter, arrived in Rio de Janeiro in 1866. For a year after the war ended, they hid in the Bahama Islands until they could immigrate to Brazil. Communication with the Southern states was terrible in that time. They lost contact with their family in South Carolina. Like many immigrants in that era, our Gordons had to let go of the past to concentrate on making a new life. When you arrived from Charleston, I thought perhaps you are a link. Perhaps together we can solve a one hundred fifty-year old mystery."

Lizbeth goes very still. The back of her neck prickles. She pinches her leg hard under the table, forcing her thoughts into a calm, rational mode.

"This is impossible serendipity!" she says, in an excited whisper. "In April, my cousin Charlotte and I discovered the grave of Angus Gordon in First Scots Presbyterian Church cemetery in Charleston. The epitaph on his stone said he was survived by three children: Jeanne, Robert, and Laurette." Lizbeth takes a deep breath to keep from rushing her words. "My family is descended from Jeanne Gordon. Growing up, we didn't know Robert and Laurette existed, although our Grandaddy Gordon had vague tales of lost family. We grandchildren loved his tall tales, but we didn't consider them God's truth. Every Southern family I know has stories about people who never returned home after the Civil War."

Lizbeth's heart is pumping. Oh my God . . . Oh my God. . . . Robert and Laurette went to Brazil?

"Just before I got the job offer at Leblon, I'd spent weeks digging in libraries looking for information about Robert and Laurette and found nothing."

Ana Maria claps her hands in delight and gives Lizbeth a radiant grin.

"I think you've found them. Come for lunch next weekend and meet my family. My daughter and her family live in Rio and my son will be in town for business all next week."

ॐ

Back at the apartment, Lizbeth reviews lunch. Intuition, like a magnet, draws her to warm, intelligent Ana. But since Dan's betrayal and then Joao, she second guesses herself, scanning people from a safe emotional distance like a telephoto lens scoping for danger. She doesn't want to identify with the Confederado Gordons if they were scoundrels. She's had enough disappointments this year and it's only half over. Somehow, in Charleston, it felt safer to look for missing branches from the family tree.

Never-mind, she decides. One Sunday lunch with Ana Maria's family can't hurt.

CHAPTER TWENTY

C ounseling at a multicultural international school is a delicate political dance. Fortunately, Lizbeth dances well. She's festooned her office in an upbeat vibe: bilingual inspirational posters from Universidade Federal bookstore and colorful corkboards with announcements on groups and activities for new families. Her students from North America are flummoxed by the Brazilians' deep family connections and indirect conflict-resolution style, yet they have an academic advantage because the school's core courses are taught in English. The greatest hurdle is helping students from countries like Korea or Israel who don't have a good grasp of either English language or Latin culture. Teachers and administrative staff notice Lizbeth's gift for connecting with adolescents and calming anxious parents. In no time, she's swamped, happy to be counseling kids again.

 e-ro

Monday, after Ana Maria's disclosure of their family connection, Lizbeth stands at her school mailbox sorting her mail: coupons for businesses, adverts for vacations she can't afford—and one pale blue envelope with her name in elegant script that must have been delivered to school by hand. No stamp.

"Dear *Senhora* Gordon. I need a consultation. Please call at your earliest convenience." Respectfully, *Senhora* Monica Lopez."

Part of the counselor's obligation at Leblon School is to accommodate parents who want a private consultation away from curious eyes. Rio may be a city of six million, but a small cadre of well-connected families live in a labyrinth of relationships. Intrigued, Lizbeth returns to her office and dials the local number. She listens to the Lopez phone ring and ring without going to voice mail and is about to hang up when a woman answers, "Lopez residencia."

Lizbeth navigates the usual screening questions, feeling a lick of pride that her daily hour or two on Portuguese language lessons is bearing fruit.

"Apenas um minuto, por favor," the woman says and drops the receiver with a loud clunk. Lizbeth pulls a face. Probably the housekeeper assumes Lizbeth is nobody important. Receding steps echo on a tile floor and disappear. Lizbeth waits and is rewarded when Monica Lopez picks up. They agree to meet that afternoon.

∾

Monica Lopez leads Lizbeth to a patio surrounded on three sides by a flowering oleander hedge. Coffee and sweet biscuits are laid out on a tray. They weave through the usual subjects of weather and school events until Monica's beautiful face crumples as she broaches the subject of her son. "I'm sick with worry over Angel," she whispers, noting the approach of a uniformed maid to retrieve their dishes. Monica returns to light conversation until they are alone again.

"Last week I caught him stealing from Hernan's wall safe. Angel won't say why he needs money. We give him a generous allowance."

She blots her tears with a tissue.

"Hernan will be furious if he finds out. He says I spoil Angel. Perhaps he's correct. Angel is my youngest, a free spirit, full of humor, and popular with his peers. But unlike his siblings, Angel prefers sports to studies. Hernan is very disappointed."

Lizbeth is empathic immediately, thinking of her sons thousands of miles away.

"It's hard when children veer from the path we want for them."

"Yes. Hernan is a proud man: a chauffeur's son, from San Juan, Puerto Rico, who won a scholarship to Columbia University and has done very well in business. Angel is on academic probation, which my husband finds unacceptable."

Monica's hands are clasped tight in her lap as she struggles to control her voice.

"Hernan is threatening to send our son to a boarding school in Utah."

Monica grabs another tissue, folds it carefully, dabbing at the corners of her eyes, attempting to save her ruined makeup.

"I'm a Bolivian citizen. I've never lived in the United States. If Hernan sends Angel away, what will happen to him? I will be powerless to intervene."

Lizbeth understands troubles with sons. Reluctantly, she agrees to counsel Angel at school without his father's knowledge.

∽

The next afternoon in Lizbeth's office, Angel, a tall, seventeen year old with an athletic build, sits rubbing his knees rhythmically, as he confesses to stealing from his parents. He admits he's in trouble because of his affair with Francisca, a thirty-year-old personal trainer at the gym where his family has a membership.

A couple of weeks ago, he dropped Francisca for a recently arrived Italian student at Leblon. Francisca, accustomed to choosing the time to end a sexual dalliance, was furious and out for revenge. If Angel doesn't pay up, she threatened to send snapshots from their trysts to the newspaper gossip column. Angel is desperate, and miserable. He's already pilfered money from his father's safe and a pair of gold earrings from his mother's jewelry box. He's terrified of his father's wrath. But Francisca isn't satisfied. He's put her off but not for long.

Lizbeth and Angel agree to a second appointment. In the meantime, they'll both brainstorm strategies that could get him out of this mess without exacerbating the problems with his father.

After Angel departs, Lizbeth gazes out her window at students laughing in the courtyard. She stews on a few unappetizing options. Ripples from a scandal could affect Angel's future community standing and career opportunities for years. Monica has good reason to be concerned her fun-loving son is in big trouble unless a formula for damage control can be found.

⁓

Lizbeth and Ana Maria meet up to walk during the school lunch hour, keeping the conversation light as they pass people with a *"Bom dia,"* or a nod.

"We are so fortunate to have my son, Lucas, down from Benin, staying with us all week. Christina, her husband, and children are all coming on Sunday," Ana Maria reports. "Everyone is dying to meet you."

"What can I bring?"

"Perhaps a dessert from your family tradition?"

"When I was packing for Brazil, I put a copy of *The Charleston Recipes* in my bag. My mama used to make the butter milk pie from that book."

"Perfect."

"I'm nervous about my Portuguese. It's good for the basics, but I can't go deep into conversations yet. Do you all speak English?"

"I studied in the United States, so, yes, I'm the family expert, but my children do well. When they were young, we had English-only dinners three times a week. It's a Confederado tradition to speak English, although these days, many families aren't vigorous about keeping it up."

Lizbeth resonates to Ana Maria as if she's an older sister and wants to deepen the friendship. But if Robert Gordon was an exile who believed in slavery, she remains ambivalent about embracing him as her ancestor. And what criminal behavior made Laurette join him in exile? Lizbeth glances at her watch.

"We'd better get back. There'll be a student knocking on my office door in fifteen minutes."

"You're right. I'd lost track of time."

"Ana, I have a favor to ask about a Brazilian student with a difficult problem. Are you up for a consultation?"

"With pleasure."

Lizbeth relates Angel Lopez's dilemma.

"Let me think."

Ana Maria slows her pace, pondering, while Lizbeth shoots glances in her direction. On the one hand, Lizbeth's broken client confidentiality. On the other hand, she has no one else to consult with on this sensitive situation.

They walk in silence for a minute. Ana Maria turns to Lizbeth with a smile. "Angel's problem is solvable."

"What can I do? I was up half the night weighing approaches. No matter what intervention I contemplate, the fallout seems draconian."

"Trust me to work the Brazilian pathway of discretion. I need a few days."

"OK. My fingers are crossed. Angel and I have an appointment on Friday afternoon." She wonders what Ana could have come up with that she hasn't already visited and revisited while pacing her office.

Lizbeth is rather miffed when Ana Maria is busy for the next couple of days and doesn't get back to her about Angel. It's Friday. She's wracked her brain but hasn't come up with much that can help. At the appointed hour, Angel saunters in, loose-limbed and relaxed, grinning from ear to ear.

"What's got you so happy?"

"Francisca is gone. She left a note in my locker saying we're done." He punches his fist in the air. "I'm free!"

Lizbeth gives Angel the not-so-fast-buddy look she perfected on Josh and Robbie. She's sure, underneath the bravado, he's a sweet kid who's had the scare of his seventeen-year-old life.

Angel sits down.

"Francisca may be gone but you're not done with me. Here's the deal. You use the school tutoring service, get your grades up by December, or I spill some beans to your Papa and off you go to Utah."

Angel's eyes widen in surprise. "You wouldn't."

"I would."

CHAPTER TWENTY-ONE

Sunday at noon, Lizbeth stands in The Royale's lobby, holding two buttermilk pies, waiting for the driver Ana Maria is sending. She's pleasantly surprised when Antonio saunters through the door.

"Antonio! It's Sunday! Don't you ever take a day off?"

He holds her pies while she settles into the back seat of his car.

"Weekends are my own business, not school business, *Senhora*. I like the extra money. My family is saving for a larger apartment."

Lizbeth can relax with Antonio as her driver. Dr. Oliviera warned her: "Until you buy a car, *Senhora*, use only vetted private drivers." She doesn't mention hers is a public transportation budget. Fortunately, though buses are crowded, they're safe during the day and run pretty much on schedule.

A travel show she watched before she left Charleston had warned of crime in Rio's *favelas*. As Antonio skirts a steep hillside stacked with honeycomb-like buildings, she queries him, "Are favelas as dangerous as the stories say?"

"*Senhora*, it is unfair to say this about all hillside neighborhoods. Vidigal Favela, where I live, has middle-class apartments, small houses, and family businesses. We have a very good market with traditional crafts on Saturdays. I could drive you there sometime if you wish. It is also true some favelas are home to very poor people who steal to survive, gangs who terrorize people, and violent drug wars over territory. You should always be careful, *Senhora*. A woman must not be on the street alone after dusk. Call me. I will drive you."

Advice implying women don't have the sense to look out for themselves irritates Lizbeth to no end. During her years in Mexico, no one harassed her. But, as a Peace Corps volunteer, she had lived and worked in a small community. In Rio, she's a stranger with few connections. Antonio is just trying to be helpful. And he had a point. One cloudless afternoon soon after she arrived, Lizbeth spread her towel on the beach to relax after a swim. In no time, she was surrounded by a swirl of pre-teen boys hawking towels, Cokes, and sunglasses. Even after waving them away with a firm, "No, thank you," they persisted, competing for her attention, crowding in, offering deals. Lizbeth felt intimidated by their numbers. She gathered her things and moved off quickly. They pursued, begging for business. Fortunately, she passed a family she recognized from her apartment building; they came to her rescue by waving her over. In the end, it turned out well. That afternoon began a warm relationship with the Ribeiro family.

∾

Antonio arrives in Lagoa, a desirable neighborhood at one end of the lake for which it's named. He turns onto a street dappled with light from a canopy of mature trees and stops in front of a white stucco house with a traditional red tile roof. Lizbeth admires the postcard-perfect image. It's exactly how she imagined the streets of Rio would look until she found herself living in a beach neighborhood dominated by high-rise apartments and condominiums.

Ana Maria greets Lizbeth at the door with a kiss on each cheek.

"Let's put your dessert away before we join the family."

Lizbeth follows Ana to a well-appointed kitchen, relieved to grab a private minute to catch up on Angel. "Angel was on cloud nine Friday when he arrived for our appointment. A complete one-eighty from earlier in the week. Francisca left town. Weird she'd disappear when Angel was in her clutches for blackmail."

"Well, there is more to it."

"Tell me."

"My husband and Ricardo, the gym owner, have been friends since university days and meet for lunch regularly." Ana Maria gives Lizbeth an impish smile. "Of course, Ricardo was aware of Angel's affair. He keeps tabs on these things to protect his business and his clients. Francisca has a reputation for liaisons with gym members who gift their appreciation with jewelry and other indulgences. However, extortion is not tolerated. Ricardo gave Francisca a reference for a gym in Brazilia and told her not to contact Angel again. She departed knowing Ricardo has connections that could see she never works as a personal trainer again."

Lizbeth's mouth drops open. This is the first time she has personally experienced the power of multilayered family connections in Rio.

"I don't suppose I can thank your husband?"

"No."

"Well, I'll thank you, then."

"My pleasure."

"I had my own win with Angel. While he was high on escaping Francisca's clutches, I wrestled him into a deal. He's signed up for tutoring starting Monday."

Ana Maria circles Lizbeth's waist as they walk from the kitchen to the patio.

"His mother is very grateful. Come, my family is impatient to meet you!"

As they approach the patio, Lizbeth sees Ana Maria's family in animated conversation around a table set for lunch. Blooming pink hibiscus and enormous ficus trees are planted in front of the wall enclosing the garden. Lizbeth's stomach roils in a moment of panic. What will they think of her?

Ana Maria's face glows as she introduces her husband, Pedro, their son Lucas, daughter Christina, and her spouse. They spend a few minutes in greeting before Christina calls to her twin girls doing cartwheels on the lawn.

"Come meet your cousin all the way from the United States."

As the girls skip to the patio, Lizbeth can't believe what she sees.

"One of your daughters reminds me so much of my cousin Charlotte as a child, it takes my breath away."

Ana Maria laughs.

"I knew you would be excited once you met more of us. We're quite multiethnic after four generations, but the Scottish genes continue strong. And twins are common in the family."

"I have twins." Lizbeth blinks hard to hold back tears.

"You told me the day we met. I knew from that moment you were one of us."

∽

Between the barbeque course and dessert, Ana Maria takes Lizbeth to a home office, where portraits of shockingly familiar-looking Gordons hang on the wall.

"Some of your ancestors look so much like my Carolina family it's eerie." She walks from one portrait to another, then gives Ana a long hug.

"They *are* your family." Ana brushes Lizbeth's cheek with a kiss.

Lizbeth and Ana-Maria return to the patio where the buttermilk pie, with just the right balance of fresh lemon juice and grated nutmeg, gets rave reviews. Lizbeth tells stories about her sons and the family in South Carolina. The warmth of the day is waning. Christina's family departs. Lucas and his father retire to talk business over a glass of port, while Ana Maria and Lizbeth have coffee in the living room.

"When you told me at the Jardim that Robert Gordon was your great-grandfather, I wanted to believe we were related, but events in the last year have poked holes in my confidence to believe in anything. Now, I'm convinced you were right from the get-go."

Ana Maria's eyes crinkle with mischief as she sets her demitasse cup on the table.

"My Gordon grandfather used to say I was 'a little fey.'" She shrugs. "Sometimes it gets me in trouble, but I trust my intuition. I knew immediately you were a link to our Carolina family, but I suspected you needed time to come to us in your own way, so I tried not to push."

"In Charleston, I had a fantasy Laurette and Robert Gordon were romantic figures. Then when you told me they were hunted, country-less refugees, I thought perhaps maybe I'd better 'let sleeping dogs lie,' as my granddaddy used to say." Lizbeth laughs. "Well, I've changed my mind. I want to know everything!"

"You will."

As Lizbeth gathers her things, Ana Maria goes into the home office and returns with a thick manila envelope.

"I've saved a precious gift for the end of our evening." She hands a fat, legal-sized envelope package to Lizbeth. "My Great-aunt Suzi, our Gordon matriarch, gave me permission to make you copies of these Civil War-era family documents."

"Truly?" Lizbeth's eyes widen. "Just for me?"

"Yes."

"I'm honored." Lizbeth hugs the envelope tight to her chest.

"Aunt Suzi is Robert and Moira Gordon's granddaughter. What you hold is Laurette Gordon's diary with entries from 1863 until early 1866 and letters Robert Gordon wrote to his sister, Laurette, when he was living in Scotland and Nassau, the Bahamas. As you can imagine, the originals are fragile, faded, and difficult to read. Back in the 1950s, Suzi typed transcriptions of everything so the originals could be stored, carefully preserved.

Ana Maria nods her head toward Lizbeth's chest. "The copies have the original letter or diary entry on one side and Suzi's translation on the other. Unfortunately, what we have is not a complete record of our Confederados history. There are large time gaps between some of Robert's letters. We guess there were other letters, lost or destroyed over the years. In Laurette's diary, some pages have been torn out close to the spine. It was not uncommon for people in the nineteenth century to edit a diary years later for reasons of their own."

Overwhelmed, Lizbeth squeaks out, "Thank you."

"We revere our brave pioneers. I warn you though, their stories are hard to read. Our Confederados lived through very difficult times."

Ana Maria and Lizbeth hug hard at the front door.

Lucas drives Lizbeth back to Copacabana making light conversation she won't remember in the morning.

Lizbeth lets herself into her apartment, makes a cup of herbal tea, settles into the living room easy chair, and opens the envelope. She never makes it to bed that night.

PART TWO

"Anyone who is not satisfied with the war should go see Charleston."

William Tecumseh Sherman, 1865

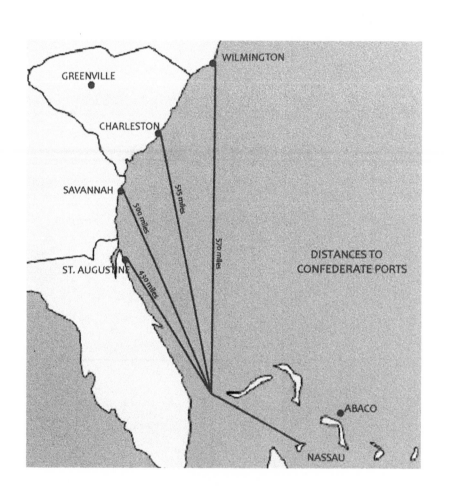

GREENVILLE

WILMINGTON

CHARLESTON

SAVANNAH

535 miles

500 miles

570 miles

ST. AUGUSTINE

430 miles

DISTANCES TO
CONFEDERATE PORTS

ABACO

NASSAU

CHARLESTON, SOUTH CAROLINA, 1863-1865

Laurette Gordon's Diary

December 25, 1863

The Charleston Mercury *declared Christmas Day the 169th day of siege. This morning exploding rockets of Greek Fire woke us before dawn. Damn Federals won't even give us peace on the birthday of Our Lord. I am sure that Yankee General Gilmore will burn in hell for causing the deaths of thousands of innocent citizens. The Federals fire on us, though they know our soldiers are up the peninsula, well out range of Yankee cannons located on Morris Island.*

We Gordons refuse to sink into despair over shortages during this dreadful war. Jeanne and I prepared a delicious Christmas dinner. Jeanne traded Mrs. Dunne five pounds of rice and two of Mama's winter bonnets for a well-fed hen. Who would have thought that trunk of Mama's things, packed in the attic after her death years ago, would have such precious bargaining value.

We baked cornbread, of course, although we are weary of it day after day, and collards from the winter garden. Flour and sugar for pies is nowhere to be found so I drizzled baked apples with honey. Everyone around the table, especially dear little Ned and Eliza, gobbled my dessert up in seconds and begged for more.

We set an empty place and chair for James in the traditional way, like many friends and neighbors are doing this year. How I miss his smiling face and good humor. No matter how dreary a circumstance, James always made us laugh. I cannot believe he is never to be with us at Christmas again. But I must not dwell on that sorrow, not tonight.

After dinner we lingered around the table telling stories of happier times until there was a huge commotion in the vestibule. It turned out to be the best Christmas surprise imaginable; Robert and his bride, Moira, safe and sound all the way from Nassau!

It's been over three years since Robert left for Glasgow. He is so attractive with his new mustache, fit as a fiddle and pleased with himself. When he described the evasive tactics they use to dupe the blockade, Robert sounded quite unlike the peacemaking brother I grew up with. Moira attempted to calm our concern, telling amusing details of how they snuck under the nose of a Federal blockader in the early morning fog outside Charleston harbor.

Robert and Moira brought out a trove of treats: candy for the children; quinine and chloroform for the hospital; gingham for Jeanne; whiskey for Papa; and bottles of ink and this lovely leather pocket-sized diary for me!

⁓

Laurette rose and put her diary away, feeling stiff after a day begun before dawn. She used her bedroom chamber-pot chair and washed her face in a bowl on the dry sink with homemade lye soap. She sighed, remembering the rose-scented variety Papa used to import before the war. Now her hands were rough and chapped from chores that included boiling laundry in the cookhouse. If she had a suitor, he would have an unpleasant surprise when he took her hand and felt her horny, callused palms. She touched the cloth of her clean, threadbare night dress, pulled a face, and lifted the gown to flow over her head and down her body. Before the war she had something new and pretty every Christmas.

Papa had been his effervescent old self with Robert and Moira by his side this evening. Laurette and Jeanne had been fussing for months, worried Papa would get apoplexy over the war. For years, Papa had preached emancipation was inevitable and should be planned for. He called greedy planters that wouldn't negotiate an end to slavery 'a gaggle of fools' that would crush the life work of honest businessmen like himself. His fears were coming to fruition. Angus Gordon's imported textiles from Scotland had third-rate shipboard status, as companies importing military ordnance took priority.

This Christmas night was brittle cold and clear; the street iced white like a cake sifted with powdered sugar. Laurette rolled on darned, mismatched wool stockings before she climbed into bed and yanked the quilts to her chin. As she settled into the cotton-stuffed mattress, she heard a quiet murmur drift through the shared wall with James's bedroom. Always a restless sleeper, James was talking in his sleep again. No, her heart clenched, it was Robert and Moira talking on the other side of the wall. Her sweet younger brother James had been shot dead at Vicksburg in July. A kindhearted letter arrived from his commanding officer extolling James's courage, saying they'd buried him a mile from the battlefield, under a live oak tree with a beautiful canopy.

Before the war Papa used to brag to whomever would listen that he was one of the luckiest men in Charleston. He'd massage his ample belly and expound on how he'd arrived in 1830, a skinny immigrant with nothing but a few pounds sterling and what he'd called his Scottish nose for business. He told and retold how he'd fallen in love with Michelle Bucot, a book publisher's youngest daughter, and married her within a year.

These days he brooded in his office rather than tell success stories. Before the war, he lost his wife and young daughter to diphtheria. And now, two sons gone to the war—the younger never to return.

Laurette pulled the blanket to her neck wishing she could wake in the morning to breakfast of fresh sweet bread, eggs, and real coffee—and everyone content around the table like before the war. She heard more murmurs and soft laughter from Moira and Robert on the far side of the wall. She pictured them lying in James's bed, inches from where she slept alone and wondered if she would ever know the intimacy of marriage, a home of her own, a child of her own. She turned on her side, faced away from the shared wall, and put her pillow over her ear. Her jealousy shamed her. A tear angled across her cheek and into the pillow.

"Goddamn Yankees," she whispered.

December 31, 1863

This week has been a delight with the house full of family, time to catch up on news, and time to make a fast friend in Moira. While Robert worked with the crew of Emily *making repairs to the boilers, Moira accompanied me to the Taylor hospital every day. We've found we are not only sisters-in-law but also kindred spirits. Moira wrote letters for patients and read to them while I made my rounds with herbal medicines and organized meals to be prepared in the cookhouse.*

We still have our hands full with changes to convert the Taylor house into a proper hospital. We have been rewarded with excellent help thanks to the support of our neighbors and Pastor Paul who comes regularly to comfort the men. But the long hours have taken a toll on John, who limps badly by day's end. I plan to increase my hospital hours to help lighten his load.

The Good Lord must have taken note of our need as well. Mrs. Johnson and Mrs. Sutter organized our Bible study group to share what they could spare. They arrived with gifts of food and serviceable clothing for our wounded soldiers far from home and missing their families desperately during the holiday season.

At today's mid-day meal, Robert told us Emily *is loaded to capacity with bales of cotton, and weather is favorable. How I wish my dear brother and Moira could stay longer. Robert tried to ease our fears about the blockade saying the cloud cover tonight will obscure light from a new moon. He said* Emily *will slip through the Federal blockade slick as waxed thread through a needle.*

I will be brave and pray for Emily, *all her crew and cargo until Robert sails into Charleston Harbor again.*

⁓

Laurette's brother-in-law, John, had traveled with the Confederate Army as a battlefield doctor until the fall of 1862, when a broken ankle became gangrenous. His leg was amputated below the knee. He remained feverish and was sent home to Charleston on a hospital train with a dicey chance for survival. Laurette, Jeanne, and Tilly, a free Black herbalist, nursed John around the clock until he was out of danger.

When he was well enough to practice medicine, John joined the medical team at the Charlotte Street hospital. In late July of 1863, the siege of Charleston began. People who could fled the cannon fire in what became known as 'the Grand Skedaddle.' The Taylor family was among them, retiring to their plantation near Columbia and offering their Charleston home as a hospital for the duration of the war. That night at dinner, Angus announced the Taylor's generous gesture.

"Ha!" Laurette said. "I'm not surprised the Taylors joined 'the Grand Skedaddle,' running from the Yankees." Laurette had harbored a secret wish to see snobby Mrs. Taylor trip on a pile of horse pucky crossing the street.

Angus gave his younger daughter a *behave-yourself* look.

"Bless their hearts," Jeanne added, her voice dripping with sarcasm. "Truth be told, Mrs. Mary Taylor spread the word about their Christian charity when what they really get by offering their house for a hospital is protection from squatters."

Angus pulled his eyebrows into a warning frown.

"Nevertheless daughter, it was a generous offer."

John's face glowed, like a child on his birthday, thrilled at the prospect of much needed hospital space.

"Charlotte Street Hospital has wounded men lining the halls. The Taylor house has bedrooms to segregate patients who are infectious, as well as a walled garden and outbuildings to store needed supplies when we can find them." To soften his excitement in front of his wife and sister-in-law, John cut another piece of cornbread, giving the task strict attention. "Angus and I went to look the place over and found two of the Taylors' slaves, Elijah and Florence, hiding the cookhouse."

Laurette didn't bother to quash her opinion. "Slaves run off every day and who can blame them for grasping a chance at freedom?" If looks could kill, the one John gave Laurette would be a painful wound.

"Not all slaves run off, Laurette. My parents' slaves have sturdy cabins, good clothing, holidays and Sunday afternoons off, and the same medical care as our blood family."

Laurette dug her fingernails into her palms and restrained herself from a poisonous comeback. She loved everything about her brother-in-law except his willingness to accept the institution of slavery. "What if we pay Elijah and Florence to cook and clean the hospital house and garden?" She looked to her father for a rescue.

"Elijah and Florence aren't free Negros," Angus replied with regret in his voice. "We haven't money to pay them if they were. But we can allow them to remain in the slave quarters until they can plan an escape from the city."

Laurette had heard about the brutal workhouse where escaped slaves were taken. She had another solution in mind. "I imagine they might stay at the Taylor house and work for us until something better comes along if we offer a comfortable room and food. People will assume we own them. They will be safe for a while."

"With a mind like yours you should have been born a man. Elijah and Florence could be a big help at the hospital." John gave his sister-in-law a wide smile. Laurette drew her brows together, ready to spew a caustic remark, but winced instead when Jeanne kicked her under the table.

"I think you've arrived at the perfect solution, dears," Jeanne said.

Laurette wanted to pinch Jeanne for her innocent smile.

When they were alone, Laurette confronted her sister. "John treats all his patients in hospital equally regardless of race. Why does he continue to justify slavery?"

"From the time we met, John has defended how well his farming family treated their slaves, compared to people like the Taylors." Laurette felt her sister's warm hand on her arm and had to grit her teeth to keep from pulling away. It galled her; since Jeanne married, she bowed to her husband's every opinion.

"Papa raised us to abhor slavery. I always have and I always will."

"Please be reasonable, Laurette. John's a good man. He never wanted to go to war, but he gave his all, in tents near godforsaken battlefields. Every morning he straps on his wooden leg. I can see it's painful no matter how carefully he wraps his stump with clean cotton—but he never complains."

Laurette saw the conflict was going nowhere. She got up, kissed her sister on the cheek and retired to the kitchen house to use a mortar and pestle and vigorously crush dried herbs for medicinal tea.

February 14, 1864

Last year, for St. Valentine's Day, Jeanne and the children made sweet cards for all of us. This year, paper and ink has become so precious it would never be used for such frivolity. Presently, we take our little bits of pleasure where we can. A letter from Robert, or the lavender Tilly and I pressed into oil yesterday. The divine concoction seeped into my blouse sleeves. Most bottles went to the hospital of course, but I put aside one for my own bathing.

I took the afternoon off from nursing to attend a meeting led by Pastor Paul at Mrs. Mary Anne Lamont's home. In addition to prayers for the fallen, we beseeched our Heavenly Father to help us secure fresh food for our children so thin and vulnerable to illness. So many of our women who are expecting a little one lack healthy nutrition. More tiny headstones appear in cemeteries every month. With ladies dressed in widow's weeds on their daily errands, one might think black and gray are the new fashion colors.

We must stay strong! Our Bible study group is collecting ersatz coffee recipes. I'm pressing a clever one using grape seed oil between these pages. Our routine is to gather on Wednesday afternoons to bake bread with a little honey for our men near the battlefields. When the warm, sweet cornbread cake came off the hearth this week, I was reminded how James loved it! Remembering my dear brother in an unmarked grave in Virginia, I had to turn my head away to hide my grief.

Without meaning to be self-important, I can honestly say I am getting quite a reputation for my herbal teas. This week I contributed dried chamomile and Saint John's Wort for tea, which was much appreciated. I am sure our brave soldiers would prefer whiskey. I would gladly give it to them if we had any. Because our men in gray are giving their all, we never breathe a word of what we lack at home.

⁓

Laurette blew the ink dry and slipped her soft black leather diary into the generous pocket of her skirt. Sometimes she leaves it there all day, reaching in to fondle its sleek sides, knowing her dearest confidences are close at hand.

She and others who didn't flee their homes were well aware fear of mortar fire in the city kept farmers in the near countryside from resupplying Charleston. Yesterday Laurette traded peaches she and Jeanne dried last summer for black-eyed peas and stale peanuts they would not have considered suitable for their family a year ago. Her heart wrenched when Jeanne, who usually has the patience of Job, snaped at her children when they complained about dull, unseasoned food.

With bare necessities in short supply, Laurette was thankful for the much-needed gifts of thread, buttons, muslin, morphine, quinine, a bottle of Scotch whiskey for Papa that Robert brought when Emily slipped into Charleston on a moonless night. Laurette kept her brother's visit secret from Bible study friends and neighbors. There are deserters around town who betrayed former comrades for food and Federal spies numerous as fleas on a dog. Before Robert departed, Laurette had hugged her brother desperately, fearing it could be for the last time.

Laurette returned to the present when Tilly called from the foyer. "Miss Laurette, I've brought dried apples and sweet potatoes mama collected when visiting in Mount Pleasant yesterday." Laurette smoothed her unruly ginger hair and called out "I'm coming." At the bottom of the stairs, Laurette burst into smile at the sight of Tilly's loaded basket. "You're going to be the hospital heroine today sharing this bounty!"

In the courtyard, Elijah had loaded the handcart he'd built from wood scraps with jars of strong chamomile tea wrapped in bits of cloth destined for bandages. Laurette noticed he was anxious as a man who happens on a mother bear with cubs. When challenged he confessed, he'd lost his 'slave badge'. These days, armed citizens challenged strangers in the street. Everyone knew non-White people without a badge were assumed to be runaway slaves looking to join up with the Federals. They were usually taken to the workhouse, beaten, or hung. Laurette, Tilly and Elijah frantically searched the garden and yard where Elijah had been working. Thanks be to providence; he found his badge half buried in the dirt by the privy and they went on to the hospital.

March 21, 1864

Today was the first day of spring and the Good Lord provided us with a warm and sunny one. Tilly and I admired the herbs we've cultivated for the hospital's garden. The English lavender is budding; the yarrow, thyme and rosemary we transplanted from elsewhere wintered over well. The marigolds are up. In addition, this year we will have space for a scent garden of blue tansy, mint, chamomile, dill, and more. In a few weeks, we can harvest an early crop to dry.

I am forever thankful Papa let me apprentice with Marion when she was training Tilly in the secrets of herbs and flowers. Grandmere Bucot gave Papa many a cross look when I was allowed to study with a former slave, but Papa said people in Scotland sought out country healers and their wise council, so herbal remedies learned from elders born in Africa certainly had important knowledge, too. When Mama and little Annette became ill, we couldn't save them, but medicinal plants helped ease their suffering and that helped us all. I don't know what I'd do to keep despair away if I couldn't continue to study and make my medicines.

It seems each new week brings evidence of how the siege puts us citizens ill at ease. Ruined buildings housing vagrants keep people fearful of the vengeance of runaway slaves. I can't blame the runaways for being resentful. I am incensed when Negroes on the street are treated even more shoddily than before the war. Tilly was confronted in the street today. I defended her, but I won't forget the rude, unsettling experience.

The constant clouds of war have an occasional silver lining. My good news is John's interest in herbal healing has been piqued. He's obtained a copy of naturalist Francis Porcher's book, Resources of the Southern Fields and Forests *and shared it with me. I've finished my first reading of this remarkable tome, and now I'm reading it aloud to Tilly.*

❧

John observed Laurette use snapdragon for skin rashes and tea of slippery elm for whooping cough with good results. When quinine became unavailable, Laurette knew to use the inner bark of dogwood as a substitute. John became curious about native Carolina plants and ordered Dr. Porcher's book. He raved to Laurette about the scientific history lessons; for instance, the ancient Greeks used yarrow as a coagulant. Laurette's heart sang when her brother-in-law treated her as a peer. Gradually, with the help of Dr. Porcher, John was won over to the value of herbal medicine. After dinner, she and her brother-in-law often sat in the drawing room and discussed where when and how to gather local plants and herbs.

ری

Over the winter of 1864 Laurette developed a master plan for an expansive herbal garden within the walled Taylor house's half-acre of land. Her idea was to expand her stock of herbal medicines and trade the surplus for necessities like cloth suitable for bandages.

In January, she directed Elijah to dig up roses along the tall brick wall adjacent the house. He collected manure anywhere he could find it in the street and prepared the soil for a new herb garden twenty-five yards long and eight feet wide.

Elijah grizzled and complained under his breath as he pushed his shovel into the earth, turning and pulverizing hard hunks of soil into small pieces.

"Old Master's not going to like this when he come home. No, he is not. I best be gone by then." Laurette knew, as everyone in the neighborhood did, that William Taylor was not a generous man.

"I'll take full responsibility for ruining his garden," Laurette said. But by the look Elijah gave her, he wasn't convinced.

In February, Laurette insisted they replace the azaleas along the side of the house with onions, sweet potatoes, garlic, and carrots. Laurette planted tomatoes in old split half barrels on the second-floor piazza where they could remain covered in early spring. Never mind if they didn't ripen, she thought, green tomatoes fried in corn meal were tasty and there were plenty of mouths to feed at the hospital.

In early March, it was time to populate the new herb beds. Laurette and Tilly strolled through neighborhoods taking note of burned-out abandoned homes with unkempt gardens. Vacant homes bombed out by mortars at the southern end of the peninsula and buildings abandoned since the fire of 1861 were the best candidates for foraging.

Harvesting plants on private property was risky. They were careful to avoid city "plantations" like the Taylors—walled acreage with large houses and extensive outbuildings. Surprising terrified slaves, armed with knives, and left behind to mind the master's property was a constant concern.

At the same time, they knew, hearty herb gardens often remained healthy when neglected because they didn't require pampering like finicky roses. Laurette wanted yarrow for wound clotting, tansy and chamomile to settle the stomach, catnip and St. John's wort for the nerves and sleep. Wintered-over lavender, rosemary, lemon balm, and mint standing in overgrown gardens could be dried right away and was in abundance now. Fortunately, many of the plants they targeted were popular in Southern gardens for nosegays, food flavoring, and soothing teas. The hospital needed quantity immediately. There was no time to "borrow" seeds and start from scratch while patients were struggling for life.

Laurette and Tilly hid their spades and shears deep in large sweetgrass baskets and departed late in the day when few folks were on the street. Laurette crept through gates into private spaces, sneaking around the edges of empty houses owned by the families of girls she had known. She wondered if they were safe—or maybe dead.

Heading home with full baskets fragrant with lavender, chamomile, and rosemary, they were accosted by two men demanding to see Tilly's slave badge.

"She's a free woman," Laurette spouted, incensed.

Tilly shrank back visibly. "Yes, sir. I have my badge right here, sir." She put her baskets down and rummaged under her collar to find the braided cord around her neck with the "free" badge. One of the men grabbed Tilly roughly and peered at her badge in the growing gloom. He acknowledged the convex design and "free" mark on the stamped copper oval and grunted.

"It's curfew time. You shouldn't be out." The second man, the silent observer thus far, spoke up. "Y'all get along. And don't let us see you out at dusk again."

Laurette and Tilly walked quickly, shoulders brushing. They went a block before Laurette addressed the humiliation she'd been unable to prevent.

"They were horrible to you."

"Worse if they find me alone."

"I'm sorry. I didn't know it was that bad."

Tilly nodded and they hurried on toward the Gordon house in silence.

ↄ

August 25, 1864

We buried our dear Papa yesterday. He was hit by shrapnel from an exploding mortar and bled to death in the street with none of his family present to hold him in his last minutes. Although John and Jeanne are opposed to it, I am determined to seek out the men of the Charleston Fire Brigade and get the entire story from the mouths of those who tried to comfort Papa as he lay dying.

We did our best to honor our beloved Papa. With most our able-bodied men away at war, it was a small funeral. Pastor Paul gave an inspiring homily and a moving graveside prayer at First Scots, followed by our home reception. We served the last of our real coffee, with chicory added to stretch it so everyone could have a second cup. Jeanne and I begged and borrowed enough sugar to make a real cake in honor of Papa's sweet tooth.

By the grace of God, Emily *docked at Addison's wharf the day before the service. It was a ray of light in a sorrowful event that Robert and Captain Burke could attend the funeral. Papa would have loved the men telling stories in his library with healthy drams of his horded whiskey.*

After the reception, Emily *slipped out of Charleston Harbor in the wee hours of the morning. Jeanne and I admire Robert for sacrificing his life in Glasgow to supply South Carolina in our time of need. The war has turned all our lives on end. Robert was always the scientist, the most studious of us children. While James and his friends rode fast horses and pulled pranks, Robert built sailing models to test at the mill pond on the Ashley River. Tonight, I will be on my knees praying God watches over my dear brother's passage back to Nassau.*

In the privacy of her room, Laurette clamped a hand over her mouth to conceal her sobs from Jeanne, John, and the children. At breakfast the following morning, no one mentioned her red-rimmed eyes as they sipped ersatz coffee sweetened with a teaspoon of sorghum.

"Nothing could have saved Angus," John said for the umpteenth time. "Searching out those who saw him die will not bring him back. Let us be thankful that he didn't languish in pain."

John's practical advice irritated rather than soothed Laurette. Her brother-in-law's long days spent treating patients, most of whom would not survive, had taken a toll, making him brisk. At thirty, his sandy brown hair that shone with health three years ago had become brittle and streaked with silver.

"If only I could have held Papa, comforted him, and said goodbye." Laurette sighed.

"Pastor Paul left us some scripture readings that help." When Jeanne relied on prayers to assuage her grief, Laurette wanted to holler at her more docile sister.

After breakfast, Laurette ignored her brother-in-law's advice to leave well enough alone and sought out the men who were with her father when he died. She approached Carl, a one-armed veteran, who'd run to the burning house on Church Street to help the Fire Wagon brigade. Carl hadn't seen Angus fall. He sent her to Ben, the free Black man who lived and worked at the firehouse, managing the horses and equipment.

"It was a sorrowful, terrible thing that happened, Miss Laurette," Ben said.

"Please tell me everything," Laurette pleaded.

"It's not a story for a lady, Miss Laurette."

"Tell me anyway."

"Yes, ma'am. If you are sure, ma'am."

"I want to know." Laurette crossed her arms tight across her chest to keep still and focused.

"The house afire was brick except for the second story piazza; that was burning hot. The fire jumped to next-door and we feared it would burn all the way down the block. My man, Rebus, was pumping with Mr. Carl. Me and Mr. Angus had the hose. Oh, Miss Laurette, I do believe the Yankees are in the bed with Satan. They aimed those rockets to kill us while we worked to put the fire out." Ben gave her a look that seemed to say: *Are you sure you want me to go on?*

Laurette nodded. "Tell me the rest, Ben."

"We almost had the flames out, when another mortar screamed over and burst in a cloud of smoke and stink of cordite. It was like the jaws of hell opened to take us. Pieces flew everywhere. Mr. Angus, he grabbed his neck and he fell to the ground and he roll' in the street. Blood was pumpin' through his fingers, runnin' down his collar into his coat. I run to him, and I put my hand to his neck, tryin' to stop the blood. He pass to Our Lord in my arms, lookin' surpriz' more than hurt. He was a good man, Miss Laurette."

Laurette took a handkerchief from her pocket and wiped at the tears that streamed down her cheeks. "Thank you for holding my Papa in his last minutes." She reached out to touch Ben's hand and gave it a squeeze. "Thank you for everything."

To compose herself, Laurette took her time walking home, stumbling here and there on the mortar-pitted cobblestone streets of Charleston's colonial district. Until today, she had thought the rumor of Federals targeting fire brigades was a political ploy to fan flames of Federal hatred.

Laurette wondered for what felt like the millionth time why war turned some men into godless monsters. Before the war, people who traveled to the South from up north often attended Sunday services at First Scots Presbyterian. At coffee hour afterward, Laurette remembered the visitors as kind, pious, and intelligent. Papa, always curious about people and their adventures, sometimes invited a traveler home for dinner.

Now the leaders of those very same pious people terrorized her family. Fumes from rockets and bits of grit in the afternoon sea breeze kept the risks of living in Charleston omnipresent. Until recently, John prescribed laudanum to sleepless citizens who cowered in fear of screeching missiles in the night sky. Now he saved his precious supply for dying patients, so local ladies learned to manage with prayers and chamomile tea if they could get it.

Laurette's nephew, Ned, whom the war made wise beyond his eight years, remarked at dinner one night: "We don't have to be afraid. Saint Michael's was hit, but the Yankees can't take it down. We're smarter. We painted the steeple black, so no light reflects in the night sky. God protects the church, and he will protect us."

∽

October 15, 1864

With every loss during this war, the good Lord gives us strength to find ways to cope. We don't inquire where people come by what they have. The other day, a man came to our door wanting to trade a heavy, rolled-up canvas awning he said had come off a storefront on Queen Street. He was happy to exchange the sturdy material for a jar of sorghum and dried apples from the cellar. The canvas was too heavy for shirts or pants or skirts or undergarments, but Lord be praised, Jeanne and I decided it was more than adequate for shoes.

Ned and Eliza had run barefoot all summer. Now it's cooler, they have to put on last year's shoes that pinch badly. Jeanne and I practiced making canvas shoes on the children. We made paper patterns of the children's feet, cut the shapes, punched holes through the canvas with a nail, and sewed the soles to the uppers with twine Robert brought on his last trip home. We saved the striped portions of awning canvas for Eliza and ourselves. Though faded, the blue and white stripes are quite attractive on the female foot. Even with a double bottom, canvas can't compare with leather for street wear, but canvas shoes are more comfortable than paper stuffed in holes of worn-out boots.

We've plenty of the plain canvas left for patients at the hospital. Many men lose their boots when wounded or have them stolen in the evacuation train to Charleston. Tilly and I created haute couture shoes for men at the Taylor hospital and were very popular for our creativity with a needle.

∽

Laurette put her diary aside and laughed like she hadn't done in a month of Sundays. Who would have imagined two rolls of canvas awning that had seen better days would be like manna from heaven? She walked to the window that overlooked Charlotte Street. It seemed like a quiet fall afternoon before the war on this block until she noticed a Black man bumping along the cobblestones, his heavy handcart loaded all catawampus with pieces of wood debris from wrecked buildings.

Mrs. Ames, who lived on the corner, appeared at her door and called out for him to stop. With coal for fireplaces nonexistent, everyone was on the lookout for something to keep a room or two heated in evenings. Laurette watched Mrs. Ames and the man converse and nod, appearing to arrive at an agreement. The man carried a load of wood up to her porch. She disappeared inside and returned with something to trade tucked under her shawl. Laurette wondered, could it be a piece of silver, a silk blouse, or perhaps tinned meat. Bartering was the common currency now that printed Confederate bills were of questionable value. Laurette turned away, embarrassed at having witnessed an intimate transaction.

∞

December 20, 1864

We are coming up on another lean Christmas, but I have a wonderful secret! I was home alone when Mrs. Madelaine Scott came by wanting to trade a serviceable piece of muslin for dried lavender and chamomile for tea. She was bursting with pride. Her boys had arrived home for the mid-day meal with one of them wearing an old-fashioned top hat. Mrs. Scott said she shook the younger one until he confessed, they'd found trunks of clothes in the burned-out Emory house attic! She unrolled a sumptuous, fine cotton shirtwaist and held it up to her bosom. I gasped with envy when Mrs. Scott told of the matching skirt at home.

We agreed children have no business playing derring-do in that neighborhood south of Broad, but with our schools closed, and the teachers gone for soldiering, boys get up to all mind of things. I was quite bold with Mrs. Scott, insisting on the entire story, including what her sons said about the wrecked staircase leading to the attic, so I could go later myself.

At the Emory house an hour later, while John was at the hospital and

Jeanne and the children were visiting friends two blocks away, I slipped out through the back garden, my hair and face mostly hidden with an oversized bonnet. I wore a winter cape with deep pockets to hide whatever treasure I might find.

The Emory home was a lovely building of red brick before the war, but today it was steeped in shadow, its grand staircase open to the air and resembling bad teeth. Mortar had flattened the adjacent kitchen house. But what I found was indeed treasure. The garments spilling out of trunks the Scott boys opened looked to be a decade old, but oh, my goodness, every piece below the top few was still brushed and packed away, good as new. The Lord doth provide, as Mama used to say.

Slap me down if I sound critical, but Mrs. Mary Emory never left home wearing anything but the latest mode. So perhaps I can be forgiven taking a few things left in the attic when her family fled to their plantation near Edgefield.

I've no colorful paper to wrap my presents, so I'll have everyone sit with their eyes covered while I bring in the folded gifts. I can hardly wait to see their surprise!

⁊

Laurette put her diary away and smiled. Hadn't she been the clever one to carry such treasure home. As she left the Gordon house, she'd thought to don that old, oversized cape. Just as she'd imagined, it turned out to be the perfect disguise to hide what she was after. In the wreckage of the Emory's attic, she had worked fast and chosen carefully. The cape's bulk obfuscated two fine old fashion linen shirts, one wrapped around each of her upper arms. She had tightly rolled three muslin dresses and secured them under her skirt. Then she tied two pairs of stockings around each leg. Back on the street, to all appearances, she was a woman great with child, on her way home from an afternoon errand.

She smoothed each garment and folded them carefully before putting them out of sight in the bottom of her clothes press. As Laurette left her room, she shook her head to clear the memory of inching down the that dangerous staircase, her back pressed against the wall of slick moss that left a deep green streak on her cape. Her last vision of that once grand

Emory home had been the vestibule stripped of every stick of furniture. Even the molding had been pried from the doorways for firewood. Still, she thought, as she left her bedroom, the risk she'd taken was worth the prize.

の

February 19, 1865

I haven't wanted to write for some time, but I feel I must put some words down. My heart grieves great sorrow over the last terrible days. Two days ago, General Beauregard ordered our fighting force to withdraw from Fort Sumter, Fort Moultrie, and the city of Charleston and march to fight near Columbia. As our soldiers departed, they scuttled the gunboats Charleston *and* Chicora *tied at the wharf and torched the Lukas Mill and the munitions near the train depot. The vibrations from the exploding spiked cannons at White Point blew out windows on East Bay and Battery streets. Oily smoke wafted three stories into the sky, fouling the air all day. Those of us who remain in the city pray and try to stay courageous.*

After the troops left, people of every kind and color swarmed the Northeast Depot hoping to find tinned food, crackers, cornmeal, kerosene—anything of value the departing soldiers hadn't time to destroy or carry away. At eight in next morning, there was an explosion. Fire broke out, trapping more than one hundred fifty people as the depot collapsed.

Yesterday, Mayor MacBeth surrendered our city to General Alexander Schimmelfennig, ending 567 days of cannons firing on the citizens of Charleston.

Today, John, Jeanne, and I stood on the second-floor piazza with our arms around Ned and Eliza as the Negro 55th infantry from Massachusetts, led by their White officers astride sleek horses, marched down Meeting Street. They stomped and shouted and waved flags aloft singing "John Brown's Body."

Families in Charleston remain in their houses behind bolted doors. We discovered quickly the Federal army is a school for bad morals! We had hoped for Christian kindness. While officers turned a blind eye, triumphant Negro soldiers broke down doors to liberate their "brothers in bondage." Some freed slaves danced in the streets, while others ran back inside to cower in the only homes they'd ever known, asking only to be left in peace. We feel a vindictive spirit descending on Charleston; it vibrates in the air like a plucked fiddle.

_∾_

The Gordons retired inside to watch the mayhem from behind the piazza windows, as White and Negro troops barged into homes. Some officers joined the looting, while others averted their faces as their men exited homes to show off booty of pocket watches, wedding rings, and earrings ripped from terrified women's ears.

Ned's friend, Ike Johnson, banged on the door, begging John to come quickly. Bertha, nursemaid to three generations of Johnsons, had been stabbed with a bayonet because she wouldn't disclose where the family buried their valuables. Fearing the entire family would be treated in a similar way if they remained silent, Ike's mother told the soldiers where to dig in the garden out back.

Shortly after Ike and John departed to tend to Bertha, a raucous group pounded on the Gordons' door. Someone in the street shouted, "That's a doctor's house, leave it be."

"We are spared like the Biblical Passover for doing God's work regardless of race." Laurette said as she hugged Jeanne and kissed her cheek.

John sent Ike back to the Gordon home with a message. "He won't be home until late. Another neighbor, Mrs. Miller and her month-old daughter are doing poorly. Please send Ike to the hospital with Saint John's Wort tea to calm her."

"What happened?" Laurette asked the boy with trepidation in her voice.

"A Federal officer and his men wanted her house. Mrs. Miller and her child were turned out into the street with nothing but the clothes they were wearing when she refused to become their housekeeper and cook."

Jeanne put a hand to her mouth in horror. "Poor woman. We all hoped her sweet baby girl would lift her spirits after losing her son to diphtheria last year. And no news for a month from her husband, who rides with Wade Hampton's Brigade."

Laurette forced her mouth into a weak smile. "I'm going back to the hospital with Ike. The hospital was already full after the depot fire, we're low on medicine, and now, three new patients." She pursed her lips tight to keep from crying. The sisters hugged. Laurette left for the hospital with Ike as her escort, preferring not to voice further fears of what else would change under martial law.

ॐ

February 26, 1865

We waited in line to sign the onerous "United States Loyalty Oath" today. The Oath directed us to attest we never aided or encouraged those who engaged in armed hostility against the United States. If the document was purposely worded to cause the most humiliation possible, it certainly succeeded in doing so. It makes liars of all of us. Those who refuse to sign are denied citizen rights, their property may be confiscated, and they may be jailed or hung as traitors without trial. We live at the mercy of Federal soldiers who seek revenge.

John's position as a doctor means our family is more fortunate than many, for which I am grateful, but I feel guilty when I observe what befalls others. The Federals need our hospital and our healing skills as they add their men to ours at the Taylor house. Tilly and I work tirelessly making medicines. Thank the Lord that the garden Elijah built in '64 produces abundantly.

We've had no news from Robert since Emily's last run into Charleston Harbor February first. Emily's cargo of food and ammunition was unloaded quickly. She was scheduled to depart a few short hours later, in the early morning hours. Just before slack tide Robert came by the house. We hugged and cried until he stepped back with a wave goodbye. We all knew that day the war was lost, and Robert will be hung if apprehended. We've had no further news. Our dear brother and Moira are constantly in our prayers.

ॐ

Laurette picked at the frayed sleeve at her wrist, wondering if the fragile fabric would shred, or if it would bear turning and hemming again. The war was finished for Charleston, but it didn't appear things would improve for the citizens of the city any time soon.

John, Jeanne, and Laurette talked in whispers after the children were in bed.

"The Federals have a list of names, and sketches of ships and officers, all drawn by their spies in Nassau. Robert will have to be very careful," John said.

"He will go into hiding," Laurette added, trying to sound positive.

John rubbed his leg rhythmically just below his knee, where leather straps held his prosthesis in place. "I overheard an officer say Confederates with silver or land to trade are buying their freedom from the gallows."

"So wealthy scoundrels from the planter class who hid money overseas will escape scot free while Robert will be hunted and the rest of us take the brunt of Yankee ugly treatment?" Laurette slammed her cup of chamomile tea down, nearly breaking the china.

Jeanne sucked in her breath with such force her sister and husband noticed.

"Maybe we should close up the house, leave a Federal doctor in charge of the hospital, and join your upstate family for a while. It might be safer for the children."

"The Federal doctors are already in charge, my dear. I work at their mercy." John's mouth turned up in a rueful smile. "I cannot leave my patients. The bright spot is, the Federals have morphine and anesthesia, blankets and clean bandage material, supplies such as I haven't seen in two years. And men who've worked in field hospitals have been assigned to help in my surgery."

Laurette rubbed her eyes gently, as if doing so could erase the shadows beneath them. She agreed with her brother-in-law about staying in Charleston.

"I too feel I must be at the hospital, so patients are treated fairly. After all their preaching for men to be free and equal, the Yankee patients who arrive complain if a Negro's in the next bed."

April 14, 1865

We feel waves of ugliness crashing on our shores. Yankees from New York and New Jersey have arrived on chartered steam ships, dressed in their finery, to attend the flag-raising ceremony at Fort Sumter. This week they swarmed over Charleston with the most deplorable behavior. I saw some streaming out of the library on King Street with paintings and books I am sure they did not borrow. Pastor Paul said several men barged into First Presbyterian Church, and left with the communion challis among other things.

I attended patients at the hospital with John early this morning, but we didn't dare leave the house again after lunch. Tilly visited late in the afternoon to tell us everything. She said Colonel Robert Anderson presided at Fort Sumter, raising the very same United States flag he'd lowered exactly four years ago when he surrendered the fort. She told us about the speeches by abolitionists Henry Beecher, and William Lloyd Garrison, so filled with pride at their achievements. Mr. Robert Small, the Negro river pilot who stole the gunboat CSS Planter *and delivered her to the Federal navy in 1862 was honored. I must say hearing of his daring and courage reminded me of Robert, yet Mr. Small is considered a hero and Robert is now a pariah.*

We heard there was a faux funeral parade organized by Charleston's Negroes that included a real coffin to bury the institution of slavery. Tilly told us about the brass band and hundreds of former slaves dancing in Marion square. I wish I could have seen it.

We have no idea what to expect in the coming months. Every night I am on my knees praying for peace and Christian decency for all.

⁓

Laurette put her diary aside and reflected on the conversation that afternoon in the parlor.

"Mama was doin' a jubilee jig today." Tilly's face had been aglow with pride. "We buried our 'badges' in the ground. No one can put any of us in the workhouse ever again."

Lickety-split, the South was changed. Blacks celebrated freedom and White Southerners were afraid to go anywhere in public for fear of being accosted. Laurette still couldn't quite take in this new reality.

"Mama is so happy." Tilly had continued. "Since my body grew to a woman, she's been worried for me. She told me stories of how she hid from your granddaddy Bucot, after he'd had his whiskey. She always told me to be careful about men, even though I be free."

"Has Marion resented us all these years and we didn't know?" A mild headache Laurette had been ignoring all day suddenly pounded in her temples.

"No, Miss Laurette. Mama always praise Mr. Angus for granting her freedom when she come to him and Miss Michelle as a wedding gift. It be your Mama's people that she cannot abide."

"I never knew my granddaddy did such things." Laurette's cheeks were crimson.

Tilly's eyes flashed. "Plenty of White people kick me and my family like we be dogs that don't hunt. But y'all are good people." Tears filled Laurette's eyes as Tilly's secrets rolled out. Tilly reached out to touch her friend's shoulder.

"You pay no mind. You an' me been friends since we was girls; we be friends forever."

လ

At the hospital, most of the Federal patients appreciated Laurette's ministrations. She'd trained herself to be patient and pleasant in close spaces that reeked of suppurating wounds and male sweat, but from the day he arrived, Corporal George Larson was a different kind of patient. Her dilemma with Corporal Larson began with his first compliment about her ample bosom. She responded with a stern look, silently vowing to avoid time alone with him whenever possible. Though Laurette was not known to engage in gossip about patients, she asked one of the new male nurses about the Corporal. She learned he had harassed a farmer's wife and she returned the unwanted attention by peppering his thigh with buckshot. The male nurse laughed, saying Larson surely deserved it.

Laurette did her best, but there were occasions when she couldn't avoid Corporal Larson's groping hand. She'd slapped him away but didn't mention the insults to John. She'd gained her brother-in-law's respect as a healer. Would he question her competence to manage patients alone if he knew she couldn't demand proper respect from a wounded patient?

⁓

May 6, 1865

I have been uncertain whether to disclose what happened in the street, but because I am the only one to read these pages, I decided I must be honest about my life during this difficult era. My bruises from the assault to my person by three men are fading. Last night I pleaded with John to allow me back to my nursing duties where I can be of use, and free of ruminating on my shame. Caring for patients will be a poultice on my heavy heart and violated body. Being housebound for a fortnight is driving me wild with memories I'd like to forget. Jeanne hovers about, with sorrow in her eyes, a constant reminder of unthinkable experiences a few short weeks ago.

⁓

Laurette's images of that afternoon were a fog of humiliation. She and Willy, a boy of twelve who did errands for the family, were on their way from the Gordon house to the Taylor hospital, arms loaded with baskets of lavender and citrus oil to sweeten rooms and bedding. As they rounded the corner to Alexander Street, three Federal soldiers confronted them: a White sergeant and two Black privates. The three men began off-color teasing that quickly turned mean when Laurette rebuffed their over-friendly advances. The sergeant grabbed Willy by the scruff of his neck and threw him hard to the ground. The child struggled to his feet; scared, he ran off.

Reeking of sweat and sour breath, the men circled Laurette slowly. They called her "pretty girl" as they reached out to touch her hair with dirty hands and jagged nails. The sergeant trailed his index finger from her shoulder to wrist, circled her wrist, and pulled her close with a hand rough as sandpaper. One of the Black soldiers pulled at her skirt and lifted it to see her legs. She spat in the sergeant's face and wrenched free. He caught her by the elbow and swung her back toward him. He slapped her across the mouth, split her lip, then backhanded her, opening a wide gash in her cheek with his ring. He slammed an elbow into her stomach. She bent double. They dragged her into a weed-filled garden through a gap in a fence. One of them hooked a leg behind her knees and threw her to the ground. Her head hit the packed earth hard, making her dizzy. The sergeant went first. He pulled her skirts over her face, stuffing material into her mouth. She gagged and choked and tried to breathe. He moved quickly; he ripped her small clothes and rammed into her, pumping hard. She thought she surely would die. He finished with a grunt, and said, "Your turn, Bobby."

She struggled with no success. Bobby pinned her shoulders to the ground and raped her violently. She could feel his spittle dripping on her hair. Sighing, he pulled out. "You next, Thomas."

"I'll pass," Thomas said.

Through the fuzz of her shock, Laurette heard the sergeant challenge, "Ain't you a man, Thomas? We got you a buttered bun, ready to go." Without a word, almost gently, Thomas dropped down on her body and finished quickly.

⁓

Jeanne heard a scratching at the front door and opened it. When she saw Laurette collapsed on the doorstep, her face froze into a Greek tragedy mask. Suspecting what happened without having to ask, Jeanne hooked a supporting arm around her dear sister's back, half-carrying her through the foyer. She called upstairs to John, where he and a neighbor were deep in discussion on the piazza. Jeanne held Laurette's hand. "Malcolm is a friend. He will carry you up the stairs. I'm here Laurette. You are safe now. We'll take care of you."

Malcolm, lean as a willow switch from four years in the cavalry, ran to scoop up Laurette and carry her up the stairs with John limping behind barking orders about hot water.

"She's in shock," John said as he gently examined his sister-in-law.

"Jeanne, my dear, stay with her and talk softly about something pleasant. Malcolm, go out to the kitchen house. There's Epsom salts on the left shelf by the hearth. Add a handful to boiling water, cool it a bit and bring it up in a bucket. Knock before you enter. Laurette doesn't know you well. At this moment, any male voice she doesn't recognize will deepen the shock."

Malcolm went to stoke the kitchen stove, while John sought out his precious supply of laudanum. Laurette lay shivering, though the night was warm and unseasonably humid. Jeanne smoothed her sister's hair away from the deep gash on her cheekbone. Laurette's eyes were open but unfocused.

"It's all right, sweetheart. We're going to get you warm and clean in no time." Tears streaked Jeanne's face while she stroked her sister's arms softly, singing a favorite childhood song.

Carefully, Jeanne tried to relieve Laurette of the bundle of dried herbs she clutched in a vice grip, so she could remove her sister's torn clothing. Laurette screamed, "No, no! It's for the patients; you can't have it," and thrashed about.

"It's going to be all right." Jeanne whispered, as much for herself as for her sister. "I'm here, my darling," she crooned. "You've had a terrible time. I'm going to take care of you."

The quiet rhythm of Jeanne's voice invited Laurette back into her body. Tears began to flow. Finally, she was able to whimper, "I know they hate us, but I never thought this could happen to me."

"Shush, sweet sister," Jeanne murmured. "Say no more and rest now." She tucked a blanket around Laurette and lay down next to her, waiting for Malcolm to bring warm water. John stood outside the bedroom, allowing the sisters time alone.

Laurette turned her face to the wall. "It's all my fault for being bold. I counted on a boy for my escort instead of waiting for John or another grown man to walk me to the hospital."

Jeanne rose up on her elbow, to look into Laurette's eyes.

"It's not your fault. Ugly Yankee soldiers take revenge because they lost many of their own, and Charleston is where the war started."

"What will people say? I am ruined, tainted for life."

"No neighbors were outside when you arrived home. We'll tell everyone, including the children, that you are in bed with a fever. Malcolm is John's dear friend. He'll keep mum. No one except the four of us will ever know."

June 1, 1865

This diary is the only witness to my confession. I have failed my mission to remain impartial as a healer. In a moment of rage, I lost control of my senses. I am quite sure I killed Corporal George Larson. I cannot know until I meet my maker if the Lord will forgive my sin.

I purposely avoided George Larson and his inappropriate attentions since the first day I attended to him, but John pulled me aside today to say the Corporal's leg wounds had become gangrenous, please make him as comfortable as possible. Be compassionate. John said the Corporal became angry as a snake when he learned that surgery to amputate at the hip was scheduled first thing in the morning.

I entered the room to freshen George Larson's bedding. When I bent to straighten his sheets, he squeezed my nether region. He knew better. I had chastised him repeatedly each time he tried to touch my person without permission. He smiled, and said he knew I wanted him. Though he was weak with fever, he surprised me by pulling me onto his chest. I pushed away, but he squeezed my bosom, hurting me. It was as if Satan himself took control of me. I took the corporal's pillow, covered his face and sat on it, until he stopped thrashing. I left him in that little room, once a bedroom closet, and walked home with John shortly thereafter without mentioning a word about the Corporal.

෯

A Federal captain, David DeVos, collected Corporal George Larson's possessions and sought John out for permission to speak to Laurette, the last person to see the Corporal alive, before writing the soldier's family in Columbus, Ohio.

Laurette was in the kitchen house behind the hospital, stirring a cauldron of salt pork and vegetables while Tilly mixed a batch of corn bread. The captain strolled through the door and coughed to get their attention. The women turned to find a tall, finely built man his lips set in a formal half smile. They noticed immediately, unlike some, this officer paid attention to his toilette; his beard was neatly trimmed, and his well-worn uniform brushed clean. A dangerous-looking man if you cross him, Laurette assessed. She turned to face him, smoothing her skirt as shards of icy fear sliced through her body.

When the captain spoke, his tone was respectful. "What can you tell me about Corporal George Larson? I want to put details of his courage in my letter to soothe his family in their time of sorrow."

Laurette was frozen speechless. Was this another Federal trick? She managed a cough to find her voice. "He had a good sense of humor." Laurette continued on for a few sentences, making up a story on the spot ending with, "He was quite ill, and I didn't know him long."

The captain narrowed his eyes at Laurette; seconds dragged by as sweat rolled from her armpits down the inside of her blouse.

"Thank you for your time, miss." He dipped his head, turned on his heel, and walked away.

Tilly gave Laurette a wide-eyed look but didn't utter a word. Laurette turned back to the soup and worried the contents in the cast iron pot as if she was expecting the mayor for dinner.

Later, Laurette sat in her room whispering the names of patients she'd healed, as if hundreds of hours changing bandages, applying poultices, writing letters home, and mixing teas to help with pain or sleep could purge the sin of snuffing out a life.

❧

July 3, 1865

Captain DeVos invited us to a Fourth of July picnic. I find it uncomfortable to accept such a party invitation. It seems disrespectful to our neighbors, some of whom have had their homes commandeered by Federal troops and are sleeping in the servant's quarters in their own kitchen house. John says we must be practical, take advantage of Captain DeVos's access to medicines, nutritious food for our patients, and male nurses who lighten our work at the hospital.

I find the captain to be a decent man. He seeks me out in a most gentlemanly fashion for conversation when he visits his men. He asks intelligent questions about the science of my herbal medicine, saying he will send notes about our remedies to his brother, a doctor in New York. The captain asked me to go walking on Sunday. I declined his offer. I don't want a beau. I am thankful for my role creating herbal medicine, and nursing at the hospital allows me a freedom that married women of my social group do not have.

Tilly and I have increased the hospital herb garden manyfold in these last three years, and I've planted another in our enclosed courtyard at home as well. I am gaining quite a reputation for my knowledge. People come to the house to purchase my remedies or ask advice. Although I am proud of what I have learned, I wish to remain humble and share my knowledge as the Good Lord intends us to do.

☙

After that first encounter in the kitchen house, Laurette retreated when she heard Capitan DeVos's baritone voice echo in the foyer of the hospital house. Gradually, she noticed he shared fresh fruit and other rare delicacies with Southern patients, rather than hording the best for his own men alone. If he caught her unawares, he tipped his hat and greeted her respectfully when they passed in the hall. One afternoon the captain stood in the doorway unseen by Laurette, listening to her read Rudyard Kipling to patients. When she finished, he clapped, smiled, and said, "Well done, Miss Gordon." Without thinking, she flashed him a smile. She wondered if they could become friends.

☙

John's status as a doctor provided a security that came at a cost. For the time being, the Gordons' escaped the fate of losing their home, but privilege brought challenges. Laurette and Jeanne ignored the slights by jealous citizens and did their best to unite with families who had resources to share. Their group prepared cornbread, sweet potatoes drizzled with molasses, peas, and greens from backyard gardens for distribution to those who had little.

A daily reminder of losing the war were the countless widow's and children without the soldiers pension their taxes paid to the widows of Federal soldiers from Ohio or Maine. The homeless slept where they could find shelter in ruined buildings. Orphaned children roamed the streets,

ducking in alleys to avoid Federal patrols, reemerging to rifle though trash
and overgrown gardens for edible fruit, greens, or seeds. Stories circulated
about families with homes in ashes, land salted, animals slaughtered, and
no money to pay land taxes. Those who'd lost so much seethed in shamed
anger and sold what was left of their property for pennies on the dollar
to carpetbaggers. If they had a mule and a wagon, many headed west,
looking for a new start.

၈

September 15, 1865

*I've avoided writing what I am sure of now. I can no longer deny I am a
soiled dove. At the war's end, we were all lean as bean poles. I did not take notice
when my monthly visitor, unpredictable for three years, did not arrive. I buried
the atrocity to my person months ago the way I would a poisonous plant. Until
recently, I believed my ample bosom and the pinch at my shirtwaist were results
of nutritious food arriving at the wharf on supply ships. But I could not deny
the butterfly flutters in my female belly that caught my attention today. I had to
admit, the gentle rolling sensation I felt several times during the afternoon was
not gas or indigestion due to spoiled meat. It forced me to calculate the time since
my last monthly visitor. Around four months. Is the good Lord punishing me for
the sin I wrote of months ago? When people notice I am with child, it will be the
ruin of me and will bring shame to our honorable family.*

၈

At the hospital that afternoon Laurette saw John standing in the
doorway, watching as she cupped her belly. Their eyes locked, acknowledging
the truth.

"What am I going to do?" Laurette asked, blinking back tears.

"You're going to be a mother." John cocked his head and gave her a
warm smile.

"I don't want this baby," she said, her eyes wild with terror.

"Jeanne and I have noticed your body changes. Out of respect, we have
been waiting for you to tell us. You know we believe new life is a gift from
God."

There was a shout, "Doctor! You're needed!" from a male nurse. Before John hurried down the hall, he pulled Laurette close and said softly, "Go home. Talk to your sister. She understands and will be a great support."

Laurette fell into her sister's arms and let her sobs loose, until, at last, she collapsed on the sofa, spent. Laurette had always been one for creative solutions to problems, but this time Jeanne took the lead. They decided to build a story of Laurette's whirlwind romance and marriage to a wounded officer she met at the hospital: a fine man who returned to his unit only to die at the battle of Petersburg, Virginia, the last month of the war. It was a plausible story.

There would be curiosity about Laurette's mysterious husband, but no one would dare a direct confrontation. Strange alliances and compromises happened in wartime. People did what they had to do to get by. Laurette's reputation would be preserved.

∽

Laurette's labor was long but not complicated, thanks to Jeanne's support and Tilly's mother, Marion, as midwife. John brought chloroform from the hospital in case they needed to call on him to do a Caesarian section. Fortunately, Laurette, at twenty-six, was tall, strong, and healthy. Her baby emerged into the world with a vibrant wail.

Marion placed the healthy infant wrapped in bunting on her mother's chest. Laurette stroked the silky cheek, cooing "my sweet Rosalie," and smiled as her baby's turned her head searching for a nipple. From her first hour of birth, Rosalie was vigorous with life, unaware of the complications her unorthodox conception could bring to the family.

∽

January 31, 1866

I did not truly comprehend what Jeanne and my women friends meant when they said a mother falls in love with her baby on the day she gives birth. Now I do. Never, ever in my wildest imagination did I think any human could have such a precious soft cheek, and such a beautiful Cupid's-bow mouth. My baby Rosalie is perfect. She came into the world with curly dark hair and skin

darker than my Scottish skin that freckles so easily. Now that she's two weeks
old I believe she will have Papa's green eyes. Rosalie has thrived at my breast
since the day of her birth. I can't believe why I was terrified of the miracle of
motherhood. Already, I cannot imagine life without my Rose.

Jeanne and Tilly have been spoiling me while I rest and regain my strength.
I feel ready to be up and about, but Jeanne insists I rest a few more weeks "lying
in." Notes from friends who want to see my baby come nearly every day, but
Jeanne and Tilly have been strange, keeping Rosalie in seclusion, saying she's
too young for viewing. I suppose they know best.

Still, there is so much work to be done as Charleston recovers from the
wreckage of war. I need to return to my herb garden and the kitchen house to
dry and crush plants. People call at the house daily for my teas and medicines.
Jeanne has been taking orders and collecting money until John allows me to
do it myself. I'm saving every dollar taken in for Rosalie's future.

Tilly has promised to find me a girl who will care for my precious little
one in trade for herbal medicines for her family. I feel fortunate I will soon be
able to work and study for some hours every day.

❧

When Laurette's pregnancy became obvious, custom demanded she
retreat from the public eye. To keep her mind occupied, she spent hours
reading Porcher's book on healing plants, and adjusting formulas for her
medicines. Jeanne acted as a go-between, taking orders in the parlor and
collecting payment. The sisters abhorred the arrogant, Yankee neighbors
who've purchased foreclosed properties. But acquiring United States dollars
to tuck into her clothes press was a financial necessity Laurette would not
pass up.

❧

When friends wanted to meet Rosalie, John and Jeanne told them the
baby was born sickly. No visitors were allowed. With women just beginning
to secure healthy nutrition after the long siege, and infant mortality high,
no one questioned the wisdom of his edict.

Tilly teased Laurette about giving birth to a well- mannered baby that
slept so well from the day of her birth. Laurette used the quiet moments to

re-read Porcher's book on healing plants taking copious notes for additions to her garden. She had big plans. Although she and Jeanne abhorred the arrogant Yankee neighbors who bought up foreclosed properties, they had United States dollars to pay for Laurette's medicines and Laurette had a child to raise.

e๛

One afternoon Laurette sat softly singing to Rosalie, who, sated with milk, was asleep at her breast. Through the bedroom door left ajar, she listened in horror to a conversation in the hall.

Jeanne's voice shook with emotion.

"Laurette chooses to be oblivious, but the reality becomes more apparent every day. Rosalie's father has to be one of the Negroes who violated Laurette, not the White man."

Her voice cracked, ending in a stifled sob. "What will we do, John? We know mixed-blood infants can look White at birth and darken in a few weeks. Rosalie's skin has become dusky. If she doesn't darken more, she'll have an easier time, like Tilly. She'll be able to find a good job, a skilled trade, and perhaps a good marriage, too. But if she becomes very dark, her future could be terrible."

Laurette's eyes grew round as saucers. She hugged Rosalie tight to her chest.

"What will be, will be," John muttered. "It's important to protect Laurette. The ruse of a brief marriage to a Confederate officer who died in battle will be exposed if people see Rosalie now."

Laurette heard anguish in Jeanne's voice that didn't begin to match her own. "It's what we most feared for my dear Laurette and her baby. They will be pariahs. The politics of Federal Reconstruction make Rosalie's position worse. Resentment is high from Charlestonians who have lost property or position to former slaves. Laurette's my only surviving sister; we must help her."

John's voice in the hall sounded resolved. "Perhaps Marion or Tilly know a good Negro family who can adopt Rosalie. We can pay for the child's education."

"Laurette has fallen in love with her baby, and I can't blame her. My sister is proud and stubborn. I don't know if we can convince her to give up Rosalie."

"Your sister is postpartum, dear, and not thinking clearly about the shame this will bring on all of us, including Ned and Eliza. We'll let it be another week or two. Given time to adjust to the idea, Laurette will be reasonable about a solution for her baby. We can tell friends Rosalie succumbed to fever and let the child be adopted by a family where she can have a future of acceptance."

Laurette tightened her grip on Rosalie, who woke and emitted a shriek of objection. Laurette hugged her baby and whispered, "Over my dead body."

↜

The next day, Laurette wasted no time giving Jeanne a piece of her mind.

"I heard you and John last night." Laurette's hazel eyes flashed like daggers in the sun. "How can you think of separating me from my beloved baby. Never mind who fathered her!"

Jeanne took Laurette's hand between hers. "Please be practical, dear one. Tilly has told us about Pastor Greene from the Baptist church and his wife Louanne. They're light-skinned Negroes who haven't been able to conceive a child. They want a baby so badly and would make wonderful parents."

"How can you be so unfeeling, sister?" Laurette's chest heaved with indignation. "You've birthed two healthy children and want another now the war is over. You know a mother's heart."

"You could stay close, dear, and watch your Rosalie grow to womanhood. You could be her guide, teach her your gift with herbs and plants. We could pay for her education at the new Negro college."

Laurette snatched her hand away and gave her sister a determined look. "You all betray me. Even Tilly, who when asked confessed she told the Greens she knows of a baby who needs a good family. Can't you see? Without Rosalie I have nothing to live for."

"How can you say that, Laurette? You know we love you and want the best for you."

Laurette's breath came in gulps. "So much has changed since the war's end, including my work at the hospital. Yankee military nurses help John with surgeries, and I am relegated to changing sheets and writing letters for patients. Yes, I can make medicines, but it will be here at home, not at the hospital where I used to work directly with patients. I resent being pushed home, to become the spinster needlepointing pillows while other women smile and nod in church, thankful they are married with children."

Jeanne rose to face Laurette, struck by her younger sister's passionate response.

"You do have possibilities, my dear sister. That handsome Captain DeVos is interested, and you know it."

"The captain is a nice man. But you must understand I would never marry a Federal Officer and live among Yankees after the violation I experienced from one of their own."

"Please don't act rashly, Laurette." Jeanne reached out to brush a wisp of ginger hair from her sister's forehead.

Laurette softened and gave her sister a sympathetic smile. "Please listen, Jeanne. I have an idea I didn't take seriously until now. There is an alternative choice. Robert's written he plans to join other former Confederates immigrating to Brazil." Laurette's eyes filled with tears. "The idea of leaving you, our family, and my home breaks my heart. But for Rosalie's sake, sailing to Brazil with Robert, Moira, and their little Angus may be the only option for me and my child."

&

April 21, 1866

This is my last diary entry as these are the last pages in my little book. Here I am with an apt ending and a new beginning. It is a relief to be done with these three months spent in seclusion, making and selling medicines, saving every penny, and refusing social engagements using the ruse that Rosalie is sickly.

Tomorrow my sweet little one and I are bound for Nassau. Then on to

Brazil aboard the Emily *with Robert, Moira, little Angus, and two other men and their families, officers Robert knew during the war. The good Lord must have forgiven this soiled dove, to afford me and Rosalie this hope of a fresh start. We will be immigrants just like Papa who found his true love and became successful in Charleston. I will be a pioneer, too, making medicine to support myself and my darling daughter in a new land.*

Jeanne and I shed oceans of tears as we packed my two steamer trunks and two valises for Rosalie and me. John traded Mother's large silver water pitcher to the ship's captain for assurance Rosalie and I will have a favorable cabin on our voyage to Nassau. I will miss my dear sister, brother-in-law, and darling Ned and Eliza so badly it is beyond words. Tears pour from my eyes as I ponder, when will I see my family and Charleston again?

શ

Laurette closed the diary and wrapped it carefully with a leather thong before placing it in her valise. Her steamer trunks were to be loaded in *MaryAnne*'s hold this afternoon. The mail packet would depart for Nassau on the morning tide. Laurette glanced over at the two small cases packed with necessities she and Rosalie would need on the first leg of their voyage.

Lightning streaked through a dark mountain of clouds, followed by a torrent of spring rain, scented by the tall climbing jasmine under her bedroom window. After a last look into the deserted street below, Laurette rose and checked on Rosalie, asleep on her stomach with her tiny bottom in the air.

Glasgow and the Bahama Islands, 1859-1866

September 10, 1859

Dearest Laurette,

I don't have your affinity for letter-writing. But, as promised, I will keep you apprised of my adventures crossing the Atlantic and my news from Glasgow when I arrive. To prove I mean what I say, my first letter will be on the return passage to Charleston.

We are two weeks out of port with four more before we dock. Today, we are making excellent time through heavy swells. The sea is gunmetal gray with a sky of equal color, making it nigh impossible to determine where the water meets the heavens in the distance. When I walked the deck this morning, white water was breaking over the bow. You would have laughed when a thick spray hit me full in the face. I'm not complaining. This weather is a welcome relief from the last few days becalmed, wallowing in troughs, keeping most passengers below deck with a bucket handy. If you'd been aboard, you would have had plenty of patients to nurse!

We in second class are required to prepare our own meals. Thankfully, Mrs. Miranda Tait, Mama's friend who used to live on Vanderhost Street, is aboard with her children and has agreed to cook for me. I dine with them in exchange for entertaining her sons, Daniel and Ralph, who are quite a handful. They dog me everywhere begging for sea stories. If I run out of tales from Two Years Before the Mast *and* Moby Dick, *I'll have to invent some pirate tales. To escape the Tait boys and other tiresome passenger conversations, I volunteer for evening watches, which I quite enjoy. In fact, I will end now as I am due on deck shortly.*

Fondly,
Robert

⁃⁃⁃

Robert slipped Laurette's letter into a large, waxed canvas envelope that kept his trove of personal papers dry. He bent down, pulled hard on the below-bunk drawer, winced at the screech of swollen wood, returned the waxed envelope, then muscled the drawer closed.

Stretched out on the narrow bunk, his fingers laced behind his head, Robert thanked his lucky stars that, at slightly under six feet, he inherited the Bucot family build, not the barrel-chested Highlander body of his father and his brother, James. The top of Robert's head brushed the forward end bulkhead, and his feet braced against the aft end next to the cabin door. Snug as a bug in a rug when *Evangeline* pitched. Rolling was another matter. Since leaving Charleston Harbor, he'd been tossed to the floor more than once in the early morning hours, rising to wipe the grime from uneven floorboards from his cheek and lips.

Etiquette expectations were relaxed at sea, which suited Robert well. No one dressed for dinner. Passengers averted their eyes when a cabin door swung open exposing a lady or gentleman in any form of dishabille. Robert was curious how the women onboard, with multiple petticoats under their skirts, coped with the staterooms with two hooks, no clothes press, and two meager under-bunk drawers. It would have been ungentlemanly to ask.

Robert was in his element at sea. As a boy, he rowed a johnboat out to fish. As a teenager, he sailed with river pilots, collecting cargoes of rice up the Ashley River. As a university student, he sketched the graceful lines of old Clipper ships moored at the wharfs on Bay Street. In recent years, he'd become obsessed with the new steam-powered merchant ships so fast, so sleek, and so elegant.

It had taken a year of carefully crafted conversations—and one especially dramatic whiskey-laced evening—to gain Papa's blessing to pursue his dream of studying ship design in Glasgow.

"It's an outrageous indulgence," Angus had growled.

Robert nodded and clapped his father on the shoulder.

"You always told us to think of the long-term advantages and take calculated risks, Papa."

His father's raised eyebrow of doubt hadn't swayed Robert's passionate focus for a second. He continued. "Southern ship construction is antiquated. Charleston is at the mercy of northern middlemen. Almost every shipment of cotton, tobacco, and rice goes first to New York on sailing barges, then across the Atlantic on fast, efficient northern steamships. We should invest in ship design and steam power construction, and profit from a direct route from Charleston to ports in England and France."

Angus leaned back in his chair, put his whiskey down, and lit a cigar. He squinted at his son through a thin veil of fragrant smoke. "You're working me hard, son. If you put half the energy into ship design that you put into convincing me, I'm inclined to agree. Why not take a couple of years in Glasgow? Just remember, I expect a return on my investment."

Robert had suppressed a whoop of joy. "You drive a hard bargain, Papa." The very next day, Robert wrote to his Uncle James, asking for connections to secure a naval architecture apprenticeship at Darsey Brothers Shipyard.

ఌ

A sharp double rap on his door alerted Robert to the time. He grabbed his jacket and slipped down the narrow passageway, up the ladder onto *Evangeline*'s main deck for his four-hour watch. The clouds had lifted, the sea had lightened, and stars were emerging. It was a beautiful evening to be on watch, as the ship ghosted along to the northeast under courses and topsail.

ఌ

November 15, 1859

Dearest Laurette,

I miss you all tonight, as I send my love from Glasgow. Uncle James, Aunt Margaret, and our cousins have been welcoming and generous. I wish you were here to dine with me at their home in the new West End neighborhood. You would be delighted by the view, high on a hill overlooking the city.

Thank you again, dear sister, for always being my best advocate. Since we were young, you have helped me convince Papa that summers sailing with riverboat pilots was educational, not just a youthful dalliance. Without your support I might have lost my resolve dogging Papa until he gave his blessing for Glasgow.

The Darsey shipyard is near Meadowside Wharf, close enough to my lodgings to be convenient. The training here is everything I hoped for. The shipyard owners have wasted no effort acquiring the latest in design and construction excellence. Darsey's steam-powered side paddlewheelers carry passengers and goods across the Irish Sea—to and from Dublin and Ulster—as well as to Liverpool and London. I'm training in both engineering and in supervision of practical matters of construction.

In the yard, I had expected shipyard workers to have an arduous life, but some of the conditions they live and work in are quite appalling. You must remember Papa's stories of lack of opportunities, the workers' strikes and violence in Glasgow that made him decide on immigration to Charleston. I always thought he was exaggerating. Now I know he was not.

I learned quickly not to put on airs—like some engineers from wealthy families do. I get along well with the laborers in the building slipways and I've already been invited to observe on sea trails twice. You would be amused to see me working outside: dressed in a long, waxed coat, knee-high rubber boots and slouch hat pulled down over my ears protecting me from the frigid November elements.

Mr. Robert Napier's famous foundry is upriver from Darsey Brothers. You would be impressed with his science and the five-hundred-horsepower engines. Recently, Mr. John Elder, a student of Napier's, has been creating even more innovative engine design. It's thrilling to be here and be part of it all. In addition to design work, if I train as a steam engine specialist on sea trials it will give me another skill to bring home to Charleston. Can you imagine being aboard at speeds of over thirteen knots in a ship 230 feet in length, a twenty-five-foot beam, and a knife-edge bow?

After church on Sunday, I would love to take you to the steam ferry races "doon the watter" as they say here. Competition between ferries is so fierce for an afternoon on the Clyde, the tickets are practically free. You would enjoy the decks crowded with every kind of people waving and calling out to those on the shore.

I miss you, dear sister! Papa sends letters full of advice but your letters are like a cool, fresh glass of water on a hot July afternoon. Please write often.

Fondly,
Robert

The Gordon children had been raised on Angus's stories of wealthy mill and shipyard owners who made fortunes on the backs of the working class. They'd heard about the crowded, reeking, tenements that sprung up along the greasy, polluted Clyde. Angus told his children that by 1830, the year he left Glasgow, The United Society of Boiler Makers and Shipbuilders used factory walkouts and riots to force wages up and improve safety practices. But improvements were few and far between. Suspicion continued in the mills and yards; any small thing sparked confrontation with management.

In 1859, Scottish factory owners and politicians broke into cold sweats when they observed union and abolitionist advocates unite into a formidable force to right what they determined were abuses of power by the privileged class. The threat of Southern state succession snuck into Glasgow boardrooms. Factory owners were well aware over a million jobs depended on regular Southern cotton transport to mills in Scottish Lanarkshire and northern England. Any significant interruption in the delivery of raw product would bring widespread riots, production slowdowns, and then recession, followed by more rioting as out-of-work men with hungry families took to the streets.

☙

One afternoon, Robert was summoned by Mr. Darsey. "Tell me young man, as a citizen of Charleston, will the Southern states secede?"

"I hope not, sir. But it's possible. My father writes that prominent men like James Pettigrew, Dean of the College of South Carolina, oppose secession. Father and other merchants and farmers believe slaveholding labor must be phased out in a planned, rational way. But many in the powerful planter class disagree. The 'peculiar institution' assures their wealth grows."

Robert paused, thinking how to say what he needed to say next.

"You should know, when abolitionists preach morality, Southerners can't abide Northerners who act as if they own the Christian high road. Meanwhile, Federal tariffs favor northern industrialists with another layer of profit to their corrupt pocketbooks while people in their factories work like slaves and live in squalor."

℘

The meeting with Mr. Darsey made Robert ache for an evening's discussion with Papa, soothing his frazzled nerves in the library with a cigar in one hand and a glass of whiskey in the other. As he walked to Uncle James's house in the gloaming, Robert was blind to the burnished leaves and gardens ripe with late fall color. He ruminated on his years at Carolina College where many classmates were spoiled young men from influential families whose fathers manipulated the state legislature with divisive rhetoric. Secession might be legal according to the United States Constitution, but he doubted the powers in Washington, DC, would tolerate such a bold move. At dinner, his cousin's light conversation about the unusually fine weather and a new production at the playhouse on Queen Street, gave him some solace. Perhaps he worried too much.

℘

February 20, 1860

Dearest Laurette,

To entice sweet thoughts of me so far from home, I am sending a package of Scottish sweets with this letter. The biscuits are so delicious you will want to hide them from Ned and Eliza lest they disappear in a day.

Mr. Darsey has the work ethic of a true Scot. He requires me at the shipyard from eight in the morning until dusk, checking drawings and observing construction in the graving dock. We are launching a ship every eight months! Some evenings I fall into bed without washing and sleep like the dead until morning. The knowledge I'm gaining keeps my spirits up, when I can hardly put one foot in front of the other at day's end.

I'm preparing a presentation for Papa and his friends. I think Charleston's deep-water shipyard on South Battery would be a prime location for steamship construction. If Papa's friends put together a consortium, they could build fast steamships to sail directly to Glasgow or Liverpool. Imagine how that would challenge the Fraser and Trenholm Company's monopoly on transporting cotton to England via New York!

I have a new concern here in Glasgow. Abolitionists shouting from soapboxes

*in George Square believe violence against slaveholders is the only solution. I
feel they speak with ignorance that would bring harm to our country. They are
impatient and do not consider other solutions, like phasing out slaveholding
through education and skill building in trades to earn a living.*

*Last week I went to hear Frederick Douglas, an escaped slave, speak at
the John Street United Presbyterian Church and was fortunate to squeeze
into a packed pew. The evening venue was a debate between Douglas and
the Scottish Quaker, William Smeal, over the validity of the United States
Constitution. Mr. Smeal declared our constitution "a covenant with death"
written by slaveholders. Mr. Douglas eloquently presented his interpretation,
saying the United States Constitution, written and ratified by men, many
of whom were slaveholders, does indeed intend for all men to have the right
to life, liberty, and the pursuit of happiness. Would that you and Papa had
seats next to me. What a lively time we would have had at supper afterward,
discussing the Douglas-Smeal debate!*

*After the debate, I strolled in the church garden and chanced to meet
a charming young woman, Moira MacDonald. She teaches at the United
Presbyterian Church School, and lives with her brother and his family not far
from Uncle James. She let me know she and her sister-in-law are in the habit
of walking in the new park, Glasgow Green, on Sunday afternoons. I know
where I will be after church next Sunday.*

Please convey my love to Papa, Jeanne, John, and the children.

Fondly,
Robert

Uncle James had repeatedly warned Robert to give soapbox abolitionists
at Glasgow Green and George Square a wide berth.

"If those ruffians find out you are from the American South, you
would be fortunate to get away with your limbs intact."

When the subject of abolition came up in conversation at the shipyard,
Robert walked a narrow line. He agreed with men who believed enslaved
people were no worse off than steel or mill workers with no negotiating

power, and also with colleagues who said all men should have freedom to choose a life path, whether wisely or ill begotten.

Moira, influenced by her father's preaching, crossed her arms on her chest and declared, "It's immoral to own a human being."

Robert, who grew up with an opinionated sister, wasn't put off by the ferocity of his new lady friend's feelings. "You don't understand the American South," he said with a deep sigh. "Slaveholders are, unfortunately, vocal and powerful. But there are other points of view. Many Southerners believe slavery is a sin and would never own another human being. Others who currently own slaves would be pleased with a cash recompense for their 'property,' like the English government offered slaveholders when that institution was abolished in Great Britain in 1833." Robert gave Moira a half smile. He wanted this very special woman to understand that the Christian home he was raised in believed in hard work and fair treatment for all people.

Robert told Moira how his father freed Marion, an enslaved woman who was a wedding gift from his in-laws, and later hired her as midwife and family healer.

Moira, still not convinced, gave Robert a cross look. "Where does your family stand now?"

"My father advises friends to free their slaves and hire them back at a competitive price, but he doesn't publicly criticize the wealthy planters who could crush the business he's worked so hard to build."

Robert turned his head to the open window, wishing he could join the crows squawking on the roof across the street rather than discuss the subject of slavery. He turned back to face this intelligent woman and tried again.

"When I was a child, my parents did their best to protect us from the ugliness of 'the peculiar institution,' as it's called, but of course that wasn't entirely possible. One day when I was around ten, and running errands for my father, I was very late. I took a shortcut past the Slave Market on Chalmers Street, where I'd been forbidden to go. Loud shouts and an auctioneer's gavel drew me to the open door. A young woman clad only in a translucent cotton shift was standing barefoot on a raw planked stage, weeping. I ran home, ashamed by what I'd seen. I never told a soul about it until now."

Moira put gave Robert's forearm a gentle squeeze and looked into his face. "What a horrible thing to witness as a boy."

"As I got older," Robert continued, "I learned more about the economics of people owning people and the sins of slaveholding."

Robert paused, concerned Moira would not understand. He shook his head to clear it.

"I used to hang around the wharfs. I made friends with Negro sailors—both free men and slaves. Papa wanted me to join his business eventually, but also encouraged me to understand the life of working men."

Robert lightened up briefly while he told his new love silly stories of hounding river pilots for work as a summer deckhand for a day or a week. He loved the sound of Moira's laugh.

He took a deep breath and continued. "Thaddeus, a pilot who taught me to read the water and navigate the shifting sandbars, was like an older brother. His master was a free Negro, who allowed Thaddeus to use the sloop *Belinda,* and keep the cash he made on his time off. Thaddeus told me how he saved every dollar until he could purchase his wife's freedom. The law states, children born of a free woman are free, even if the father is a slave. Thaddeus was so proud his children went to the school for free 'colored' on John's Island."

"Negroes don't own slaves!" Moira withdrew her hand and stared at Robert like he was a lunatic escaped from the asylum.

"Yes, indeed they do. There are several thousand free former slaves in South Carolina; some of them are successful businessmen, and slaveholders themselves."

Robert tried to keep frustration out of his voice as he continued his story.

"On the river, I was Thaddeus's helper, but when we tied up at Twelve Oaks wharf, we acted otherwise for his protection. The plantation overseer was a hard man who swung a willow switch, striking the thighs of sweating Negroes as they shouldered man-sized bags of rice up the gangway. Once the boat was fully loaded, we'd cast off and tack downriver, and Thaddeus became my superior again."

"How could you say nothing? You are White and could confront that overseer."

Robert ran his hands through his ginger hair and gave Moira a smile with a bit of chagrin in it.

"Much as I would have liked to, if I had intervened, it would have endangered Thaddeus's life and my own—and we both knew it. I was a powerless youth, standing on land owned by a powerful man." Robert's green eyes flashed in irritation at Moira's naiveté. "As for your point about freedom, I don't see equity as a priority in Glasgow. Slavery is illegal, but race and class rules keep many Scots in abject poverty, and women are second-class citizens with freedoms restricted in every way."

Moira huffed out her response. "I still say there is no excuse for owning a human being—class differences are not the same."

They locked eyes in a stubborn standoff for a long minute and then laughed after they said simultaneously, "Let's talk about something else."

⁓

October 15, 1860

Dearest Sister,

I have the best news imaginable! Moira's brother, William, has given us his permission to announce our engagement. I have a standing invitation to dine at their home on Wednesday evenings. On Sundays after church Moira and I have a walkabout. I've purchased a copy of Hugh MacDonald's book Rambles Around Glasgow. *The book is rife with suggestions on inexpensive places to take an educated lady.*

I expect an increase in salary soon. If I follow Papa's edicts on thrift, in a year I can afford an apartment in the fashionable West End, a suitable residence in which to start married life. It is my fondest hope that all of you will come for our wedding and meet my bride. I know you and Moira will become fast friends. She is as outspoken as you are!

It was very good news to hear from you that James finished his studies at the Citadel and has accepted a commission as a lieutenant in the United

States Army. Papa must be a very happy man with James settled on a career that suits his adventurous spirit. Give James my congratulations and I will write soon with my brotherly advice that it's time to leave his pranks behind and be a serious, proper military man.

Please relay my love to everyone.

Fondly,
Robert

એ

Engineers at Darsey's earned a generous bonus for overtime work. With saving for an apartment in mind, Robert stepped up immediately. For thrifty evening meals, he purchased pasties from a vendor who rolled his cart to the shipyard gate at the end of the workday. Robert spent long evenings checking drawings for errors. Mornings, he arrived early to discuss design changes with shipwrights before they took up their tools at the blast of the workday whistle.

Sundays were a reprieve to enjoy the new neighborhoods in Glasgow, the proud examples of modern science and engineering. Robert and Moira joined the growing middle class out and about, dressed in their best to see and be seen. After church, they took circular walks down Argyle Street to Buchanan and round to Jamaica Street. Shops in fine, new granite buildings rose several stories with marvelous large glass windows at street level, and winding stairways inside that led to multiple small shops. This new way of shopping had a name—*department store*. Inside one found the most wonderful things: ready-made clothing in the latest mode with quite affordable designs and textures; shirts and ties for gentlemen; and women's bonnets, shoes, and handbags.

Other enterprises sold baked goods; some even offered a sample sweet treat to entice customers into the new tearooms. Moira raved to Robert about these tearooms as acceptable venues where ladies gathered to show off a stylish hat and talk among themselves about women's suffrage.

February 25, 1861

Dearest Laurette,

The Glasgow Guardian reported the most disturbing news today! I read that a total of six Southern states have now seceded and Governor Pickens has ordered the seizure of all Federal fortifications in South Carolina. It's hard to believe that Forts Moultrie and Johnson are now in the hands of General P.G.T. Beauregard and that the Federal officer, Major Anderson, has surrendered Fort Sumter to the Confederate Army. The word around Glasgow is, the new president, Abraham Lincoln, will not tolerate this secession.

It appears our Southern politics are having an impact on my future with Moira as well. Dear sister, your counsel has always been sound, and I need it now. Moira's father is of the opinion South Carolina's secession is the work of the devil. Moira told me he was an itinerant preacher who championed workers' rights in Ayrshire, but I didn't understand he was such a firebrand on abolition as well. He has written Moira he no longer considers me a suitable candidate for her hand. He could demand she return to live in Ayrshire. Fortunately, her brother, William (with whom she lives), has become a friend. I know he trusts I am a man of honor. Like many in the Glaswegian business community, William's sympathy lies with the Confederate South and the philosophy of States Rights.

Moira and I have talked it over again and again and decided our love can weather these difficult times in spite of her father's fuss. I haven't yet attained adequate savings to support the woman I love in the way she deserves in Glasgow. But I have a plan I hope you will not discourage. Please tell me I am not so besotted with love I have lost my reason.

Moira and I want to marry quietly and be away to Nassau in the Bahama Islands in a few months. There are many opportunities there for a man with knowledge of steam engines.

They say the Port of Nassau was nothing more than a coal depot for the British Navy with the pet name "the dusty pigeon in the colonial office," until this last year. Now merchants from around the world are setting up offices, expecting Southern secession will lead to a new country or a civil war. Either way, it's to their benefit to have a foothold in Nassau, where goods from Great

Britain, Europe, and the Northern States can be warehoused. Goods can then be transferred to smaller, faster steamers, bound for deep-water Southern ports, primarily Wilmington, Charleston, and New Orleans. Preparations are well under way. I understand that warehouses, ship maintenance yards, and hotels are erupting like mushrooms. They say fast steam merchants can cross from Glasgow to Nassau in little over a week and cross from Nassau to the ports of Charleston or Wilmington in three days!

I hope to secure a position as the engineer on one of the new steamers carrying goods between Glasgow and Nassau. The Lady of Arran, a state-of-the-art, single-screw 260-foot channel class vessel, is currently in the Darsey graving dock. My capability as an engineer on sea trials has been noticed. I have a good chance of securing a position. I will continue to pray for a negotiated peace over Southern secession that can avert hostilities. In his letters, Papa reminds me that if war is declared, it will be my duty to use my skills to serve my family and my home state of South Carolina. I have grave concern about a war between the States, but you can all rest assured I will do the right thing should peaceful negotiations fail.

Please convey my love to all the family and write at your earliest convenience.

Fondly,
Robert

Born fifteen months apart, Robert and Laurette shared a strong bond with their mutual love of the natural world. As children they escaped the house to the narrow marshy inlets on the Ashley River, where Laurette collected flora and Robert tested model boats for stability and speed. Since Robert can remember, when either sibling encountered conflict, they sought the other's trustworthy advice. He was on pins and needles waiting for his sister's next letter.

Crushed about the secession of his home state, Robert was relieved when a lead article in the *Glasgow Herald* hailed the British Government's official neutral stand on Southern secession. However, graphic political cartoons depicting the United States as a youthful bully trying to intimidate a solid, mature "John Bull" implied more sympathy for the South than neutrality.

On the street, Robert heard entrepreneurs, shop owners, and politicians express empathy for the new Confederate States of America. He listened to Scottish worries about recession if Scottish employers were forced to lay off millworkers because Southern cotton didn't arrive on schedule.

At the same time, soapbox abolitionists called on brothers and sisters working in factories and shipyards to fight Great Britain's neutrality toward any state that tolerated men and women in bondage. Because Moira abhorred the abolitionists relish for violence, Robert was relieved he and his beloved were in agreement that taking up arms for civil war was not the answer.

The board of directors at Darsey's met behind closed doors, entertaining consortiums of merchants anticipating fat profit margins if war was declared in North America. Faster, sleeker single-screw vessels would pay for themselves in two or three passages, as the price of quality cotton cloth, leather, madeira, and medicine would surely spike in the American South.

Robert was introduced to Captain Douglas Davis, hired as *Lady of Arran*'s captain. Davis was one of many British naval officers taking a leave of absence from Her Majesty's service, eyeing the coming conflict in North America as a golden opportunity to fatten their wallets. When *Lady of Arran* completed sea trials, she would carry the usual cargo of finished clothing in the latest styles, perfumes, handmade bonnets, and whiskey. But, concealed in crates in the belly of her hold would be Enfield rifles, barrels of gun powder, percussion caps, uniforms, and boots for the Confederate Army.

ల

Sunday afternoon Robert and Moira sat in a pew at Saint Mungo's Cathedral, hands entwined. They admired the tall stained-glass windows with scenes of sacrifice and hope and discussed their future in Nassau in excited whispers.

After leaving the sanctuary, they climbed the hill to the necropolis adjacent the cathedral. The stern-faced statue of John Knox atop Glasgow's highest hill didn't detract from its popularity with the people of Glasgow.

Couples sat on benches enjoying the view across the River Clyde, walked among the ornate mausoleums of the rich and the tiny headstones of the middle class. Graceful trees and early flowering shrubs were a perfect place to steal a kiss. Moira told Robert the story of St. Mungo, the pet name for Kintegern, who performed miracles and converted Glaswegians to Christianity in the seventh century.

"The cathedral has been rebuilt more grandly to sit on the very spot of Kintegern's first church. I always feel at peace here," Moira said. A tear trickled down her cheek. "I will miss my Glasgow desperately."

"Would that we could entice Mungo down from Heaven, to provide another miracle to avoid a Civil War," Robert added as he took her hand in his.

享

August 30, 1861

Dearest Sister,

I have wonderful news to begin this letter. Last Sunday, Moira and I were married in the chapel at Saint Enoch's Presbyterian Church. William, his wife and children, and two of my friends from Darsey's were our witnesses. After the wedding, we had a fine celebratory dinner and good wine for toasts. Moira was disappointed but not surprised her father declined to attend. She and William concur; their mother's death and his evangelism have greatly changed him.

You and the family are in my prayers every evening. I was incensed to learn Abraham Lincoln authorized a blockade of Confederate ports. Mr. Lincoln is a fool to believe this aggressive maneuver will quickly bring our proud Carolinians to heel. My heart aches as this turn of events forces me into war against people who, a few short months ago, I considered my countrymen.

Captain Davis has assured me, my position as Lady of Arran's *second engineer remains secure in spite of my inexperience during wartime. The ship is a magnificent double engine, single-screw deep-water ship; sleek and fast, she will fly across the Atlantic. Moira is to be one of three passengers on the voyage to Nassau that should, if the late summer weather holds fine, be completed in a week.*

My compensation disappoints, but Captain Davis assures me that if I prove my mettle on the next voyage between Glasgow and Nassau, it will redouble fast. Moira has been gathering necessities we may find difficult to purchase in the Bahama Islands. The exact date of our departure I cannot reveal. The Captain is cautious about our details due to the nature of our cargo.

I understand housing is difficult to come by with construction in Nassau dedicated to commerce on the waterfront. I will not subject Moira to a residence near the sailor's boarding houses and rowdy pubs. I have been given the name of a family with rooms to rent in a quieter neighborhood until we can secure a home of our own. Those who have been to the island tell me the new grand Victoria Hotel hosts tea parties and dances regularly. I am relieved Moira will be able to meet other recently arrived wives as well as the island residents who've been there since colonial days. I shall be at sea a good deal and want my dear Moira to have proper friends to socialize with as soon as possible. Knowing my sweetheart as I do, in no time she will be organizing a book group for the ladies and educational projects for the children.

Please give my love to all the family. Moira reminds me to tell you we keep every one of you in our nightly prayers.

Your loving brother,
Robert

Before he signed a contract as engineer on *Lady of Arran,* Robert met with officers off ships, who educated him about the Bahama Islands, assuring him the shallow harbors around Nassau were ideal for a steamship like *Lady of Arran.* One young lieutenant had a raucous story about a deep-draft, heavy Federal warship led aground near Hog Island off the port entrance while in hot pursuit of a lighter, faster British merchant vessel.

Robert was told international law states no merchant may be boarded at sea and confronted as a belligerent unless she is armed with cannons. That, the men warned Robert, did not mean boarding and confiscation of cargo wasn't a risk—which was why firemen poured on the coal when the Captain spotted a Federal warship. A merchant ship's crew had good reason for fear.

At Johnson's Island in Lake Erie, there was a barren three-hundred-acre prisoner-of-war camp. Men off captured blockade runners were sent there to die of malnutrition or freeze to death in northern winter temperatures.

Merchant mariners who visited Darsey's shipyard had told Robert about Conchs; Bahamian descendants of pirates, smugglers, and Tories who left the United States after the American Revolution. The mariners said, before war was declared, the Conchs were inclined to favor the gallant, courageous Southerners over the haughty, often offensive U.S. government representatives and spies who had been posted to the islands.

⁓

"*Lady of Arran* can outrun any Federal warship," Robert told Moira to calm her frazzled nerves. "And remember, we fly the Scottish flag; international neutrality is in our favor."

"Don't try and pull the wool over my eyes, Robert Gordon!" she replied. "I was present at the dinner when, after a few drams, your captain told stories about boilers exploding at high speeds and swamped ships running aground."

"Captain Davis served fifteen years in the Royal Navy and never lost a ship my dear. Trust me, I am not a rash man."

He could tell by the look on Moira's face she was skeptical about that comment.

"And remember, as an engineer with the privilege of personal baggage, I can bring something from Glasgow every trip, to make ours a more comfortable life."

What Robert told his bride was true. Yet, in the wee hours of the morning, he tossed and turned, wondering what he had gotten himself—and the woman he loved—into.

September 15, 1862

Dearest Sister,

I hope you and all the family are managing well. Your letter about John's leg saddens both Moira and me. We thank the good Lord the amputation was below the knee. He should be able to get along with a prothesis once he is fully recovered.

We've recently learned the Federal Navy captured New Orleans. The loss of that deep port will make the supply chain to the South more challenging. Papa writes the reduction in ships to carry his imports to Charleston is crushing his decades-long relationships in Glasgow. I know only too well the consortiums like the Trenholm Company have huge profits from military ordnance and fancy luxuries for the very wealthy, so they carry fewer civilian necessities, like leather for shoes and cloth for clothing. I find it shocking a Charleston company's greed would take such advantage of their own. Every night Moira and I add an extra prayer for the survival of Papa's business.

Please dear sister, let me know small things you need: buttons and thread, paper and needles, or a bottle of fine Scotch whisky for Papa. I have a friend, an engineer on the blockade runner Cassandra, *that regularly docks at Addison's wharf. He's willing to add a few things to his personal luggage for you and the family. I despair that I'm not able to personally do more for the citizens of Charleston in these difficult times.*

With loving regards,
Robert

∞

Robert pined for a fortnight's visit home. But, as things currently stood, it wasn't possible. To visit his family, he would have to pay the captain of *Cassandra* a hefty fee to accept him as supercargo. In Charleston, he would not be able to linger on the streets, visiting people and places he missed. Able-bodied males from fifteen to fifty were conscripted on sight, given a pair of marching boots and assigned to a regiment. Robert was not a marksman like his brother James—but try and tell a Confederate officer who had lost half his men in battle you were more valuable aboard ship than on the front lines.

෧

In Nassau, Robert and Moira attended dinner parties with merchants and Confederates who held fast to the fantasy that the war would end soon, leaving the Southern states secure as an independent nation. Robert was a realist. At home, he and Moira had sat up late talking about what had become, for them, a very uncertain future. In Great Britain, support for the Confederate States was waning in tandem with no easy Southern victory in sight. Robert and Moira feared if they returned to Glasgow, his role blockade running for the Confederacy would generate a cold shoulder for employment. And his dream to be a leader in the shipbuilding renaissance in Charleston looked like a holiday balloon popped by a bully.

෧

As the Federal blockade tightened, shipyards in Glasgow and Liverpool continued to build sleeker, faster, low freeboard steamships that burned 160 to 180 tons of coal between Nassau and Charleston or Wilmington. Prices skyrocketed for the preferred, smokeless anthracite coal that kept a heavily laden vessel hard to spot. If a captain miscalculated the quantity of coal he needed for a return voyage to Nassau, Bahamian pilots were known to save the day by guiding a blockade runner into a shallow bay on one of the hundred small islands in the Bahamian archipelago. There a vessel sat, safe but trapped, until a supply of coal from Nassau could be delivered.

Complicating matters, the competition of Confederate agents vying for quality new crews escalated as ships were captured or sunk. The financial compensation offered by shipowners grew with the risk but couldn't accommodate for the paucity of experienced sailors. An experienced pilot got seven hundred pounds per voyage and the engineers got five hundred. The deck crew and firemen got fifty pounds each, better pay by far than any of them ever saw in Great Britain.

Robert didn't enlighten Moira about the extent to which *Lady of Arran*'s voyages are fraught with danger. In defiance of international law, more Federal warships boldly challenged merchant vessels off the Scottish coast. On their most recent run from Glasgow to Nassau, a Yankee warship fired across the *Lady*'s bow, warning the captain to stop her engines and prepare to be boarded. Captain Davis ordered the firemen to pour on the coal and run. The *Lady* sprang ahead, into a safety blanket of fog. When they arrived in Nassau a week later, the captain's first order after unloading cargo was to go directly to the shipyard and repaint the *Lady*'s topsides the color of a winter sea.

⁓

July 30, 1863

Dearest Laurette,

I long to receive a letter letting me know all the family is well. The current unreliability of mail packets troubles me terribly. We hear devastating news about the Federals on Morris Island, with their cannons trained on Charleston. Have you and Jeanne considered traveling upstate with the children for safety's sake? Ned and Eliza might find it quite an adventure to visit their grandparents and spend time on John's family farm in the Piedmont.

My trips across the Atlantic are fraught with surprises of bold Federal blockaders. That said, our ships remain faster and better designed. And I have a new opportunity! I have become acquainted with Captain James Moffitt, a most intelligent and remarkably skilled seaman with a wealth of knowledge about Southern ports. Ten years ago, he surveyed the Eastern seaboard for the United States government, including the ports of Charleston and Wilmington. Here in Nassau, he's responsible for scheduling blockade runners, as well as hiring and replacing officers and crews.

Captain Moffitt has offered me the position of first engineer on the recently delivered blockade runner Emily. *I've heard the run from Nassau to Charleston can scare the stripe off a skunk. But the moment I saw* Emily, *I knew she was exceptional. She is a magnificent 230-foot side-wheeler with a long, low, molded iron hull painted the color of fog and capable of carrying eight hundred bales of cotton. She has 180-horsepower twin vertical double oscillating engines, making her capable of an amazing eighteen knots! For extra stealth, she has the new telescoping funnels that can collapse to a few feet above deck if a*

Federal blockade patrol is spotted. For further security, her steel turtle-back bow prevents swamping in rough seas. I've included a sketch of Emily *in this letter. Captain Moffitt tells me our primary destination will be up the Cape Fear River into Wilmington, but there will be runs to Charleston as well. I may arrive at Addison's wharf before you know it and hope to bring Moira along as supercargo, at least once, so you can meet my bride.*

Fondly,
Robert

&

Robert didn't disclose he knew the tenacious United States consul in Great Britain was pressuring London to sanction blockade running into Confederate ports. The political tide in England has turned from laissez-faire to honoring the vocal British abolitionists who had lobbied against the Southern states since secession in 1860.

Fortunately, the Conchs in Nassau assured Confederates they wouldn't be abandoned by the Bahamians. To flummox Northern spies and journalists, warehouse workers carefully relabeled boxes of munitions as shoe leather and preserved meat, obfuscating how the neutral island aided a war effort. Everyone from ship owners to firemen on blockade runners knew: the higher the risk, the higher the profit for consortiums in Liverpool, Glasgow, and Charleston, and all those who sailed for them. If a ship only made three successful trips through the blockade, investors still pocketed up to seven hundred percent on their investment in her construction.

The sentiment toward the United States was embarrassingly obvious to the citizenry of Nassau on July 4, 1863. W. G. Thompson, acting consul for the United States, refused to raise the Stars and Stripes and play the national anthem because the Federal government had become the subject of ribald jokes.

Even so, men like Robert were ever conscious that Northern sympathizers lurked around docks and shipyards, where captains and engineers supervised their ship maintenance and repairs. Federal spies

sought to document ships and their officers and prepared a list of men
who would soon have bounties on their heads.

Robert prayed for a negotiated peace. But after the Federal victory
at Gettysburg, and Lincoln's Emancipation Proclamation, he suspected
deep losses for the South were inevitable. When blood-filled nightmares
woke him, Robert slipped out of bed careful not to disturb Moira as he
poured himself a stiff whiskey in the parlor and paced the floor for hours.
Like Papa, he never wanted this war, yet his brother was a young officer
fighting somewhere in Virginia. Every letter from home contained news of
one more friend dead in battle or from disease, buried in unmarked graves,
far from grieving loved ones. Although Laurette wrote about shortages of
medicine at the hospital, when her letters turned to the discovery of new
herbal remedies, she sounded almost buoyant.

But Southerners were suffering dearly. Only the very wealthy could
purchase basics like muslin for clothing or paper and ink. Fear for his
family in Charleston helped push aside thoughts on losing his life at sea.
Emily was a state-of-the-art ship. Robert refused to entertain thoughts of
what would happen to Moira if he left her widowed far from the land
of her birth. He felt he had no alternative than to do his part to support
the Confederacy; blockade running meant keeping a lifeline open for the
people and the land he loved.

೧೨

September 30, 1864

Dearest Laurette,

*I pray this letter finds you all well. It gave me great pain to stay so briefly
for Papa's funeral and to see the city in such dire straits. I understand now why
you and John believe it's un-Christian to leave your patients at the hospital,
but I do hope Jeanne and the children might still consider a visit to his family
in Greenville County away from flying rockets and debris.*

*We had quite a high time on our return trip to Nassau. We departed
the wharf at one in the morning, with eight hundred bales of cotton. With
minimal freeboard, we needed the best wind and sea conditions, and we were*

in luck. Cloud coverage was excellent, the moon was new, and the tide near slack. Thank the good Lord we had an experienced, native Charlestonian pilot, who knows the men of the signal corps on Sullivan's Island. One of the beauties of Emily's *shallow-draft is, we can ghost along just beyond the breaking surf near Fort Moultrie, no more than fifteen feet from the beach, and make an escape out to sea.*

After we cleared Charleston harbor, we were not able to let our guard down long. Two miles beyond Fort Sumter, we were spotted by a fast blockader. She sent flares skyward in our direction to get a better bead on our course. We evaded them by sending up our own flares angled away from our intended course and confused the Federals further by zigzagging back to the safety of shallow waters. Unfortunately, our clever maneuvers wasted precious coal. We had to dump bales of cotton, stoke the boilers with turpentine-soaked cotton, and run back out to sea on an altered course. We limped into Nassau harbor with all hands safe. I don't relish another trip like that one.

There is something I want you to know. I've wrestled with how to tell you and decided that being direct, giving you an honest assessment of my thoughts about my future, is sensible under current circumstances.

At a coffee hour after Sunday service a few weeks ago, Moira and I chanced to meet two men from Aiken, South Carolina. They had recently returned from a several-months visit to Brazil where, apparently, a group of families from their town plan to immigrate. In a few months, the folks from Aiken plan to sail to Cuba, then on to Brazil. A Mr. Saylor gave me his card. I plan to keep appraised of the group's travel and settlement in Brazil.

The more Moira and I talked about the community Mr. Saylor's Aiken group is planning Northwest of Rio de Janeiro, the more interesting immigration becomes as a solution for us. The Federal government considers my role as an engineer on Emily *a hanging offense. And I would be unemployable in Glasgow now that the United States government and abolitionist politics have swayed Great Britain against the South. Brazil could be a new beginning, like an Old Testament exodus to 'promised land' for us Confederates who have no homes to return to.*

I am trying to find hope for our future, not let bitterness overtake me.

It is difficult to accept how loyalty and love for my homeland has made me a criminal in the land of my birth. Pray for the best outcome for me and Moira and our unborn child.

Moira and I await family news. Please post a letter when you can.

With Love,
Robert

☙

Robert never revealed to his wife that, pouring on coal and testing *Emily's* knife-edge hull on a race through well-armed Federal warships was the thrill of a lifetime. In the heat of the chase, he had no time to fear for his life as he monitored *Emily's* gauges, flying along just beyond breaking surf in six feet of water off Sullivan's Island, or diving into a fog bank off Cape Fear. Every escape was discussed in detail by the captain and crew for lessons learned, and new evasive tactics emerged.

In addition to his pride as the chief engineer on a state-of-the-art steamship, for risks taken, Robert received a big bonus from the owners each time cargo arrived at its destination in good condition. Although reward for each success helped, *Emily's* captain and Robert had risk aplenty to concern them. The more industrialized northern states continued flush with raw materials and money, while the Confederate states were short on both. The Federal shipyards had acquired the technology to build fast single-screw steamships rivaling those constructed in Liverpool and Glasgow. Federals ships now captured or sank one in three blockade runners.

Robert and Moira grieved over the untenable options for a future in Charleston or Glasgow. The Federals could win the war within months, and word was the United States government would sue Great Britain in international court for aiding the Confederacy. Feeling like they were already exiles from their native countries, Robert and Moira decided the best option for their family was to take Mr. Saylor's advice and join others immigrating to Brazil.

February 26, 1865

Dearest Laurette,

I write with grave concern for your welfare and that of the family. We've heard Charleston has fallen; people here have lost all hope for the Confederacy. Nassau is a madhouse, with war time residents frantic to get on the next ship to Liverpool or Glasgow. Anything valuable is being removed from homes and warehouses and loaded aboard ships bound abroad. I would not believe this island could go from backwater to boom town to backwater in four years if I had not seen it happen with my very own eyes.

The island is no longer safe for us. Very soon, Moira and I will leave Nassau for the Abacos Islands, one hundred miles to the northeast. A Conch friend, Lloyd Allen, and his family remain sympathetic to the Southern cause. The Allens own a small shipyard on Man O' War Cay. Lloyd has told me of a narrow cove surrounded by a thicket of mangroves where Emily *can anchor unnoticed and as long as needed until repairs can be made for our voyage to Brazil. Our swift ship sustained damage to one boiler and the port side wheel paddles on our last run back from Charleston. The captain gave me permission to scrap her or repair her as I please. He and most the crew departed days ago for England where they will rejoin the British Navy.*

Please write when you can and post your letters to Lloyd Allen at the address enclosed. He will see I get my mail. Moira is as well as can be expected during these trying times of heartbreak and hard decisions, but she and I do have some wonderful news. Our little one arrived safely and is growing strong and healthy! We named him Angus. Papa would be pleased if he could see his namesake, already sitting up, holding a little boat I carved from driftwood in his chubby hands.

I miss you all dearly. Moira sends her love.

Your loving brother,
Robert

Robert walked the docks, noting most ships rode dangerously low, packed with cargo, their captains well aware that time was of the essence for one last shipment east across the Atlantic. Traders, investors, and hangers-on with plump wallets from the spoils of blockade running reserved cabins on the steamers back to the great ports of London, Liverpool, and Glasgow.

Watching the wild departures, Robert asked himself: If he had known five years ago what he knew now, would he have become a blockade runner? Yes, he thought, his face splitting into a huge grin. Definitely! He had been the engineer on one of the fastest ships ever designed and had the adventure of a lifetime, using his wits to keep *Emily's* machinery running perfectly at a hell-for-leather pace. Now the game was over, and the consequences were his. Robert raked a hand through his hair, cropped close for convenience at sea; there was a bounty on his head, and he had a family to support.

He tried not to wallow in self-recrimination over his naiveté for thinking he and Moira would have a grand adventure in Nassau for a year or two and return to a quiet life in Charleston or Glasgow. In 1861, he'd thought secession might mean a skirmish followed by a negotiated peace, not a bloody four-year conflict. He thanked God for Moira's love. She'd stood by him through it all, strong, independent thinking, and resolved. She'd embraced the difficult decision to immigrate.

The job at hand was to remain focused on each strategic step to leave Nassau, then the Bahamas and on to Brazil to ensure his family's survival. He'd drawn up plans and a list of supplies for *Emily's* repairs and refitting. Given time, he knew he would find a buyer in Brazil for a fast, light, shallow-draft ship, perfect for ferrying goods and people in the islands south of Rio de Janeiro.

ॐ

April 2, 1866

Dearest Laurette,

It's been over a year since I last set eyes on you! Moira, little Angus, and I anxiously await you and Rosalie. My friend, Lloyd, will meet your ship in Nassau and escort you here. It will be a tight squeeze in our small cottage on

Clearwater Cay, but it won't be for long, as we must depart for Brazil by early June to avoid hurricane season.

    I grieve fearing I may not see dear Jeanne, John, and their sweet children again. I wake in the wee hours furious I'm refused amnesty when criminals and wealthy planters can buy theirs. Sometimes I sit on the porch and stew until dawn. Were it not for the love of Moira and Angus, I would be inconsolable. I'm relieved Papa, so proud he became a citizen of the United States, can't see the vindictive Federal sanctions against citizens like me, born and raised in Charleston.

    You can be confident Emily *will be shipshape for our voyage to Rio de Janeiro. I have found a seasoned captain, and I, of course, will serve as engineer. Two additional Confederate officers and their families, as well as a few strong men to act as firemen, will join us on the voyage. I have been corresponding with prospective buyers and feel confident* Emily *will fetch a good price in Brazil. We will land at Guanabara Bay, the port that serves Rio de Janeiro. I am told Rio is a city with a hospitable climate and magnificent beauty. Moira is looking forward to finding a proper home, and I can't blame her. She showed great fortitude enduring raucous Nassau and now the opposite—a quiet out-of-the-way bay with no educated women to socialize with.*

    Mr. Saylor has written that most Confederate exiles in Brazil are farmers, but professional work is plentiful in Rio de Janeiro for those with an education or a skilled trade. Moira hopes to open a school. Pack your herb seeds and medicines; your skill as a healer will be welcomed.

    I have written to two shipyards and received information that naval architects are in demand, though I am concerned about learning Portuguese. Remember when you Jeanne and I had a French tutor who rapped my knuckles for having a dull ear for languages? Perhaps I will get by using drawings, mathematics, and sign language in the beginning.

    Give everyone a fond embrace from me before you and Rosalie board ship. And please know your arrival will be a great celebration for us all.

Fondly,
Robert

Robert closed his laptop writing desk, relaxed back in his chair, and admired the bucolic view before him. At moments like these, he felt his family lived in paradise with the warm sun on his face and a favorable wind freshening. It was a perfect afternoon for a sail in the small sloop tied to the dock a short walk from his chair. If they were to stay, in a couple of years, Angus could sit in the stern to trail a fishing line, drifting on the bay. Yes, there had been moments when Robert was tempted to settle in the Abacos, supporting his family designing and building beautiful small boats. Moira could teach Angus, Rosalie, and any future children. Maybe they could build a small community school.

A buzzing mosquito drilled into the back of his neck, jerking Robert out of reverie. Swift as a snake, his hand killed the bug with a practiced slap. He returned to reality and the list of Civil War traitors with his name on it. His hands fisted and his eyes narrowed to slits.

Things sounded grim in Charleston. It would be a soothing bit of family and home when his favorite sister and her baby arrived. One of Laurette's letters reported Major General Daniel Sickles, the Federal officer now in charge of martial law in the Carolinas, had a foul character. She wrote that his infamous reputation was filled with monetary indiscretions, drunken brawls, and womanizing. Apparently, Sickles was a man from a wealthy New York family who'd bought himself into the Army early in the war by recruiting and paying for a regiment from his home state. He'd disgraced himself—and was nearly court-martialed—disobeying orders at the battle of Gettysburg, resulting in the loss of twelve thousand men under his command.

Robert had heard tales of Sickles' personal scandals with women from Conchs who visited Charleston. Despite his own penchant for infidelity, it was said Sickles couldn't abide it in others. In 1859, he shot dead Barton Key, the son of Francis Scott Key, with whom his wife was having an affair. With the assistance of a panel of eight attorneys and his family money, he'd won the first ever acquittal a jury awarded for temporary insanity. Now he was using his authority in South Carolina too strenuously, allowing his troops free rein in a most vindictive fashion.

Robert gritted his teeth in frustration over his inability to help his family in Charleston. Only one realistic choice remained: leave the Bahama Islands and begin again.

A creaking door made Robert turn his head as Moira approached with her dimpled smile and Angus on her hip, squirming to be let down. Robert folded his letter to Laurette into an envelope and opened his arms. In spite of the trials of the last four years, he felt blessed to have a loving wife and a fine son. Angus was a healthy rascal, toddling about and into everything he could get his chubby hands on. His son had a striking resemblance to his younger brother James, right down to the laughing blue eyes.

"Why so serious at your desk on this glorious morning my love?"

"I have been thinking of the adventure ahead, finding a new home and perhaps some difficulties for Laurette and Rosalie. Our mulatto niece may have a hard time in Brazil." He gave his wife a worried look.

"Have faith my dear. We'll make ours a merry little family."

"Would that Jeanne, John, and their children could join us."

"I agree. But John could never leave his patients, regardless of who is in command of the hospital. Jeanne understands that."

Moira scooped Angus back up and plopped him wiggling into her husband's lap. The baby lifted his hands to Robert's face. "Da, Da, Da," he said, and got a fond kiss from his father in response.

"I pray the good Lord will bless our new beginning my dear."

"Great adventures are in our blood, my love. My grandparents left the highlands because of the clearing. I grew up on stories of being cast off the land our family lived on for centuries. Your Papa left home for opportunity. We'll be like our ancestors, venturing into a new land of promise."

PART THREE

"You wanna fly, you got to give up the shit that weighs you down"

Toni Morrison

CHAPTER TWENTY-TWO

Rio de Janeiro, August 2010

I f Lizbeth's T-shirt had buttons, they would have popped off with pride and washed away with her tears as she read Laurette's diary and Robert's letters twice and then a third time, taking notes. The courage of her Confederado cousins has left her awestruck.

Her eyes burn from a sleepless night. She grimaces at the cold cup of tea with its curdled cream abandoned on the coffee table sometime during the night. Lizbeth hasn't pulled an all-nighter like this one since college. She glances out the window at the dark Atlantic and notices the thin line of dawn breaking over the horizon. She picks up her cell, dials Charlotte, and hangs up before the call completes. It's still too early to call the States.

Under the shower spray, fresh tears merge with the warm water streaming down her body. First World problems, whatever they may be, seem inconsequential compared to the dire circumstances her ancestors suffered after the American Civil War. Wrapped in her robe and fuzzy slippers, Lizbeth reads through her notes again and drums her fingers on the table in a peak of impatience.

Why is it that war victors get to revise history with impunity, highlighting atrocities made by the losing side and obscuring equal atrocities of their own? Plenty of Southerners didn't support slavery, but once the war began, they were pulled into it out of loyalty to their homeland, or because they were drafted whether they wanted to fight or not. After the Civil War, helping former Confederate states recover was not a United States government priority. No wonder her grandparents preferred not to dwell on childhoods with lasting effects of ruined land, poverty and Jim Crow. Lizbeth's stomach roils thinking about how people she knows in the West and North sooth their shame over United States history of slaveholding by demonizing the South while ignoring racism in their own backyards.

With the sun off the horizon, spilling red-orange and gold streaks into the morning sky, Lizbeth phones Charlotte. Waiting for her cousin to pick up, she stirs sugar into a fresh cup of coffee, slopping some on the counter. After the fifth ring, Lizbeth sucks in a long breath for a dramatic message that will get her cousin's attention.

Just before the voice mail message kicks in, Charlotte picks up with a throaty croak, "Hey, Lizard, it's five a.m. I need my beauty rest. Did you forget I have a business to run? Oh, wait . . . Is this an emergency?"

"Yes—I mean, no. Actually, yes."

"What are you talkin' about, girl?"

"I know it's early. But I couldn't wait any longer. Remember how we're probably related to Ana Maria Gordon de Sousa? Well, it's not probably. Ana was right on from the get-go. I've been up all night, reading Laurette Gordon's diary and Robert Gordon's letters. They're our people for sure. Charlotte, dear cuz, we've found our lost family!"

"Whoa, give it to me slow. Let me pull myself out of bed and brush my teeth, get rid of the sleep cobwebs. I'll call you right back."

"Yes, ma'am. Call me RIGHT back."

Lizbeth paces the floor taking sips of coffee, organizing her thoughts for ten minutes until her cousin calls back. The phone doesn't complete a full ring before Lizbeth is on it.

"What's so important it couldn't wait till dawn, cuz?"

"Ana Maria gave me permission to scan and email you everything. I'm going to the Copy Mart as soon as it opens, so when you open your inbox later today, it'll all be there. You can read everything yourself!"

Lizbeth's talking too fast. She sits down on the couch, crosses her fingers so she can be clear and not come off like a babbling nut case.

"Yesterday I met Ana's family, our cousins. They're lovely. And, oh, my God, one of her granddaughters could be your sister! She's pretty as a peach."

"Ana Maria has a fifty-year-old granddaughter?"

"No, dummy. Ana Maria's granddaughter looks like you did when you were six, doing cartwheels on the lawn like you used to. I wish I'd thought to bring my camera and take pictures!"

"Lizard, it's grand you found these long-lost relatives but get a grip! We're talkin' four generations since the Civil War. This stuff is interesting, but it can't be life altering."

"To me it is! Read the diaries and letters and you'll see. Our Confederados were amazing, brave people we can be proud of! It's so cool to finally find them!"

"OK, darlin'. After my meetings today."

"Come on, Char, get into it." Lizbeth is putting on her most convincing tone, the one that works every time she and Char are off on an adventure.

"This is the real stuff we've been trying to solve. The more I think about it the more the diary and letters solve oddities in our family history I hadn't taken seriously before. Remember Granddaddy's story about Confederate ancestors hunted by the Yankees after the war? He was pretty vague about it. He thought they disappeared south somewhere, probably Mexico, but he was wrong. They went to South America."

Lizbeth is up again, striding around her apartment, voice rising to punctuate each point she makes. "As little kids we took Granddaddy's tall tales as gospel but by the time we were through grade school we thought he was just havin' fun with us. In high school I remember teasing him unmercifully. Now I wish I could apologize."

Lizbeth's heart squeezes. She stops in front of the window giving out onto the Atlantic. Please, please, Char, listen to me, she mouths silently. "Our Rio de Janeiro Gordons have embraced us Char! I feel a deep connection in my bones to our ancestral Confederados and Ana Maria's family in Rio."

Lizbeth taps her foot impatiently. How to get her cousin onboard? "Wait till you hear this! I've been invited to great Aunt Suzi's ninety-fifth birthday in Santa Barbara D'Oeste in September. Suzi is Robert and Moira Gordon's granddaughter. How about that!"

"Take a break from sipping the Kool-Aid, cuz. Slow down."

Lizbeth imagines Charlotte's eye roll and face full of skepticism. "Trust me, Char."

"I'm tryin', Lizard."

"Hey, in the middle of the night while I read, I was working the family puzzle. Remember Jeanne Gordon's photograph taken ten years after the Civil War? Remember we didn't follow up your mama's invitation to dive into Grandmama's chifforobe because we thought all the clues were in Charleston? The way Aunt Sarah talked, other than the picture she found, that old wardrobe held Bucot family history. At the time, that chifforobe didn't seem relevant."

"Yeah. We kinda dropped digging in Mama's closet for more on the Gordon history, huh. Besides, I was distracted by a new man, and you left determined to comb the libraries in Charleston for anything juicy on Robert and Laurette."

Lizbeth winces remembering how adamant she has been; safe, sterile, academic research was the preferred path to trustworthy results. "Better later than never cuz. Go rifle through that old piece of furniture in your Mama's closet and see what its hoarding. Aunt Sarah said the vague story passed down was that Jeanne, John, and the children arrived upcountry with practically nothing but the clothes on their backs. We are still in the dark about why they left, and what happened to make them lose touch with Laurette and Robert."

Silence stretches across the miles. Lizbeth takes a deep breath and continues.

"Isn't it odd our branch of the Gordon family has this connection with pre-war Charleston that seems to have dropped off the family consciousness? Jeanne, John, and their children left the city mysteriously after the war and didn't set foot in the Low Country again until Grandaddy, a young Marine on a weekend pass from Paris Island, met Grandmama in Charleston? Why did our Gordon family get split up, Char?"

Dead air dangles between continents. Lizbeth's fingers are crossed so hard they are beginning to cramp. Come on Charlotte, take the bait.

"Alright, I'm getting curious. Your druthers are my druthers, darlin'. Deep dark secrets have a way of getting my juices flowing." Charlotte laughs. "OK. We're on Lizard. I'll checkout Mama's closet."

⤬

Before ending the call, they negotiate dates for Lizbeth's Christmas trip to the Carolinas. She needs to plan months in advance to take advantage of airfare deals for the twin's flight from Bellingham, Washington to Greenville, South Carolina and her own reservation from Rio during the high-volume travel season.

⤬

The Leblon International School year terminates in mid-December, allowing Lizbeth to take a six-week holiday in North America. Charlotte has invited the entire Carolina family for Christmas; Aunt Sarah, Char's daughter, Penny, and Josh and Robbie will stay for ten days. Charlotte's brother, John, and his family will come from Raleigh for a few days at Christmas to include an old-fashioned barbecue with all the fixin's. Lizbeth's mouth waters anticipating Southern comfort food. John's slow-cooked ribs are second to none.

There *are* a few people she'd like to see in Port Benton if she dares return to Washington State near the first anniversary of Dan's death. Just the thought of dark, December weather and sympathy from neighbors might send her into a nosedive. No, too many memories of twenty contented years and then betrayal she doesn't want to revisit.

Moreover, she has no desire to see Dan's parents. She pushes away paranoid thoughts of what Howard and Lillian have said to Josh and Robbie when her sons visit for a weekend. After the funeral, Dan's parents quoted scripture on marital relationships implying Lizbeth had strayed from the proper faith-based anchor their son needed. Bottom line, they blamed her, and she isn't close to forgiving the righteous insinuations her in-laws made in front of her twins. Her counselor persona warns to avoid the subject of her in-laws with Josh and Robbie. Pressing her sons to choose alliance to their mom at the expense of their grandparents could backfire big time.

But with Charlotte, she's free to vent.

"Dan's parents blame me for Dan's gambling."

"Addiction is addiction is addiction, cuz."

"I thought he loved me."

If Charlotte suggests another self-help book or Al Anon, Lizbeth will pitch a fit. To keep from saying something she'll regret, her knuckles go white in a tight fist. She wants to get down and dirty, rant about how Dan Keller did her wrong. She wants sympathy for all the years she thought they were carefully planning their future, when it was only her.

"Recovery groups are great for some people, but my fatal flaw is public confession. It humiliates me."

"Yeah, yeah. I get where you are coming from, Lizard. Don't take Dan's addiction personally. Gambling became his first love; from the moment he woke, until he slept at night, it was about his next game. He couldn't help himself, darlin'. He was a sick puppy."

"I did what I needed to do to protect my sanity after he died, Char. Selling the house was part of it." Lizbeth has tried hard to erase the memory of her sons closed faces as they climbed into her SUV last January.

"You did good, cuz."

Lizbeth feels her cousin's kindness seep into her heart.

"At Christmas it'll be nearly a year since I've wrapped my arms around Josh and Robbie." She blinks back tears, aching to hold her boys close and inhale their scent.

"Stay in the present, Lizard. Christmas will be here before you know it."

☙

Char may be right about addiction, but her cousin's wisdom can't mend the rift with her sons. Lizbeth has to take deep calming breaths when she gets a flash of her manic behavior last December and the chasm of hurt it opened for Josh and Robbie. Still, she can't bring herself to apologize. She resents her sons' blind loyalty to their father.

Lizbeth sighs. Christmas in Greenville will be a safe haven in a way the Pacific Northwest could never be this year. Once the boys head back to college, she'll have a few weeks to do some self-care: shop for books in English, buy make-up in brands she misses, and take care of chores impossible to do in Brazil, like renewing her driver's license.

❧

On her next call with Charlotte, Lizbeth strikes a lighter tone.

"If all y'all send measurements, I'll bring everyone, even the guys, Brazilian bikinis for Christmas."

"That's rich, Lizard! I'd like to see my brother, John, striding into the surf in a thong." They have a good laugh visualizing the proper attorney, jumping the waves in a teeny tiny, ball-hugging swimsuit.

"It's so different here, Char. You're gonna have to come to the Copacabana. It's freeing the way people wear whatever they want at the beach, they celebrate being themselves."

CHAPTER TWENTY-THREE

Greenville, South Carolina, 2010

Charlotte has caught the sleuth bug from her cousin. After church on Sunday, she stops by her mama's condo for a light lunch and family gossip. "Mama, you won't believe the Gordon Civil War-era letters Lizbeth's found in Brazil, of all places! I have a copy. Want to read them?"

"No thank you, darlin'." Sarah gestures to the picture wall; photos of her parents, children, and grandchildren, and the adjacent Victorian sofa with matching end tables, festooned with all manner of knickknacks.

"I have my favorite family keepsakes here where I can enjoy them every day." Inclining her head toward the spare bedroom, she continues, "I've said before, and I'll say again, if you want to look into the old days, you are welcome to whatever you find in your Grandmama's favorite family piece yonder."

In her mama's spare bedroom, Charlotte removes an ancient linen sheet of unknown origin draped over the chifforobe, squeezes into the closet, and forces open the warped bottom drawer with a screech. After one whiff of the stale documents, Charlotte calls out, "Hey, Mama! How 'bout I load this entire drawer into the back of my BMW and carry it on home?"

"Do not pull apart my mama's favorite piece of furniture! You might never get it back together, and Lord knows what might break off inside when you try."

"All right, Mama. I'll go get some boxes."

Charlotte returns with a stack of shallow boxes and heads directly to the guestroom.

Sarah stands in the doorway watching her daughter. "You may not find anything you'd like to share rummaging around in an ugly era of South Carolina history."

"What are you not sayin', Mama?"

"Child, I am not responsible for the sins of my parents and grandparents though I loved them dearly. They lived in a world where people thought differently. As a child, I visited my grandparents in Greenville County where Black laborers and White farm owners attended the Presbyterian Church together on Sunday, but their Bible study evenings and cemeteries were segregated."

"I know all that, Mama."

"You know your granddaddy had romantic ideas about what he called the 'War of Northern Aggression.' He'd heard all kind of heroic stories from his papa and others, who were small children during that war. As you know, I don't repeat such hearsay foolishness. I prefer dwelling in the present."

"Aren't you just a little bit curious about how our Gordon family got separated during Reconstruction, Mama?"

"Not much. During that period of time, history that's vague or missing is better left that way."

Charlotte sighs. Her mama can be stubborn, and there is no changing her mind when it's set. Instead of pestering for further details, Charlotte fills boxes with fragile, yellowing papers and pictures, ribbons and buttons, and ancient certificates for school attendance. A few silverfish slither from the last papers she gently lifts from the drawer. Charlotte shakes the nasty insects off. "I'm not taking you hitchhikers into my place. Jesus, Mama, you've got silverfish in here. Do you have a can of bug killer?"

"Reckon I do. But don't you curse in my home!"

"Sorry, Mama."

ల

Pandora's boxes sit beckoning in Charlotte's dining room for a week before she has time to explore the contents. Some papers are so fragile she uses a spatula to lift them carefully onto the table without tearing the mildewed sheets. The array of difficult-to-read documents are faded to shades of brown and water-spotted from humidity.

She and Lizbeth have agreed to zero in on Angus Gordon's arrival in Charleston around 1830, through the Civil War Reconstruction. Charlotte lifts her gaze in a prayer of thanks that people dated letters and photos back in the day. Even so, it takes days to create a timeline in chronological order on the dining room table.

One item that captures Charlotte's attention is a tintype she carefully plucks from a heavily water-spotted cardboard folder. She holds it to the window and gives it a good squint. Unsatisfied, Charlotte carries the tintype to her home office, rifles through her desk for a magnifying glass to better examine the young couple. On close observation, the woman resembles the picture of Jeanne Gordon her mama brought to lunch in April. Could this be the Michelle Bucot who married Angus Gordon? Her hypothesis is confirmed when she looks again, and finds a wedding invitation, June 4, 1832, tucked deep in the cardboard folder's side pocket. Holy Moly. Lizard will love this! We are double related through marriage. Michelle is one of Grandmamma's Bucot kin. No wonder she had this tintype with her Bucot history!

ల

Charlotte pumps her fist in the air, calls her cousin, and leaves a voice mail.

"Hey, Lizard, I'm sitting in front of a treasure trove of stuff I lifted from Grandmama's chifforobe: letters, cards, faded out pictures left all catawampus in the bottom drawer. It's mostly Grandmama's Huguenot Bucot heritage, just like Mama said it would be. But, hey, I found a juicy clue to our Gordon mystery. Call me!" She disconnects with a chuckle. Her titillating message will drive Lizbeth nuts.

૭૦

Lizbeth is in the bedroom trying on half a dozen outfits for Aunt Suzi's birthday weekend when she misses Charlotte's call. She's packed and repacked her weekender suitcase twice and obsessed over her choice of shoes. After listening to Char's voicemail, she calls right back.

"Char, what's up? You never call in the middle of the work day."

"Hey, Lizard, glad to catch you. I thought you'd might have left for the birthday party in the wilds of that place called Santa Barbara."

"Let's hope it's a mild wild sorta place." Lizbeth answers with a smile in her voice. "Double WOW on the tintype of Angus and Michelle! You are the best, Char. I can't wait to see them. Will you send me a copy? And one for Ana Maria too? Don't you wish we could jump into those old pictures and ask our nineteenth century ancestors a zillion questions?"

"Yeah, I do Lizard."

"My flight to Sao Paolo is at three p.m. I'm starting to freak out, cuz. A taxi's coming in half an hour. Ana Maria said around forty or so blood-related strangers are gonna be at Aunt Suzi's birthday party. What will they think of me appearing out of nowhere? I'm tempted to call Ana and say I've got the flu."

"Can't never could do, cuz. Rev up your bodacious woman self and put on a smile."

"Uh-huh."

"That's my girl!"

"Distract me. Tell me about the rest of the treasure in Grandmama's chifforobe."

"Lizard, you will love this. Remember Mama said Jeanne Gordon's family Bible recorded Angus and Michelle as her parents?"

"I remember, yeah."

Lizbeth hears Charlotte inhale a dramatic breath. "Well, this is the new family wrinkle. As it turns out, Angus Gordon's wife, Michelle, was nee Bucot, from Charleston, like Grandmama. There must have been a very good reason the staid Bucot family Grandmama was so proud of allowed one of their own to marry a Scottish immigrant with no pedigree."

"Wow Char. That's more than curious!"

"Yeah tiz. I'm supposed to be in Charleston for business next week. I'll go by the Huguenot historical society and gather low-hanging Bucot fruit."

"Wouldn't Granddaddy have loved to lord it over Grandmama they were third or fourth cousins."

"Yes, he would darlin'. And our prideful Grandmama would find some juicy comeback to make us all laugh."

When Lizbeth strides out of the Riviera Apartment to meet her taxi, she feels a shade more confident. The conversation with Charlotte was just the boost she needed before Aunt Suzi's birthday party and half a hundred related strangers.

CHAPTER TWENTY-FOUR

Americana, Brazil, September 2010

The family's flight arrives in Sao Paulo late Friday afternoon. Lizbeth, Ana Maria, her husband, children, and grandchildren are all bound for Hotel Luz, a favorite overnight stop with a swimming pool to keep the kids entertained while adults have a cocktail on the patio. Lizbeth is all in for the Brazilian philosophy that time spent with extended family takes priority. They've rented two cars: a small sedan for Ana Maria and Lizbeth, who will visit the Confederado cemetery at Americana before the party; and a large SUV, with a third seat in the back, for everybody else. Tomorrow they will all take the morning at a humane pace and then meet up at Aunt Suzi's party in Santa Barbara.

❧

After a long, relaxed dinner, Ana reaches in her purse and hands Lizbeth a booklet.

"Here's your homework," she says with a mischievous smile. "It's more Confederado history. I know you've researched online, but this version is written for Brazilian tourists and includes maps and history on our festivals that you won't find elsewhere."

Stifling her initial reaction to the large Confederate flag on the pamphlet's cover, Lizbeth thanks Ana. She doesn't want to offend Ana by sharing her disturbing memories of the *Stars and Bars* displayed by White supremacist groups in the South when she was a child.

In her room, Lizbeth devours the Confederado pamphlet. She's surprised to read as many as eight thousand former Confederates arrived in Brazil between 1864 and 1880. Having read Laurette's diary and Robert's letters, the late-Civil War details of a pioneer's choice to emigrate from North America makes sense. She knows by 1864, the Confederacy was on its knees; civilians were abandoning ruined homes and farms. Undernourished boys as young as thirteen were fighting in ragtag uniforms, while the robust Federal Army drafted a seemingly endless supply of healthy men from farms and cities that had not been stripped of all crops and livestock. But her internet research had given short shrift to the history of South America during the nineteenth century.

At the time of the American Civil War, forward thinking Dom Pedro II was king of Brazil. He was a great admirer of the North American model of democracy and wanted his country to be a competitor in the emerging industrialized world. Eventually Dom Pedro II would abdicate his throne in favor of Brazil's first free elections, but during his monarchy he delighted in personally entertaining Southerners who arrived looking for land and opportunity. He supported immigrants with marketable skills, many of whom found Brazil to be a Biblical promised land, the solution to real or self-imposed exile.

People primarily from Texas, Alabama, Georgia, and South Carolina arrived in Guanabara Bay, the port area of Rio de Janeiro. They brought modern farming techniques, a far superior plough design, and expertise in training mules to work the virgin land that became Vila dos Americanos, now the town of Americana. A few settlements developed west of Americana as well, while a smaller cadre of professionals made permanent homes in Rio de Janeiro.

The booklet describes Confederado pioneer life as a struggle for people accustomed to more developed communities with public roads, schools, and churches. The new language, culture, and rules of living in a Catholic country were a hardship, as were the unfamiliar diseases that diminished the community. Early on, Confederados set aside land for their cemetery and built a small chapel for weekly services, weddings, funerals, and other community events.

Some of the wealthier Confederados—those from the moneyed planter class—found the pioneer life grueling and repatriated to the United States. Others thrived. Brazilians came to respect the yeoman farmers as honest, hardworking people with valuable knowledge. Some Confederados became land managers and consultants introducing modern farming and animal husbandry throughout Brazilian farm country.

The pamphlet also describes how the community evolved over decades. The first generations and their children kept to themselves, protective of their culture, language, and Protestant religion. In the twentieth century, descendants began fanning out over Brazil and became the multiethnic descendants of today. In April, descendants of Confederados return to Americana for a reunion celebrating their heritage with stories, music, and dancing. Since the late 1800s, the Fraternidad Desendencia Americana has been responsible for raising money for the Festa as well as caretaking the chapel and cemetery at Vila Americana. Deep pride in their pioneer history remains to this day.

இං

In the morning, Lizbeth rises thankful for the blue sky and fluffy cumulus clouds visible clear out to the horizon, where low-rise apartment buildings in this Sao Paulo suburb disappear into flat farmland.

She dresses in layers, a cotton sweater for the fall morning chill over a floral sleeveless blouse. By early afternoon, the temperature will be in the mid-eighties and feel ten degrees warmer thanks to the humidity two hundred miles inland from a sea breeze. In the breakfast room, she grabs a few minutes at a small corner table before meeting Ana Maria in the lobby. Pushing her plate of half-eaten banana cake and fruit away, Lizbeth takes a last sip of rich dark coffee. She notices an uneven cuticle and is tempted to nervously pick at it but restrains herself. She'll treated herself to a manicure for this weekend. Don't mess it up!

⁓

Lizbeth buries her anxiety as Ana greets her with double cheek kisses. They load their overnight bags and drive out of the parking lot onto the highway. Ana begins to speak as if she's read Lizbeth's mind.

"The early Confederados clung to their identity with pride, and some of their traditions may seem strange or extreme to you. But, please, ask questions before you judge us."

"If there's a lot of Confederate flag waving, I will find it hard."

Lizbeth is ashamed of her ignorant foreigner's perspective when Ana Maria's tone sounds like she's addressing a small child.

"Many North Americans attach racism to the Confederate flag, which in the nineteenth century was not about slave holding or racism. For us, the flag's a symbol honoring courageous people who lost everything: homes, family, and United States citizenship in a bloody Civil War. We're proud of our pioneer ancestors and the Confederate flag was part of their identity."

⁓

Ana Maria pulls into a packed-earth parking area with a view of row after row of headstones, dotting an acre-size cemetery of former Confederates. Lizbeth's heart clenches at the hundreds of men and their families, whose war-ravaged farms were lost to carpetbaggers or who emigrated rather than face a hangman's noose. They'd faced exile for nothing more than defending their homes from looters or refusing to sign a humiliating loyalty oath that made them liars. Why was the United States so shamed by the atrocities of post-war civilian suffering that they sanitized events out of history books?

Lizbeth bites the inside of her cheek to prevent tears from overflowing and gives Ana a weak smile. She reaches into the back seat for her wide-brimmed sun hat and follows Ana into the cemetery. A few birds call to each other without much passion as Lizbeth's shoes crunch on the gravel path shaded by tall palms casting shadows over weathered headstones. Most are embossed with Confederate flags above names: Captain Donald Williams, born in Texas, died in Americana; Corporal Ebenezer Lamont, born in Alabama, died in Santa Barbara; and on and on. Surnames are English, Irish, French, German, and Scottish, descendants of people who had fought for freedom in the American Revolutionary War, forced to leave the land their ancestors won from the British.

"I never thought there'd be so many," Lizbeth whispers as she swivels her head to catch Ana Maria's eye.

"There are more than five hundred graves here. The majority are first-generation Confederados and some of their children."

Lizbeth stops at a headstone and reads the inscription aloud. "'Jonah Greene, born into slavery in Texas, died Free in Americana 1883.' You mean to tell me some Confederados were Black?"

"Yes, of course. There are stories of former slaveholders and former slaves arriving on the same ship and ending up as neighbors."

"I'm amazed any Black person would leave the United States after 1865 when the years of Reconstruction supported Black education and businesses."

"I think the chance for a new start in a new land may have been hard to resist," Ana said with a smile.

"Wasn't slavery legal in Brazil when the Confederados arrived?" Lizbeth has been to the slave museum in Charleston where visitors can listen to voice recordings made in the 1930s; stories told by elders who were enslaved children before the Civil War. The stories she heard made her skin crawl with shame knowing some of her family had once been slaveholders.

"Yes. Slavery was legal here until 1889. Some who arrived here with money bought large parcels of land and purchased slaves. But cultural differences and the Portuguese language made recreating plantations like those in the American South nearly impossible. Most of that planter class gave up and returned to the United States within a few years. We don't consider them part of our clan."

Ana brushes moss off the headstone of another once-enslaved man.

"Confederados pulled together, regardless of race and social class. All the children shared the same classrooms, and everyone attended church together in the first generations. Keeping customs and the English language alive was the highest priority. Wait till you meet Great-Aunt Suzi. She speaks English with a nineteenth-century Southern accent!"

"Really? I'm looking forward to hearing it."

They walk on for a minute, alone in the cemetery, then Lizbeth blurts out: "You were right to pull me up short on being quick to blame. All along I assumed Confederados were the stereotypical racist people from the antebellum South."

"Some must have been. But in small settlement communities, everyone had to cooperate to survive. That doesn't mean we don't have racism in Brazil, though. You've seen it."

"I have."

"Come this way." Ana Maria leads Lizbeth toward the peach-colored chapel in what looks like the oldest part of the cemetery. The canopy of branches overhead is thick with leaves, casting soft, dappled shade on the manicured gravel path. "Our Confederado association employs a caretaker family to look after the chapel and cemetery. You can see the house from here." Lizbeth looks in the direction Ana Maria is pointing and spots a small, tidy cottage at the northern edge of the cemetery. "We're comfortable knowing our ancestors are well looked after."

"Why did Robert and Moira's children bring their parents all the way from Rio to Americana for burial? The long journey over unpaved roads must have been grueling in the early twentieth century."

"Early Confederados believed it imperative to bury their loved ones in a proper Protestant cemetery, where descendants could visit. Catholic Brazil did not allow Protestants in their cemeteries."

Ana Maria stops in front of a cluster of tombstones, mottled with age but free of moss and lichen. She brushes a silver string of spiderweb from between two stones. "Here they are, Robert, Moira, two infant children, and Laurette."

Lizbeth squats on her haunches so she can better gaze at the headstones of Robert and Moira: Robert Bucot Gordon, born Charleston, SC 1837 died Rio de Janeiro, 1918 beloved husband of Moira. Moira Mary MacDonald, beloved wife of Robert, born 1840 Glasgow, Scotland, died 1924 Rio de Janeiro. Laurette Michelle Gordon, born Charleston, SC

1838 died Rio 1875. She presses her fingers along the epitaphs and feels deep sorrow for how the Civil War separated her family. Her heart aches for Laurette's terrible choice; to keep her mixed-race child, conceived in rape by occupying soldiers, meant leaving her family and native land. And Robert's courage, a man who could not return home, brought his family to Brazil to start over where they had no connections, didn't speak the language or know the culture.

"Being here makes their stories live for me." Lizbeth feels goosebumps cover her arms in spite of the still, midday heat.

"It's my pleasure to have you here in the bosom of your Brazilian family." Lizbeth feels Ana's arm go around her shoulder with a quick squeeze and has to swallow multiple times to keep her tears at bay. Ana Maria stoops to place flowers they've brought between the headstones of Robert and Moira, her courageous ancestors who made a new life for their family far from home. She extends her hand to Lizbeth and squeezes. They stand together in reverent silence.

"I'm going back to the car," Ana Maria says. "When you are ready, join me. But take your time. It's only a half hour drive from Americana to Santa Barbara and we're not expected at Aunt Suzi's till after four."

Lizbeth wanders the rows of early twentieth century headstones, locating the graves of Robert Gordon's oldest child Angus and his spouse. Tightening her sweater around her waist, Lizbeth continues to read and stroll. The still air is so thick with moisture it feels like a blanket. She's thankful for the shade of twenty-foot palms and the subtle, sweet fragrance of flowering lobelia that softens the musk of damp dust on the packed gravel walk.

Returning to the stones of Robert and Moira, her throat goes tight, imagining the trials they endured as pioneers, halfway across the world from family, language, and culture. Lizbeth was proud of how she'd weathered every challenge during her Peace Corp years in Mexico, but truth be told, she knew missing hot showers and variety in her diet was temporary. And if there had been a health emergency or political unrest, the United States government would have evacuated her and the other volunteers in a nano-second.

Lizbeth stoops to rub at the sticky dirt to read the names on the little headstones of Thomas and Amelia, Moira's babies who died in infancy. Laurette's grave is just to the left, a simple headstone with birth and death dates, but no endearing epitaph. What was Laurette's life like in Brazil and where is Rosalie?

Lizbeth rises and walks to Ana Maria's air-conditioned rental car while searching her shoulder bag for a tissue to clean the tears from her face and the dirt from her palms.

CHAPTER TWENTY-FIVE

Santa Barbara, September 2010

On the twenty-mile drive from Americana to Santa Barbara d'Oeste, Ana Maria gives Lizbeth a rundown on who she can expect to meet at the party.

"There are a few cancellations and additions from the original list I sent you. Turns out it's not a Gordons-only party." She turns her mouth down in a mock frown. "Aunt Suzi couldn't resist inviting some favorites from her deceased husband's side of the family."

"How will I ever keep everyone straight?"

"Don't worry. Enjoy being a guest."

Lizbeth watches tall prairie grass and low hills roll by, wondering again, what she's getting herself into. As an only child, a shy introvert, she learned to be a skilled observer of others. Stepping into the role of being a standout, long-lost cousin-guest, makes Lizbeth cringe. She takes a few deep breaths to block any crazy notions of escape.

"Aunt Suzi has been living with her son, my cousin Juan, and his wife, Estelle, for a decade. Theirs is not a large home, but the garden is magnificent. Although Estelle and her daughters are gourmet cooks, we cousins chipped in to have an outside party tent and catering, so no one will be stuck in the kitchen."

"You rescued me from making a dozen buttermilk pies!" Lizbeth laughs.

"Absolutely!" Ana Maria smiles back. "No one works this afternoon! Suzi is our family celebrity, but you are number two today, and I am number three: the heroine bringing a mystery relative from South Carolina!"

Lizbeth gives her cousin an anxious glance. "Relax!" Ana says, then moves on. "Aunt Suzi is an inspiration to us all. She's frail, but her mind is sharp. She reads two newspapers daily and quizzes the rest of us on current events. You won't get much time with her at the party, but she's invited the two of us for brunch tomorrow. That's when she'll bring out her stories about Robert and Laurette."

⁓

Juan greets Ana Maria and Lizbeth with kisses. He holds both Lizbeth's hands in his and smiles into her eyes. "Estelle and I are delighted you were able to come and Mama is ecstatic about reconnecting with our Carolina Clan."

Juan escorts them on a brief tour through his home and out to the patio. Lizbeth scans the garden redolent with flowering jasmine and moves toward a spot in a less crowded corner. She's tempted to pluck a *caipirinha* off a tray offered by a passing waiter, thinks better of it, and grabs a tall glass of lemonade. Before she can take a sip, curious Gordon relatives surround her firing rapid bilingual questions.

"Tell me about Charleston."

"Voce tem filhos?" Do you have children?

"Did you bring pictures to show us?"

When her Portuguese falters, Lizbeth finds Ana Maria at her side.

"Bem-vida prima!" Welcome cousin. Lizbeth is enveloped in a group hug three people deep. Eventually, she lets go and sobs like a baby as she is folded into one embrace after another. Lizbeth feels an uncanny resonance with this crowd of blood-related strangers. Her heart sings as cousins pat her shoulder and offer tissues until Lizbeth can smile again.

She glances around the crowded garden and notices people with the

Gordon height and build. A few have hair similar to her own, frizzing in the humidity. A few folks have bright green eyes the exact shade as her father's, set in faces with mixed ethnic features. She rifles in her purse for pictures of Josh, Robbie, Charlotte and Penny, Aunt Sarah, her parents and grandparents and passes them around the circle. *Ohs* and *Ahs* surround Lizbeth as cousins pull pictures from wallets laughing and pointing out generational family traits.

Overwhelmed by the attention, Lizbeth takes a break, saying she needs to use the loo. She discovers a bookshelf-lined office next to the bathroom. She hides out perusing titles of classic literature in English and Portuguese until Ana Maria seeks her out.

"Aunt Suzi wants to greet you. She's holding court on the patio under the jacaranda tree." As they approach, Lizbeth tries not to stare. Suzi's white hair, expertly cut in a short bob, peeks out below a blue straw sun hat that exactly matches her eyes. Her face is freckled and deeply wrinkled. Something she can't quite name in Suzi's face reminds Lizbeth of an older version of her Aunt Sarah.

Suzi extends her hand. "Come closer, darlin' child. Let me look at you. Yes, just as Ana Maria told me, your face is stamped with Gordon."

Lizbeth sits close to her great-aunt. Good Lord, Ana was right. Suzi does have that distinctive Charleston accent.

"Thank you for inviting me. It's an immense pleasure to meet you, Aunt Suzi."

"You sweet thing. Please enjoy my birthday party. I reckon we'll have time to get better acquainted tomorrow." Suzi lifts her cheek for a kiss as Lizbeth stands to go.

Ana Maria ushers Lizbeth to a table and whispers in her ear, "I asked Estelle to stack your table with good English speakers, so you'll have more fun." Lizbeth gives Ana a grateful wave as she departs to sit with her husband and children.

Family anecdotes roll out in high-spirited humor as Gordon clan members stand and toast Suzi. As favorite stories are re-told, Raoul, seated on Lizbeth's left, gets her attention with his wicked wit. She hasn't laughed with such abandon in ages. It turns out he's a psychologist who taught ten years at Universidade de Sao Paulo and has recently relocated to Rio de Janeiro. As their table is served dessert, Raoul leans in toward Lizbeth and quietly asks her if she'd care to go for coffee next week. Feeling comfortable in the embrace of the family party, Lizbeth scribbles her number on the back of a grocery list dug from her purse and slides it over.

CHAPTER TWENTY-SIX

Santa Barbara d'Oestre, September 2010

Estelle greets Lizbeth and Ana Maria at the door. "Aunt Suzi is exhausted from the party, but she wouldn't hear of canceling brunch with the two of you." Estelle gives a small shrug and smiles at the unmanageable 'Gordon stubbornness.'

"Suzi says her time on this earth is precious and she's not going to waste a minute of it napping."

"We promise not to overstay our welcome," Ana Maria reassures her cousin's wife. "Our flight to Rio is at four and you know what Sunday afternoon traffic between here and Sao Paulo is like."

Estelle nods and escorts them to a quiet corner of the patio, fragrant with violet bougainvillea dipping through the overhead trellis in bunches. Suzi, sitting with her feet propped on a stool covered in floral needlepoint, waves them over. "I've got phone calls to make," Estelle says, turning toward the house. "I'll be in my study if you need me."

Slices of quiche, a bowl of fresh-cut melon, and a pot of aromatic coffee sit on a sideboard. As Lizbeth fills her plate, Suzi says, "Take that chair directly across from mine so I can see your face, child."

Susi chuckles softly. "I heard Estelle tell you I'm worn slap out. But when a person is ninety-five, there is no time to dillydally. I slept well and I'm fit as a fiddle this morning."

Lizbeth can't help smiling at Suzi's old-fashioned Southern expressions. "Your accent is just like my grandmama, who grew up in Charleston."

"I reckon it is. My parents insisted we speak only English at home. Today, it seems the young who speak good English are scarcer than hen's teeth."

Ana Maria pulls a chair up next to her aunt. Lizbeth kicks herself mentally for forgetting a notebook or a tape recorder for stories.

"I've some things to show you both." Suzi opens a cracked leather photograph album. "This photograph is the Gordon family in front of the fine Georgian-style brick house Robert designed. Ana Maria may have told you the Gordons' first years in Rio were lean ones crowded into a run-down rented place. But between Robert's design work, Moira's English school, and Laurette's herbal medicine, they did quite well over time." Suzi's pride in her pioneer ancestors radiates in her smile.

Lizbeth can't take her eyes off the first photograph Suzi pulled from the album. The Gordons are dressed in their Sunday best. Moira has her arm around a teenage Rosalie, who she recognizes for her skin, noticeably darker than the rest of the family. Two young children stand in front of Robert and Moira. Their eldest child, Angus, head and shoulders taller than his siblings, stands next to his father.

"Angus is much older than his siblings. Wasn't he born in Nassau?"

"Yes, darlin'. Angus and Rosalie were peers and best friends. Robert and Moira lost two babies in their early years in Brazil and later had two more children born healthy and strong. I imagine you saw the babies' headstones yesterday."

"Yes, ma'am."

"I see you noticed Rosalie's color. Laurette and Moira created a plausible story about Rosalie's father before the voyage from Nassau to Brazil. The Gordons told the Confederado community Laurette nursed a wounded mulatto officer who passed for White. Don't you agree, it was perfect. No one can resist a tragic war romance." Lizbeth and Ana exchange a look and nod their agreement.

"The story Moira manufactured was, a pastor married Laurette and her handsome officer, and shortly thereafter, he returned to his unit and died in battle."

"People believed the story?" Lizbeth finds it a stretch.

"Many Confederados had secrets and tragedies they did not wish to share, my dear. Out of respect, folks did not pry unnecessarily into each other's history." Suzi brushes the smallest boy in the family photograph with her index finger. "My father, James, was Robert and Moira's youngest, born fifteen years after Angus."

"Why isn't Laurette in this photograph?" Lizbeth feels a special bond with courageous Laurette and thinks of the headstone, so spare in design compared to those of Robert and Moira.

"Laurette Gordon died a horrible death." Suzi gives a slight shiver in spite of the midday heat. "She stepped in front of a carriage and died in the street when Rosalie was eight. Robert and Moira raised their niece as their own child." Suzi pats the picture of Rosalie as if she could soothe the teenager.

"How awful! But —with all the gumption it took to survive the hardships of the Civil War—how could she be so careless?" Lizbeth clamps her mouth shut, feeling rude for judging.

"It grieves me to tell you, from what I understand, whispers about Laurette's reckless demise circulated in the Confederado community for decades." Suzi takes Lizbeth's hand in her heavily veined one. "Truth be told, Robert and Moira knew Laurette's death was suicide, but they loved her dearly and protected Rosalie from shame by keeping mum."

"What happened?"

"You've read Laurette's diary. It became obvious in Rosalie's first weeks of life that her father wasn't White. A White woman giving birth to a mixed-race child was unthinkable either side of the Mason-Dixon line in those days." Susie sat back and looked Lizbeth in the eye. "One person's sin is another's salvation. Laurette refused to give Rosalie up for adoption, though Lord knows, I was told, her sister and brother-in-law wanted her to."

Lizbeth identifies with Laurette, making any sacrifice necessary to keep her baby. "How could a mother with a child she loves so much commit suicide?"

Suzi sits back in her chair with a far-away glance into the garden before she continues.

"When Grandmama Moira was elderly, she told my father the story and he told me. By the time Rosalie was seven, Laurette knew she had syphilis. She knew the disease well, had witnessed its progression in hospital patients in Charleston. The ugly late-stage markers of open sores and dementia would expose the nature of Laurette's disease. Laurette told Moira the only way she could spare Rosalie the shame of syphilis would be to make her suicide look like an accident. Moira, who loved her sister-in-law dearly, applied reason to no avail."

"After reading Laurette's diary I feel like I knew her intimately." Lizbeth is physically shaken by the tragedy of Laurette's dilemma. "What a sad end for an exceptional woman."

Suzi turns more album pages with knobby, arthritic fingers. She pauses and smiles, selecting a photograph of Rosalie around age eighteen. Working it loose from the gold leaf paper triangle holders, she sets the portrait on the table, turns more pages until she locates a sweet photograph of Rosalie at around five or six, seated on Laurette's lap. "Rosalie is darker, but you can see a strong resemblance between mother and daughter, especially the Gordon nose."

Suzi turns the photographs on the glass-top table toward Lizbeth. "Rosalie was a darling child who grew into a beautiful woman, don't you think?"

"I do."

"My papa loved his cousin Rosalie and could remember being incensed when strangers thought, because of her color, she was his nanny. He said his mama was fierce as a mother lion, setting people straight, though I reckon it took a toll on Rosalie."

Suzi opens a folder and lays a postcard next to the photographs.

"Rosalie married a mixed-race man named Miguel Boaz. I'm sorry I don't have a wedding picture to show you. Soon after their marriage, they left Rio de Janeiro for Charleston."

"Whatever for?" Lizbeth can't imagine why any mixed-race couple would immigrate to Charleston, given the Jim Crow laws of the early twentieth century.

"Rosalie was raised on Laurette's and Robert's stories of the good life in Charleston before the war. Although Robert and Moira had no letters from Charleston since Rosalie was a small child, Rosalie was adamant she'd find her Aunt Jeanne's family once she and Miguel arrived and made inquiries. She believed the children she hoped to have would fare better in North America than Brazil."

Lizbeth squirms in her chair. How could Rosalie think people in the United States were more tolerant than Brazil? But then again, she doesn't know what racism was like in Rio de Janeiro in 1900.

"What do you think happened?" Lizbeth says, thinking Rosalie's unfolding story is like a Latin American telenovela with a terrible twist.

"We don't know. I was told Rosalie wrote she and Miguel arrived in Charleston hunky-dory, but after a year, the letters stopped. I do have a clue, an address for Laurette's friend, Tilly Morgan, right here." Suzi looks wistfully at the well-thumbed, century-old postcard.

"We know Rosalie and Miguel stayed with Tilly after they didn't find Jeanne and her family at the old Charleston address," Suzi says. "This post card is proof."

"They just disappeared never to be heard from again?" Lizbeth's tone is incredulous.

"That's right," Suzi says, shaking her head.

"Moira and Rosalie were very close. Papa said Grandmama Moira took to her bed for weeks when Granddaddy Robert refused to go look for his niece in Charleston. The story was that Granddaddy couldn't go because there had been a price on his head, maybe still was, but his refusal was more likely bitterness. He maintained the US government should have paroled him for doing his duty to South Carolina and his family, like so many other officers who returned home without consequences. Grandmama Moira had only been to Charleston once and that was during the war to meet Granddaddy Robert's family. In 1900, she was no longer a young woman and didn't feel she could go to the United States alone."

"How tragic!" Lizbeth's heart aches for the many losses her ancestors suffered. Sitting here in the dappled sunlight in a flowering wisteria garden, she's in awe of what Gordon pioneer courage has created over the years.

"Sweet child, I do have a favor to ask before you go."

Suzi stacks pictures of Rosalie, the Gordon family photograph, and Tilly's postcard and pushes the grouping toward Lizbeth with a shaky hand.

"It would do me an honor if you would take these and copy them. When you visit South Carolina, perhaps you can find Rosalie's kin in the United States and reconnect our lost family."

Lizbeth swallows hard at the enormity of such a task. The thought of disappointing Suzi after being enveloped into the family fold is unimaginable. A hundred-year-old address isn't much of a clue, but it's a start. She'll get Charlotte to help, but still.

"I will do my best, Aunt Suzi," Lizbeth says with more confidence than she feels.

Ana Maria lifts her arm and checks her watch, notifying Lizbeth it's time to go. They kiss Suzi goodbye, promising to stay in touch.

When Ana Maria swings the car onto the highway, Lizbeth says, "Suzi's amazing. I want to be just like her when I grow up."

"She is our beloved link to pioneers who helped Brazil develop into a modern country."

"Suzi made me feel I belong here." Lizbeth adds with a laugh, "More than that, I'm a woman with college-age sons and it's a treat to be called 'sweet darlin' child.'"

Ana Maria reaches over to squeeze Lizbeth's hand. "You do belong here."

ↄ

The drive to the airport passes quickly with little conversation, while they enjoy bossa nova on the car radio. Lizbeth is busy in her head, organizing the weekend into a narrative for Char.

"To choose suicide, Laurette must have been desperate," Lizbeth says during an advertisement break in the music. "The chauvinism of that era makes me furious."

Ana concurs. "Rape was always the woman's fault for doing something she shouldn't or being somewhere she wasn't supposed to be."

"And syphilis was a terrible price Laurette paid in addition to her violation. Is there anything else you know about Rosalie that might help me follow her trail?"

Lizbeth is on pins and needles, thinking property or tax records might not be a resource if Rosalie and Miguel didn't buy property or pay taxes in Charleston. Aunt Suzi is counting on her. The pressure is daunting.

"Aunt Suzi told me that Robert and Moira shielded Rosalie from the truth of her conception. But, of course, her brown skin and kinky hair set her apart. I have a photograph of Rosalie as a young woman, standing with her young cousins in front of Moira's school. I'll make you a copy. My Great-Uncle Angus isn't in the picture. He would have been at Glasgow University then."

"And Rosalie who was just a year younger stayed home?"

"Robert and Moira were good Christian people who tried to be fair with their children, including Rosalie. But when it came to higher education, their sons were sent to Scotland for university, and Rosalie stayed in Rio. She became a teacher at Moira's school."

"What's fair about that?" Lizbeth's hands curl into fists in her lap. Keep cool girl, misogyny was as common as mud, even if Robert and Moira were sucked into it, it's not Ana's fault.

"Moira and Robert thought they were saving Rosalie from racism she would have encountered in Scotland if she attended Moira's alma mater, a women's college in Glasgow. They meant well."

Lizbeth is thinking about how good intentions backfire, and how complicated it is to figure out where you belong. "Yeah, I suppose Rosalie heard her mother's and Uncle Robert's happy childhood stories. And Laurette's good friend, Tilly, was a free Black woman, so Rosalie probably thought people in Charleston were openminded. She couldn't do an internet search. And she couldn't know Charleston's economy was still suffering effects of the Civil War, plus the systemic inequity of Jim Crow laws. Rosalie stepped into an ugly era in South Carolina."

Ana turns her head toward Lizbeth giving her a quick smile.

"You're right. Searching for a place she fit in must have been behind Rosalie's drive to repatriate to the land of her birth and find her people— not unlike you've been doing since we met."

A screaming siren roars up behind Ana Maria's car. She pulls over to let an ambulance pass, effectively ending their conversation.

CHAPTER TWENTY-SEVEN

Rio de Janeiro, September 2010

The seven-hour school day feels like seven hundred. When the last bell rings, Lizbeth races out the door to hitch a ride to Copacabana on the school bus. She's too antsy to wait for the city bus today. The mustachioed middle-aged bus driver, who's a terrible flirt, has a sweet spot for Lizbeth and clears kids off the seat next to his, keeping a light banter going as students disembark at stops in Leblon, Ipanema, and finally, Copacabana.

Lizbeth hustles into the Royale, gives a jaunty wave to the concierge, takes the stairs two at a time to the fourth floor, dumps her things on the chair by the door, and phones Charlotte.

"Hey, cuz," Charlotte answers. "I wanna hear about the birthday party but make it quick. I've got a house to show in half an hour, and I need my best charm on for a blowhard executive being transferred here from Raleigh. A fat commission's riding on the deal."

"OK, but you will just DIE! Here's the Cliff's Notes version." Lizbeth walks to the window and jerks it up, letting sea breeze freshen the apartment. "Laurette's daughter, Rosalie, and her husband, Miguel, immigrated to the United States around 1900. They came to Charleston to find Jeanne and John Gordon and didn't. But they did find Tilly Morgan, a friend of Laurette's, and sent Moira a post card from Tilly's. I've got the address."

"This is fascinating, Lizard, but don't spend the money you won on the lottery yet. Your only clue is a hundred-year-old address?"

"Come on, Char. It's one more family link, and besides, not only did I tell Aunt Suzi I'd find what happened to Rosalie, but I want to find the answer, too." Lizbeth's heart thuds hard, imagining the complicated quest ahead.

"OK, OK. We'll make a full investigation after Christmas. Gotta go. I'm slammed, thank God. My house needs a new roof."

Lizbeth suspects Charlotte stays upbeat to humor her. Is Charlotte right? Is this mystery fascinating because she's falling in love with the Confederado Gordons and wants to please them? Lizbeth shakes her head to clear it.

"Hey Lizard, one more thing before I go, quickly, what's the buzz on that MAN you texted me about?"

"You are incorrigible, Char! If you must know, I've still got what it takes to reel in a handsome guy." She loves keeping her nosy cousin dangling.

"Spill it, Lizard."

"Would a six-foot-tall man with a gorgeous smile who speaks English with a Texas accent pique your interest? We had chemistry the minute we met. His name is Raoul. We're meeting for coffee on Saturday."

"Ooooeee. I'm intrigued. Keep it simple till I can check him out. And remember to watch those *caipirinhas*. And be sure he doesn't have a wife he forgot to mention tucked away somewhere. Take it slow, cuz."

CHAPTER TWENTY-EIGHT

Rio de Janeiro, Brazil, October 2010

Raoul's irreverent humor reminds Lizbeth of Charlotte's older brother, her cousin John. They both have a way of teasing that makes her laugh and feel a little foolish, but in a nice way. Raoul isn't classically handsome; his hair, expertly cut to obscure where it's thinning, doesn't quite do the trick, and Lizbeth can pinch an inch or two around his middle. But Oh My GOD, when he smiles! In a bodice-buster novel, he would have the heroine swooning with desire. And he's tall. Lizbeth is five-foot-eight. When she puts on heels, she doesn't fancy towering over her escort. Dan was tall.

The day their romance took off, Raoul and Lizbeth met up at a sidewalk café; they languished for hours over glasses of Agua de Coco and *brigadiero*, a dessert that reminds Liz of an ultra-rich, double chocolate cupcake with a surprise strawberry in the center. When a waiter began resetting tables for dinner, they departed to window shop boutiques in Ipanema, ending the stroll at a quiet restaurant with a view of the beach. Raoul suggested the bartender's signature *caipirinha*, but Lizbeth opted a glass of cabernet.

Raoul looked surprised. "You don't like our famous cocktail?"

"I had a *caipirinha* meltdown my first week in Rio and haven't had one since." Her neck burns and color floods her face.

Raoul gives her a curious look, but tactfully changes the subject to his time spent in Austin, Texas, getting his PhD in psychology. "Those years were quite an adventure. My mother's family were Confederados from Texas. My American cousins took me on road trips all over the West, and we got to be close friends. We've stayed in touch over the years."

"So, you've had a roots journey too, huh." She can't believe how easy he is to be with, safe and comfortable.

"Like your Robert, my great-grandfather couldn't go home after the Civil War, but he wrote to his family, stayed in touch. Over the years, some of us continue to visit back and forth."

Lizbeth screws up courage to ask Raoul a question that's been nagging since Aunt Suzi's party. "Why did you leave a tenured teaching position in Sao Paulo for private practice in Rio de Janeiro?"

A shadow crosses his face and Lizbeth suspects, once again, she's the tactless North American. She waits, biting the inside of her lip.

"My wife died eighteen months ago after a long battle with cancer. For years doctors offered hope they shouldn't have." Raoul looks away as if considering how much to reveal.

Lizbeth holds her breath. Does he trust her?

"It was very hard." He continued. "Her doctors tried experimental drugs that had miserable side effects. Finally, she made the decision to die with dignity. It was a terrible time for me and my children."

Honored by his honesty, Lizbeth takes another risk and tells Raoul how her life in Washington State fell apart. She shares her concern about her relationship with Josh and Robbie and her twins' loyalty to their father's memory.

Now a month has passed, and Lizbeth is spending more time with Raoul in Leblon than at her apartment in Copacabana. On getaway weekends, he shows her there's more to the state of Rio de Janeiro than shops, high-rises, restaurants, and the six million inhabitants of it's capital. They drive south along the coast, to Angra dos Reis (Anchorage of the Gods) to swim in warm ocean the color of turquoise and build white sandcastles like children. They visit Parque Nationale, where exotic birdsongs waft through the thick canopy of trees. They hike till their legs feel like jelly and drop into bed at a boutique hotel.

The last week before the summer holidays, Lizbeth is slammed with year-end paperwork and preparation for her holiday in South Carolina. Raoul teases that if her work means they can't see each other during the week, he'll call every night and whisper sweet nothings while they lie in bed less than a mile apart. And he does.

On one call, Lizbeth giggles, saying she needs her lover's professional consultation. "I think I'm getting obsessed. Finding Rosalie's descendants has become more than satisfying Aunt Suzi's dream of reconnecting with Carolina cousins. I identify with Rosalie. Both of us were a bit one-off, an awkward fit in the families that raised us."

"At this point I'm not ready to diagnose you as an unbalanced woman," Raoul teases.

"Ha ha." If he were in the room, she'd roll her eyes like an escaped lunatic in an old black-and-white movie. "Realistically though, I worry about facing Suzi if we find nothing. Or worse, a bad outcome."

"Suzi will understand. She seems like an innocent elder with her old-fashioned manners, but I've known her all my life, and I can assure you, she wouldn't be the ninety-five-year-old Gordon matriarch if she didn't have steel in her backbone."

⁓

Lizbeth's suitcases are packed for her morning flight to Atlanta and she is dressed for one last dinner date with Raoul when he calls with apology in his voice.

"My daughter and son-in-law arrived fifteen minutes ago, a surprise visit to my flat for the weekend. I told them I was on my way to pick you up, and they've insisted on joining us."

The last thing Lizbeth wants tonight is to complicate her romance by folding Raoul's children into the mix. She squashes a cranky response. Her flight is at the crack of dawn. If she wiggles out of their dinner date, she won't see Raoul until February and that's a worse scenario than a meal with his daughter and son-in-law tonight.

"OK, but since we can't have our romantic evening alone, you better be treating me to an extra stupendous meal."

తూ

Raoul plays footsie with Lizbeth under the dining table to get her to relax. The evening goes fine enough, although Lizbeth never removes the sweater that hides her sopping armpits from Monica and her husband. Rather than drop her at the apartment building door, Raoul parks on a dark side street where they sit, necking like teenagers.

Lizbeth finally breaks their embrace. "I don't want to go in, but I've got to be at the airport in five hours."

Raoul reaches into the back seat for a beautifully wrapped package. "I brought you a Christmas surprise."

"Oh, Raoul, I'm a grinch. I have been so immersed in my own world. I didn't think to get you anything."

"No need," he says, as she rips open the wrapping.

"A phone?"

"It's the new Apple iPhone. I bought two with an international calling plan, so we can whisper pornographic nothings every night until you come home." Lizbeth melts inside and gives him a dazzling thank-you kiss to carry them both through the holidays.

From her window seat, Lizbeth admires Rio de Janeiro spreading out below, sparkling in the early morning sun. She can hardly wait to see her family, but after these six months in Brazil, and now Raoul, she's become confused. Where's home?

CHAPTER TWENTY-NINE

Greenville, South Carolina, January 2011

A hard, cold rain is falling in Greenville, South Carolina on New Year's Day. Lizbeth is on the couch in Charlotte's living room, thinking of the crisp sunny morning a few days ago, when she'd put blueberry muffins in a paper bag, filled one thermos with hot chocolate and another with coffee and woke her boys.

"We're goin' to Cowpens!" she'd announced. They grumbled about getting up early while on vacation but caught their mother's enthusiasm by the time they finished showering.

Visiting Revolutionary War battlefields had been a cherished tradition for Lizbeth and her father. One summer when the twins were ten, she, Josh, Robbie, Charlotte, and Penny had honored the family tradition with a trip to Cowpens National Battlefield Park near Chesnee, South Carolina.

Ten years on, the visitor experience has been upgraded to include a self-guided tour of the battle that turned the tide in the Americans' favor in the South. Lizbeth and her sons laughed at wild turkeys striding across the open fields, which have been restored exactly as they were in 1781. Something about being outside on a clear, cold, winter day—just the three of them—sparked a string of fond family memories. They talk with a depth they haven't had in a year. For the first time, Lizbeth really listens to Josh's and Robbie's grief over losing their father, without imposing her perspective.

Charlotte joins Lizbeth, carrying a tray of drinks and popcorn to the coffee table. The cousins settle on the sofa, enjoying the soft light of the crackling fire. Charlotte lifts her bottle of O'Doul's alcohol-free beer. Lizbeth leans in for a celebratory clink with her bottle of Spartanburg's RJ Rockers Amber Ale.

"We did it! Everyone behaved. All in all, a great family holiday. Happy New Year, Lizard."

They clink bottles again.

"Thanks for being the hostess with the mostess, Char. Watching Josh, Robbie, and Penny with their heads together, gossiping about college life, and Aunt Sarah beating them all at Scrabble, made my Christmas."

As Lizbeth gets up to toss another log on the fire, flames flare in a burst of heat. "Y'all get a gold medal for keeping the angst manageable around the anniversary of Dan's death. I don't know what I would have done without your gracious Southern charm." Liz gives her cousin an impish smirk.

"You're laying it on a little thick, darlin'."

"Going over the top keeps me from bawling like a baby. I miss the boys already and it's only been a couple hours since I dropped them at the airport. I mean the thanks, Char."

"The pleasure is mine."

Talking about Josh and Robbie, Lizbeth has to bite her tongue to stop tearing up. "I'm scared the twins and I will never be close like we used to be."

"They're twenty-year-old college sophomores, Lizard. Mama should not be their first priority. Give them space to come to you in their own time."

Lizbeth lets out a sigh. "Well, we did have that one magical day at Cowpens."

"You hang tight, darlin'. Put finishing touches on our road trip while I check on our soup."

Standing at the kitchen stove, Charlotte lifts the lid on a heavy cast iron pot and takes a deep whiff of Hoppin' John Soup: black-eyed peas, rice, and collards with leftover ham. A few more minutes and it will be perfection!

Most families have recipes for the traditional Southern New Year's soup, passed down over generations, and the Gordon clan is no exception. Charlotte puts a tray of buttermilk biscuits in the oven and sets a sweetgrass basket lined with a napkin to keep them warm when it's time to plate the soup.

Tomorrow, she and Lizbeth are headed to New Orleans, in search of Rosalie's descendants. Last night, while Penny, Josh, and Robbie watched a movie, Charlotte and Lizbeth had reviewed Charlotte's November research at the Charleston Huguenot Historical Library, and tea with Mrs. JoAnne Bacot. Once they had established themselves as distant cousins, JoAnne had launched into an oral Bacot family history as her grandparents had told it, including what was known of Angus Gordon's wife, Michelle. According to the story, Michelle, the youngest of four daughters, couldn't attract a suitor from the right kind of Charleston family, thanks to her father's unfortunate financial decisions. But Michelle was lively and pretty, and Angus had an up-and-coming business. Together, they were a true love match, uncommon in that era. Tragically, Michelle and their youngest daughter died of diphtheria in the late 1850s. When the siege of Charleston began in 1863, the Bacots closed their home and retired to a plantation owned by relatives in Darlington County. By the time they returned to Charleston, Angus Gordon was dead and the rest of the family gone. Charlotte politely listened to more Bacot stories until at last she found an opening for what had brought her here in the first place. Charotte told JoAnne about Michelle's granddaughter, Rosalie, and how she'd come looking for her Bacot family around 1900. When JoAnn responded, she looks directly into Charlotte's eyes: "Michelle died before the war. The Bacots never knew her grandchildren and have no record of who they might be." Her tone implied in no uncertain terms, "End of discussion."

A day later, Charlotte rapped on the door of a one hundred-fifty-year-old "freedman's house," where Laurette's friend Tilly Morgan had once lived. It was a stroke of luck when the elderly woman who answered the door was Tilly's granddaughter. Not only did she know about the Gordon family, she had a picture of her "Me-maw Tilly" and Rosalie on the front porch in 1901. They settled in for coffee, and Tilly's granddaughter began.

"My me-maw said Dr. Gordon and his family left Charleston a year or so after the war. Dr. John was out of work. The house hospital he supervised closed when the family who owned the home returned to claim it. Worse was when a Yankee officer claimed the Gordon's house for hisself and men. Me-maw had been working for Dr. John for years. They was tight. But when the Gordon's went upcountry in a hurry, Me-Maw lost touch. Dr. John knew she was close to illiterate, so he didn't write her. Laurette and Rosalie was already long gone to Brazil by then.

"That solves the question of why they left," Charlotte said softly.

Tilly's granddaughter cocked her head. "So, you Dr. John's people?"

"Yes, ma'am."

"Me-maw said the Gordons was a fine family. She said she lost all hope they would come back to Charleston when their fine home was razed after the earthquake of '86."

She looked Charlotte in the eye. "All the Gordons was gone when Rosalie come lookin' for her people in Charleston. I heard Rosalie went callin' at her grandmama's Bacot relatives too but got brushed off the doorstep like trash."

Charlotte's heart ached with empathy. What a terrible reception for Rosalie, but given the rampant racism and nationwide political corruption of the early twentieth century, no surprise.

"Where'd Rosalie and Miguel go?" she asked, feeling like she could almost touch the young couple's desperation.

"My uncle, Me-maw's son-in-law, was Creole, from New Orleans. He told Rosalie and her man, people from the Caribbean Islands live in New Orleans. As mixed-race folks from another country, they might feel more at home in that city. Rosalie and Miguel stayed with Me-maw a spell, then they disappeared to somewhere around New Orleans. I remember Me-maw Tilly said she was present, helping Laurette at Rosalie's birth, and prayed every night for that sweet child and her family."

∽

Charlotte is jolted back from that fall visit to Charleston to the present New Year's Day in her own home when Lizbeth calls out from the living room. "Where's that Hoppin John soup you promised? I'm starving out here, pondering which route to take to New Orleans."

Lizbeth knows playing the bravado card keeps her worry bug of trepidation at bay. Was she nutso to promise Aunt Suzi results?

She calls out again. "Want me to circle a couple of options where we can stop overnight? It's nine hours or more, and we aren't in a hurry."

Charlotte rounds the corner with a tray heaped with soup and biscuits. "Yeah. We don't need to book The Big Easy in advance this time of year. It will be quiet as a tomb till near Mardi Gras. We'll have us a fine time sashaying down to the Gulf Coast on the hunt for long-lost relatives. And this time we've got a correct current address, so cross your fingers."

∽

Lizbeth's phone chirps. It's Raoul. She gets up and saunters to the window, looking at crystals of frost forming on the late afternoon lawn. Its high summer in Rio, and she could be swimming in the warm Atlantic with her lover.

"Happy New Year, darlin'!" she answers.

"You too, minha querida. Do you have time to talk?" Lordy, how she loves his sexy mixture of Texan and Brazilian Portuguese.

"I just have a minute to say hey. Char and I are about to sit down to New Year's soup. How about tonight?"

"I promised I'd go to Ana Maria's for dinner. We'll gossip about you. Can I call and wake you up when I'm home?"

"Only if you whisper sweet nothings when you do." She can't believe she's become so bold. She coughs, regaining a modicum of composure and hears him chuckling four thousand miles away.

"Would you like your midnight love poem in English or Portuguese?"

"Both." If he can be pornographic over the miles, so can she. She wonders if Char has any Rumi or Anais Nin on her bookshelf.

�

At some point she'll have to tell Josh and Robbie about Raoul. But for now, with the exception of Charlotte, he remains her delicious secret. It was enough of a surprise when she told her sons she'd signed a contract for a second year at Leblon. They didn't say much. She hopes they're mature enough to understand she needs meaningful work and friends as much as they do.

CHAPTER THIRTY

New Orleans, January 2011

Lizbeth and Charlotte park on a side street near a nineteenth-century, French-style home, a bed-and-breakfast close to Jackson Park. Charlotte blows out her breath and rests her head on the steering wheel.

"Whew, I feel like Methuselah who lived seven hundred years." True to her self-care lifestyle, when they check in, Charlotte selects the best room offered, gives Lizbeth a kiss on the cheek, and retires upstairs with a sandwich and a Coke.

Saturday night is balmy for early January. Mosquitos won't be a problem for months, so Lizbeth leaves the door to her veranda ajar to enjoy the gurgling water feature in the walled garden below. After midnight, her sleep comes in fitful episodes punctuated by shouts, groans, and curses from revelers wandering home from Bourbon Street a few blocks away.

At first light Lizbeth gives up on sleep, dresses in sweats, and creeps quietly down the back stairs worn U-shaped by two centuries of servant's feet. She slips out the side door into an alley and is confronted by a raven picking at something indeterminate. He cocks his head, nailing her with a beady black eye as if to say, "Why are you here?"

Walking fast feels like a smart idea in the still dawn. The cobbled streets in the old French Quarter—festive with buskers and tourists from midday through past midnight—are anything but at this hour. Vagrants stay tucked into doorways until shop owners shoo them away. The only person sharing the street with Lizbeth is a young Black man wearing a do-rag, swishing a Clorox solution on the sidewalk in front of a bar. Lizbeth walks a few more blocks, thinking about the research she and Charlotte did at the library, trying not to script how today will go, then turns and heads back to the bed-and-breakfast for a shower.

∞

In the days before their families arrived for Christmas, Lizbeth and Charlotte did due diligence on the Boaz family at the Greenville library. They found *Times Picayune* archives and a recent article about "Jimmy Boaz, third-generation French Quarter restauranteur."

"They've got to be our family," Lizbeth said, ecstatic to find a solid clue.

Charlotte played devil's advocate. "Maybe so. But what makes you think they want to meet a couple middle-aged White chicks from South Carolina?"

"People everywhere are doing genealogy searches. It's the thing to do," Lizbeth insisted.

"Huh. Until a year ago, seems to me you were invested in obfuscating yours. Now you expect kumbaya from a family that cut ties with everyone in Brazil over a hundred years ago?"

Lizbeth attempted to lighten the conversation by wiggling her eyebrows and putting on a mischievous smile. "Well, here's how it'll go: the Boaz's will be thrilled to hear about long-lost family and envelop us in the bosom of their New Orleans clan. You and I will apologize for the racist reception Rosalie and Miguel got from the Bacots in Charleston. Then we'll share stories and plan a Confederado reunion in Santa Barbara, to party hearty." Lizbeth dropped the levity and gave her cousin a serious glance. "That's my dream."

Charlotte rolled her eyes. "Uh-huh."

"Think positive, Char. Remember that guy, James Ball, who wrote *Slaves in the Family*? His big-ass planter family had thousands of enslaved people before the Civil War. He wanted to make amends for his family's antebellum behavior, so he dug around until he located a book of family business records from three hundred years ago. He found documentation with ship's names, the ports in Africa they had departed from, and the names of enslaved people transported to South Carolina. Ball traveled around the United States finding descendants of his family's enslaved people, apologizing, and giving people documentation on their roots. Some people slammed the door in his face, but others became his friends."

Lizbeth, who was remembering the warm, welcoming, Confederado descendants gathered at Aunt Suzi's party, wants Charlotte to understand. "Ana Maria and I talked about Rosalie's father. It didn't matter who he was, enslaved or free, or where he came from. Rosalie was a beloved member of the Gordon family and embraced by the exiled Confederate community of mostly White people. I pray the twenty-first century Boaz family will fill us in on stories about Rosalie, Miguel, and their children."

⁑

That morning in New Orleans, the cousins find an office supply store and make copies of Aunt Suzi's pictures and Aunt Sarah's Greenville family photographs from the 1870s.

When they return to the bed-and-breakfast, Lizbeth pulls a slip of paper out of her jeans pocket with Jimmy's restaurant phone number and waves it in front of Charlotte's face. "Are you ready, cuz?"

Charlotte holds up both hands with her fingers crossed. "Sweet Jesus, let this go well. Dial up Mr. Jimmy Boaz and put the call on speakerphone."

After several rings, the answering machine at Chez Amos kicks in with the 1950s song "Never on Sunday," followed by a recording of Monday-through-Saturday business hours and an invitation to leave a message for reservations. Lizbeth opens her mouth to leave a voice mail and Charlotte disconnects the phone.

"Hey!"

"Lizard. Voice mail is not the way to introduce ourselves."

"I was only going to leave my name and request an appointment."

"Leaving Jimmy Boaz pondering for a day over a Gordon from South Carolina calling out of the blue might not be our best strategy." She grabs her purse off the chair. "Let's walk by Chez Amos and check out the Boaz restaurant. Then we'll get coffee and a beignet and spend the afternoon basking in the charm of the three-hundred-year-old French Market like proper tourists."

∾

Monday midday Lizbeth and Charlotte return to Chez Amos, a lovingly restored three-story stone building with a wide balcony and beautiful filigree railing overlooking the street. Lizbeth rubs her jumpy stomach as she follows directions from the restaurant hostess up the stairs, glancing at pictures in the photograph-laden hall on the way to Jimmy Boaz's office. Lizbeth turns, looking over her shoulder at her cousin. Charlotte winks.

Jimmy, a tall, dark-skinned, fit-looking older man with wary eyes, stands and extends his hand across a highly polished mahogany desk to shake with Lizbeth and Charlotte.

"Please sit and tell me why you're so interested in Rosalie Boaz."

After the usual pleasantries, Lizbeth relies on her years of putting anxious clients at ease, recounting the Gordon Confederado story succinctly. She finishes with Aunt Suzi's ninety-fifth birthday request to learn why Rosalie and Miguel disappeared—and her wish to reunite the family.

There is a long silence before Jimmy responds.

"It's not my intention to insult y'all, but we Boaz are successful in New Orleans no thanks to any blood relation to you and yours. I can understand why you might be curious about us, but I'm not sure we feel the same way."

Lizbeth and Charlotte share a look. Char lets her cousin take the lead.

"We don't know what happened after Rosalie and Miguel left Rio de Janeiro. We came hoping to learn what we can from you and gladly apologize if our branch of the Gordon family caused yours harm."

Jimmy glances down at his clasped hands on the desk and back up at each of the cousins. The only sound for a full minute is voices calling out on the street below.

Lizbeth feels like she's applying for a job, sitting across from a perspective boss, pulling out all her charm to convince him she's qualified.

"I was told the reason Rosalie and Miguel left Rio de Janeiro was because Rosalie was convinced they would have a better life in the United States. Our Aunt Suzi said Robert and Moira Gordon begged them not to go, but once Rosalie got the idea in her head to return to the land of her birth, there was no one who could change her mind. Maybe she was a dreamer like her grandfather, Angus, who immigrated to Charleston from Scotland. In the end, because they loved her, Robert and Moira Gordon supported their niece's decision."

Jimmy squints at the cousins with deep brown eyes hooded with thick lashes. "My people's early years as immigrants were, thanks in part to your White family, one tragedy after another. First, there was no trace of the Gordon family in Charleston to help when they arrived. Second, rather than the embrace Rosalie expected from her mother's Bacot people, she and Miguel were rushed off the doorstep into the street. My grandparents stayed with a family friend who suggested they would like the Creole culture in New Orleans."

Lizbeth can feel Jimmy's distrust—or is it disgust?—wafting across the desk. She didn't expect open arms, but she hadn't expected this level of hostility.

"Is there anything else about Rosalie you can tell us?"

"I remember their only surviving child, my father Amos, saying it seemed like his parents were cursed for leaving Rio. By the time they arrived in New Orleans, their savings were gone. My grandfather found a job cooking in this very building. It was a large private hotel at the time. Rosalie easily got a job teaching young ladies. She passed the paper-bag rule. You know what that is?"

Lizbeth and Charlotte nod.

"Light-skinned mixed-race women were sought after as nannies by wealthy Creoles in the city. Things went better for a few years. Then Rosalie and her baby girl died, soon after Rosalie gave birth. My father, Amos, said his daddy felt betrayed by his beloved wife's dream. After she passed, he destroyed family letters and the photographs Rosalie had saved. It was no accident the Boaz family disappeared from your Gordon family tree."

Jimmy gives the cousins sitting across his desk a dubious look. "Now you two show up."

"What a heart-wrenching history." Lizbeth feels nauseous hearing how the young couple's dreams were cruelly dashed. She takes a few deep breaths and looks to Charlotte, who jumps in.

"If he was so unhappy in the United States, why didn't Miguel take Amos back to Brazil after Rosalie died?"

"Pride, I suppose. Granddaddy was a prideful man. His reaction to racism in America was interesting though. You do notice I am a very Black man?"

Lizbeth and Charlotte glance at each other and at Jimmy, seated behind his elegant desk.

"Pride in our Black skin is Miguel's family legacy. My grandfather was a mixed-race man who identified as Black. He wanted my father and his grandsons to marry dark-skinned women so our children would not be mistaken as anything but proud Black Americans."

Lizbeth is dying a little inside, searching for how to salvage this conversation without putting her foot further into her mouth. She gives Charlotte a can't-you-think-of-something-clever-to-say look.

"It seems despite racism and terrible financial odds that confronted them, the Boaz family has been very successful," Charlotte offers.

"My father was a brilliant chef and businessman. He owned this building by the time he was fifty. Very unusual for a Black man at the time. I continued to grow the business. One of my sons will take over here, and the other manages a resort we own in the Bahama Islands." Jimmy leans forward, looks first at Lizbeth and then at Charlotte.

"What exactly do you want from me?"

"We came hoping to meet you and to convey an invitation to visit Santa Barbara d'Oeste and meet your Brazilian cousins." Lizbeth opens her purse and retrieves the photographs she and Charlotte copied and passes them to Jimmy.

Jimmy is silent, looking at the photo of Rosalie and her family in front of their home in Rio, and another of the multiethnic faces at Aunt Suzi's birthday party.

"Huh. I've never seen a picture of my grandmother, or her people."

Lizbeth reaches out and grasps Charlotte's hand under the desk. She plucks up her courage. "We'd be happy to come back and share what we know with more of your family if they are curious."

"Some could be." Jimmy's tone softens. "I'll make a few calls and get back to you."

⁓

Lizbeth and Charlotte take any distraction they can find until Jimmy arranges a luncheon. They ride the trolley to the Garden District for a walking tour of elegant homes and famous cemeteries. They explore the French Quarter for good jazz and good food. Charlotte keeps repeating her AA mantra, "let go and let God," until Lizbeth wants to strangle her cousin. In the wee hours of the morning, Lizbeth jerks awake with a gasp. She gets up and walks onto her balcony where the night air clears her head from an awful nightmare ending with Laurette's suicide. At two in the morning, she wishes she had a mantra like Charlotte's.

⁓

At the appointed hour, the cousins are ushered to an intimate dining room at Chez Amos where a spread of fragrant dishes sit on a Victorian sideboard. Half a dozen people gather around a table draped with crisp, white linen and topped with a centerpiece of showy roses. As Jimmy escorts them to the table, everyone rises to greet Lizbeth and Charlotte with handshakes.

After the usual pleasantries, Lizbeth dives into the history of Robert and Laurette, their stories of love and sacrifice, and how the siblings became Confederados. Before the luncheon, Lizbeth and Charlotte had wrestled with telling the truth about Rosalie's conception or using Laurette's lie about a brief marriage to a soldier that passed for White. In the end, they decided the Boaz family deserved the truth.

When Lizbeth finishes, Charlotte lays out photos of multiethnic

Gordon descendants from Suzi's birthday. The cousins sit silent, hardly moving a muscle, waiting for the Boaz family reaction. For long moments, the only sound is *tick-tock, tick-tock*, from a grandfather clock in the corner.

A man in a well-cut suit breaks the silence.

"How many enslaved people did you Gordons own?"

Charlotte gives her cousin a this-was-your-idea look, and Lizbeth answers honestly, "John Gordon's Greenville County family had at least one enslaved family we know of working their farm, but the Charleston Gordons were against the institution and were not slaveholders. The Bacot family, Rosalie's maternal grandparents, owned slaves in Charleston and their extended family had a plantation worked by enslaved people in Darlington County."

Some around the table ask questions about the family in South Carolina and Brazil, cool and polite—not the warm welcome Lizbeth had hoped for. As the cousins depart, they thank Jimmy for hosting lunch.

"Please keep the pictures for anyone that might be interested in Rosalie and the Confederado connection." Lizbeth hands Jimmy her contact information.

⌇

Walking back to the bed-and-breakfast, Lizbeth doesn't try to stop the tears streaming down her cheeks. "The day when people can talk to each other about the sins of the past without assuming the worst about someone of another color in the present can't come fast enough for me."

Charlotte takes her cousin's hand as they cross the street.

"Don't let that luncheon crush you. That guy, Duane, who drilled down on family slaveholding, had an iceberg-sized chip on his shoulder. We don't know his personal history. You are the one who talks about the triggered limbic brain, and distrust of another's ethnicity or social class or whatever."

"Charlotte!"

"Oh, please, Lizard. We don't have antebellum attitudes on race, or we wouldn't be here trying to connect with Black distant cousins. Jimmy got that by the time we finished lunch."

"Yeah, you're right. He did." Lizbeth gives her cousin a weak smile. "But I'm really flattened. I wanted so much to connect Rosalie's descendants with their family in Brazil. I failed."

"I'll cop to my part. I think we set ourselves up, moving too fast."

Lizbeth feels her cousin's arm circle her shoulder.

"We didn't know Miguel held a bitter grudge towards Rosalie's family. That lingering taste has remained on the Boaz palate for generations." Charlotte gives her cousin another squeeze.

"Laurette sacrificed everything to give Rosalie the best life she could. I wanted the Boaz family to know Rosalie was loved and missed by her uncle, aunt, and cousins when she and Miguel disappeared." Lizbeth sighs out a long breath.

"Don't beat yourself up, cuz. It won't help."

"I was romanticizing a large, loving multicultural family." She blinks her eyes again and again to hold off tears. "Vestiges of an only child's fantasy of a big, warm extended family, I guess." She sniffs back tears and pokes her cousin in the side. "But, hey! I've got you!"

"Yeah, we're stuck like glue, darlin'." Charlotte tries to poke Lizbeth back but can't manage to as Lizbeth dances away.

"Who knows, maybe somebody from today will get curious and contact you later."

Lizbeth feels a tightening in her chest and takes a slow, deep breath to stem off rising anxiety.

"What am I going to say to Aunt Suzi?"

CHAPTER THIRTY ONE

South Carolina, January 2011

In the morning, they load Charlotte's car for the drive back to Greenville, South Carolina. Near Atlanta, they stop at Lenox Square to soothe their disappointment with a little retail therapy. They make a beeline for the sale racks at Dillard's. Lizbeth is back in size 12 with room to spare. The twenty pounds she sloughed off mourning Dan haven't crept back, and her muscles are toned from beach walking in Rio. Charlotte takes a photo of Lizbeth modeling a slinky black dress and Lizbeth emails it to Raoul. That'll give him something to think about.

Lordy, how she aches for a leisurely call and his take on all the details of the Boaz family messed-up meet-up in New Orleans. Raoul really listens. Much as Lizbeth loves her cousin, Charlotte's support is peppered with quick slogans and practical solutions that try her patience.

∽

Back at Charlotte's, Lizbeth relaxes on the sofa over a long talk with Josh and Robbie. They sound happy and have plans for a long weekend skiing with friends at Mount Baker over the Martin Luther King holiday. Thankful the warmth of Christmas week remains alive and well, Lizbeth hints, "I could book a cheap flight to Seattle. Would you like a visitor for a few days, before I head back to Brazil?"

The twins let her down gently, saying classes are intense and reminding her that they both have part-time jobs. "We're really busy, Mom," Josh says.

"We'll come to Brazil sometime this summer," Robbie promises.

Lizbeth whines to Charlotte about playing second—or third, or fifth—fiddle in her son's lives while her cousin reminds her again, mothers are not supposed to be a number one priority to twenty-year-old sons.

"Be happy they have lives, Lizard."

"Well, OK. How about this for me? If the cottage is free for the rest of January, I think I'll go down to Folly and do some winter beach walking."

"Do it."

☙

Knowing she'll be in Brazil for another school year, Lizbeth memorizes the South Carolina landscape sliding by her window seat on the bus. Greenville's rolling hills flatten in the middle of the state to bare fields of stubble waiting for spring planting. Those, in turn, give way to Low Country flora, lush in the warmer months but looking fragile in mid-January.

After a cup of coffee and a package of Benne wafers at the Charleston bus terminal, Lizbeth steps aboard the express to Folly Island. The last stop is the Tides Inn on Arctic Avenue, and an easy walk to the cottage. Thrift by necessity has had its rewards. No car means no monthly car insurance payments. She winces at how much she and Dan used to spend on insurance for two vehicles and four drivers. After a year of practice, checking her transportation options before leaving home is a snap. It's not the draconian lifestyle she'd imagined.

Eager to relax, she climbs the cottage steps inside, unlocks the door, and swings her backpack off her shoulders. It's musty, closed up with no visitors since Thanksgiving, when her cousin John and his family were down for a long weekend. Before settling in, Lizbeth turns on the baseboard heat and clicks on the gas fireplace. Tomorrow she'll clean up the dead spiders and other beasties that slither and crawl, looking for a safe place to hide from winter in crevices of old walls.

The refrigerator is pristine and empty except for an unopened can of cranberry sauce on the second shelf. Charlotte's sister-in-law is a clean freak. Lizbeth checks the oven. Yep, spotless even after doing a full-on holiday turkey and side dish casseroles.

After a quick walk to Ken's Market, Lizbeth unpacks bacon, eggs, a quart of milk, English muffins, and coffee. She opens a cupboard to get a glass for water and finds a half-empty bottle of Jim Beam Black Label. Thank you, John! I'll have a wee dram with my omelet tonight. Then, I call Raoul.

Disappointment over the Boaz family's disinterest sits heavily on Lizbeth's shoulders. To lift her spirits, she walks out on the front porch, takes a picture of seagulls coasting over rolling swells, attaches it to a text message. "Miss you, sweetheart. Wish you were here to see my January beach."

Her phone rings immediately. "Is this an invitation?"

"I thought you were seeing patients this afternoon."

"I've got someone in the waiting room now. Just wanted to say I can hardly wait to see you! Talk to you tonight. Ciao, baby."

&

In the morning, Lizbeth sits sipping coffee in a wicker chair angled for a full view of the winter-gray sea. The thermostat on the porch reads forty-five degrees. Fortunately, it's not thirty-five. She dresses in heavy sweats and an anorak for protection from frigid spray blowing sideways off the cresting waves. Winter storms shift the sand daily, covering and uncovering sea glass and shells. Lizbeth means to find a few gems.

She sets off purposefully, head down, scanning the sand near the surf line. There are abundant green and brown glass from beer and wine bottles she tosses away, but she keeps a rare blue and a yellow one the surf and sand have smoothed to please her palm. Finding sea glass treasures remind her of Grandmama: *Glass polished by the ocean is like a jewel polished by a master artisan,* she used to say.

The shoreline birds are elsewhere today, probably hunkered down in tufts of grass covering the dunes at the county park. She cinches the anorak hood tight around her face, glad she's thought to wear a billed cap underneath it to keep the light mist out of her eyes. Alone but not lonely, she's the only human on this section of beach in the company of washed-up jellyfish, crab shells, hundreds of angelwing mussels, and a few scallops, all dislodged in last night's storm. She laughs at a courageous hermit crab dragging her scavenged shell toward the surf line.

Lifting her head to survey the larger seascape, Lizbeth is surprised she's come two miles, to the island's very north end, where Folly Creek funnels through a narrow channel between Folly Island and what's left of neighboring Morris Island. Morris Lighthouse stands proud, painted, and preserved, though there's been no keeper since the end of the Second World War.

When Josh, Robbie, and Penny were in middle school, Lizbeth and Charlotte took their children on a kayak tour of Morris Island. The guide had said Morris Island had always been low and marshy, and rich with a web of brackish creeks. But back in colonial days, there had been a meadow large enough for a couple of homesteads. In three hundred years, hurricanes and shifting currents have eroded the island into a narrow sand bar with a courtyard of shipwrecks offshore. On very low tides, it's still possible to see masts of wrecked Civil War blockade runners jutting out of the near-shore surf.

The tour guide had told how the Federal Army struck a killing blow to Charleston when they constructed an engineering feat of the day built on pilings in the marsh: an enormous Parrott cannon called *The Swamp Angel* that could land shells on homes in Charleston, a mile across the harbor. Although *The Swamp Angel* exploded after only thirty-six rounds, the siege of the city lasted 567 days and left much of it in ruins.

To lighten the mood after his talking points on death and destruction, the guide had opened his arms toward Charleston from the steps of the lighthouse and reminded his small group, "Behold, the holy city rises up, vital and strong!" They all had a good laugh.

享

The memory of that kayak tour with Josh and Robbie conjures a smorgasbord of cherished times with her family at the beach. She sends a little prayer up that her sons' happy summers will draw them back to Folly with their own families someday.

The wind is freshening. Looking out to sea, Lizbeth spots an inbound squall. Better get outta here. She takes one last look at the city across the harbor. A fat lump fills her throat. On that kayak tour one bright summer day years ago, none of them knew the Confederado story.

Lizbeth hurries toward food and warmth, thinking of Charleston starving at the end of the Civil War, and shivers. On a winter day like this one in 1864, the Gordon household would have struggled to find fuel to keep a fire going in a room or two.

Glancing out to sea as she hurries toward the cottage at a slow jog. A breaching bottlenose dolphin grabs her attention. Others in the pod are playing beyond the surf line. They remind her of the fragility of Low Country waterways; so close to streets ripe with horse droppings from carriages carrying tourists and street water runoff with chemicals containing god-knows-what-all. Articles in the *Post and Courier* reflect dueling forces of those who want to preserve the natural habitat and those who want to fill the marshland with condos and gated golf resorts. She's banking on the high cost of hurricane flood insurance to slow down greedy land developers.

Lizbeth pulls numb fingers into fists and picks up her pace. What time is it anyway? She's been woolgathering on the strand longer than she'd intended, and the temperature is dropping. The Crab Shack's just ahead: a haunt where she and Charlotte used to drink Cokes and flirt with boys every summer. Lizbeth grabs a table, pleased the restaurant, with its steamy, single-pane windows dripping rivulets of water, hasn't changed much. She doesn't care that it's the off-season, crab will be out of the freezer, not just off the boat. Lizbeth orders the she-crab soup, warming her heart as well as her body before the rest of the walk home to a hot shower.

☙

During her last days at the cottage before returning to South America, Lizbeth spends hours taking pictures of the beach and local Low Country scenes to savor when she's homesick. She visits Mount Pleasant Mall for a dozen paperbacks and new underwear, including a couple of lacy things Raoul will approve of. On Sunday, she attends First Scots Presbyterian, sings her heart out on traditional hymns and has lunch with Patsy: fried redfish and hushpuppies at *Justine's Kitchen*.

She tackles a final deep clean of the cottage. She counts out cash and leaves a note next to the landline to cover the long-distance calls she's made to Josh, Robbie, and a few friends in Port Benton. Tomorrow, Charlotte will collect her after lunch. They'll drive to the Atlanta international airport and share a meal before her evening flight to Rio de Janeiro. Although she feels it's time to leave, her eyes mist over. When will she visit Folly Beach again?

CHAPTER THIRTY-TWO

Headed for the Coast of Brazil, February 2011

Lizbeth's last load of laundry is knocking around in the twenty-year-old cottage dryer when her cell rings. Leaving the stack of carefully folded bed linens—did she really need to iron those sheets?—Lizbeth grabs her cell off the couch just before the call goes to voice mail.

"Hello?"

A youthful woman's voice asks, "Good afternoon, am I speaking with Lizbeth Gordon?"

"Yes."

"My name is Brenda Boaz. My grandfather Jimmy told me about your visit to New Orleans. I live in Atlanta, and I want to meet you."

Oh my God . . . Oh my God . . . Oh my God . . . All the Boaz' don't hate us . . . Brenda wants to meet me! Lizbeth's heart gallops like a spooked mare while seconds tick by before she can find her voice.

She coughs and stutters, "I'm booked on a flight from Atlanta to Rio de Janeiro tomorrow night, but I bet I can find a shuttle to Atlanta this afternoon." Her heart is thumping. Is this for real? . . . Is this for real? . . .

"How about dinner?" Does she sound like an overeager fool?

"That sounds perfect," Brenda answers. "My husband can stay home with the kids."

They agree on the Airport Marriott restaurant at six o'clock. Lizbeth disconnects and shouts, "Wahoo!" She pumps the air with both fists and does a victory dance around the room.

Lizbeth stuffs the last bits of laundry into her suitcase with the passion of a woman possessed and dials Delta Airlines. The only available flights are in business class. Screw the budget! She books the three o'clock flight to Atlanta and a night at the Marriott and calls a cab.

ↄ

High on anticipating her date with Brenda, Lizbeth leaves Raoul a voice mail from the Charleston airport.

"Guess what darlin'! I'm dining with Rosalie's great-great-granddaughter tonight! Can you believe it?" The final boarding call crackles over a loudspeaker. "Gotta go. I'll tell all after I have dinner with Brenda Boaz."

While hustling to the gate, it hits her. She called Raoul before she called Char!

Sitting in her generous seat on the tarmac, her plane in line for takeoff, Lizbeth calls her cousin, who doesn't pick up. Charlotte is probably showing a house or at some meeting. Lizbeth leaves a voice mail.

"You will die! I just got an amazing call! As we speak, I'm on a plane to Atlanta, going to meet our cousin Brenda Boaz for dinner tonight. How 'bout that! Drive on down, tonight, share my room at the Airport Marriott."

She chuckles as she disconnects. That should get Char's attention. Lizbeth puts her phone on airplane mode, thinking how much she loves her bossy cousin.

ↄ

Her last days at the beach, Lizbeth had taken stock, reflecting in loving appreciation the way cousin Charlotte indulged her quest to find long lost cousins in Charleston and Brazil and New Orleans. To be fair, Charlotte got hooked on the research too, but differently. For Char, the quest was curiosity more than a passionate need to identify far-flung ancestors. Char knows who she is. She examined her life when she got sober. Lizbeth is now semi-chagrinned to admit, to keep the peace in what had been a comfortable life for twenty plus years, she avoided hard questions about her family history or any blip of relationship conflict that could upset her world. Then Dan died. She squirms. Rough as this year has been, she wouldn't go back to her old life for a million dollars.

⁊

Lizbeth waits at a window table in the corporate cookie-cutter restaurant, nursing a glass of sweet tea, twisting a napkin into shreds in her lap and feeling her heart pound like a racehorse. She takes a couple of deep, slow breaths as the hostess escorts a tall, brown-skinned, thirtyish woman with the Gordon nose to her table.

Lizbeth stands, extending her hand with a tentative smile. Brenda covers Lizbeth's hand with her own. They sit, beginning with light chatter, circling like wary animals until a resonance evolves. They laugh at the serendipity of Brenda's timing; if she had called twenty-four hours later, Lizbeth would have been on a flight to Rio de Janeiro.

"I'm sorry for the reception you got in New Orleans," Brenda says. "I love my granddaddy, but his generation is steeped in the painful days of Jim Crow."

"I'd be lying if I said Charlotte and I expected what we got. We showed up assuming your family would want to know us." Lizbeth doesn't mention the warm reception she got in Brazil compared to the frost in New Orleans, though now she sees how naïve she'd been about the Boaz family experience in America. Lizbeth reaches into her tote bag and hands Brenda a large envelope. "I brought you copies of Gordon family photos. I can tell you stories that go with them if you want."

"I do." Brenda quietly pores over pictures of Gordons in Rio, especially the portrait of Laurette with Rosalie on her lap. The waitress circles back again, anxious to get their order in. They dine on the special of the day, giving little attention to food while they fill in family mysteries across the table.

"I didn't hear all of what happened in New Orleans, but I can guess it must have been tense for you. My elders remember horrific stories Miguel told as a bitter old man."

Lizbeth leans forward. "Please, it would help me to better understand Jimmy if you tell me more Boaz family history."

"I'm sure Jimmy told you how Rosalie was rejected by her White relatives in Charleston. Rosalie gave birth to Amos in a tiny house they rented in New Orleans. Miguel found work as a cook, but struggled with English while watching his bilingual, bicultural wife integrate in a way he never could."

Brenda looks wistfully at the portrait of Rosalie and her mother.

"Miguel had better employment in Rio than he ever found in New Orleans. He was ashamed of the conditions his new family endured compared to what they could have had in Brazil with family connections. From what I understand, Rosalie probably suffered from what we now call postpartum depression. Miguel must have thought he was helping his wife move on by demanding she cut ties with her family in Brazil." Brenda paused.

"Please go on." Lizbeth is breathless with curiosity and heartbroken by Rosalie's and Miguel's story.

"They worked hard, life improved, and Rosalie became pregnant again. She was no longer a young woman, and her labor was difficult. Neither she nor her infant daughter survived a day after the birth. I was told Miguel went wild in his grief. He destroyed the few photos and letters from his wife's family that he discovered among her things after her death. He never forgave her family for supporting her dream of a North American land of milk and honey. I think Jimmy probably told you Miguel insisted his son, Amos, marry a very dark-skinned woman."

"He did."

"To please his father, Amos also went to a Negro university, and distanced himself from White people except for business at his very successful restaurant."

"It's a tragedy that Rosalie returned to the land of her birth, found a cold welcome, and lost her life." Lizbeth feels shame remembering the story of Bacot relatives who could have helped Rosalie and Miguel but were too racist to bother.

Brenda looks grim as she continues. "Distrust of White people and racism festered in our family until my generation let go of that ugly past. I majored in engineering at LSU but I minored in sociology to help me understand my family history. Something I learned in one of my classes was, it takes four generations to get over family trauma. Well, I'm the fifth generation from Miguel and Rosalie."

Lizbeth reaches across the table to take Brenda's hand.

"Thank you for reaching out to me." She swallows to keep her voice from choking up. "I've been looking for lost parts of my family for a year. I felt driven to find out more about my roots after my husband died unexpectedly. I'm regretful it took that crisis to make me look deeper into my ancestry." Her tears are welling up again. Lizbeth clears her throat again.

"My ninety-five-year-old Great-Aunt Suzi in Brazil remembers how her father loved his cousin Rosalie. I promised I'd bring Suzi news about your side of the family. Pretty crazy, huh?"

Brenda pulls a packet of tissues from her purse and passes it to Lizbeth.

"Not crazy at all." Brenda takes Lizbeth's hand and holds on.

"I was excited when my Daddy told me about Granddaddy's lunch with you and Charlotte. I feel a special affinity with Rosalie because my children are mixed race."

Brenda retrieves a photo from her purse and passes it across the table to Lizbeth.

Lizbeth looks at the smiling faces of two children with light brown skin around ages five and seven, sitting in the grass, their arms around a fluffy golden retriever with a lolling tongue. The girl is missing her two front teeth.

"They are darling!"

"Stephen and I want Ellie and Nelson to be proud of both sides of their heritage. Our life together didn't start out easily. Granddaddy Jimmy pitched a fit when I brought my White sweetheart home to meet the family. He still isn't happy I married a White man, but he's no longer hostile to

Stephen. In the beginning, both our parents worried and warned our life would be filled with conflict and our children forever outsiders, but we proved them wrong and have their big-time support now."

Brenda runs her index finger over her children's faces lovingly, a protective mother bear at ease. "We have a good life in Atlanta and a circle of fine friends. Our children aren't unique in this city, though there are times when we get negative vibes, out and about as a family."

Brenda's comment hits Lizbeth's old button about the South and racism. She blurts out without thinking, "Why don't you move to a liberal city in the North or West?"

Brenda leans back and lets out a belly laugh.

"We tried that. Stephen and I met at college. We had friends and family say we would have an easier time in the Northern states, so after we married, we took engineering jobs in New York. But we missed our own people and Southern culture. Atlanta isn't perfect, but it's as liberal as they come here. We know immediately when we're not welcome. Up North, it's way more stressful. The cues for racism are subtle; you let your guard down, you get a kick from behind."

Lizbeth is chagrined. "I didn't mean to be rude."

Brenda gives Lizbeth an understanding smile. "You're not rude. Just curious and honest, and I appreciate that." She smiles again. "Besides, you're family."

"Thank you." Her tears flow, and Lizbeth has to restrain herself from leaping across the table to hug Brenda till they both burst.

"And just so you know," Lizbeth admits, "I have a reputation for putting my foot in my mouth."

"I think that's a family trait." Brenda smiles.

Lizbeth digs out her wallet and passes Brenda pictures of Josh, Robbie, and this year's photo of the Gordon clan around Charlotte's Christmas tree.

"Here's some more family for you."

They talk and laugh, and Lizbeth promises to email Brenda Laurette's dairy and Robert's letters as soon as she is back at her apartment in Rio.

It's after eight. All the tables save theirs have been reset for breakfast.

The lone waitress is straightening chairs and sending pleading glances in their direction. They agree to meet at a city park in the morning so Brenda's children can play while the cousins talk, and Charlotte can join them. They linger in the hotel lobby, fantasizing a family reunion in Brazil with Gordons and Boaz constituents from the States.

⤬

At the Atlanta airport, Lizbeth keeps her cool until her plane is airborne for Rio. Then she lets stifled sniffles loose and wipes away tears for the next half hour. Her seatmate sneaks furtive looks but doesn't intrude.

This time last year Lizbeth felt her family had imploded. Now her family has expanded in ways she'd never dreamed of, spread across two continents. It's a blessing and it's complicated. Instead of grounding her, new choices pull her in multiple directions, each with a piece of belonging. At some point she'll have to give up this nomadic life and settle somewhere. Or not.

A flight attendant offers wine and snacks. Lizbeth accepts both and soon slips into dreamless sleep. She wakes to the captain's voice inviting passengers to take in the view of colorful beach umbrellas dotting the strand as the plane descends through scattered clouds to land bathed in summer sunshine.

The baggage claim at Galeão is packed with perspiring bodies and Muzak blasting the wildly popular "Essa Mina Louca."(My Crazy Girlfriend) The double doors part with a whisper and Lizbeth exits, towing her wheelie bulging with purchases from Charleston. Humidity presses around her like a fuzzy fleece blanket. She spots Raoul crossing the parking lot wearing a big sappy "welcome home" smile. She raises her hand to wave and notices she's still holding her passport. She zips it into her pocket and opens her arms to new love.

ACKNOWLEDGMENTS

I am forever grateful for my extended family, rich with storytellers, who fired up my imagination from an early age and championed the fun of making stuff up. Unlike many authors who spent their childhoods perusing libraries, I didn't read for pleasure until my teens. I'm dyslexic. Never in my wildest dreams could I have become a writer without a community of supporters who believed in me, and computer software with spell check.

A heartfelt thank you to my deep reading writer friends; Rhoda Berlin, Maren Halvorson, Ross Mayberry, Mary Merralls, Sharon Goldberg, Sam Owen, Seattle Super Group, and Beta Readers with a special shout out to Trudy Sackey and the St George Book Club, Melinda Barbera, Vicky Horton, Jennifer Parsons, and Barbara Wohlfeil. Without your valuable feedback, generously provided, *Exiled South* would never have come to fruition.

Many kudos to Virginia Herrick, my wise and thoughtful editor who kept me on track and mentored me through revision. A big bow of appreciation to my shepherds through the publishing process; John Koehler, Joe Coccaro, and the team at Koehler Books.

Finally, *milliones de gracias* to my husband Charlie Cannon, my rock and cheerleader. With an open mind and eagle eye, he reviewed multiple iterations of *Exiled South*, and drew both the Gordon Clan genogram and blockading running map with an engineer's attention to detail.

CPSIA information can be obtained
at www.ICGtesting.com
Printed in the USA
LVHW091641171221
706497LV00014B/137/J